I wandered int
I had made the right decision to stick it
out in band. Then George popped out of
his seat, sax in hand, and started playing.
His whole body was in motion, as if there
was music in his soul. That made up my
mind for me—I'd stay in band, even though
George was a real musician and I was just
a beginner.

I wondered if there was a sub-beginner
category. I wondered if there was a category
for people who, like myself, were tone-deaf,
but in love.

I blew into my clarinet but nothing came
out, so I made the motions of playing while
I watched George's miraculous concentration and brilliant smile. I would practice
day and night, night and day, if it would
get us together!

Bantam Books in the SWEET DREAMS series. Ask your bookseller for any titles you have missed.

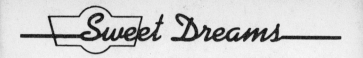

Sweet Dreams

MUSIC FROM THE HEART

Pamela Laskin

BANTAM BOOKS

NEW YORK · TORONTO · LONDON · SYDNEY · AUCKLAND

MUSIC FROM THE HEART

A BANTAM BOOK 0 553 28551 3

First publication in Great Britain

PRINTING HISTORY
Bantam edition published 1991

Cover photo by Pat Hill

Bantam Books are published by Transworld Publishers Ltd.,
61–63 Uxbridge Road, Ealing, London W5 5SA,
in Australia by Transworld Publishers (Australia) Pty. Ltd.,
15–23 Helles Avenue, Moorebank, NSW 2170, and in New
Zealand by Transworld Publishers (N.Z.) Ltd., Cnr. Moselle
and Waipareira Avenues, Henderson, Auckland.

Made and printed in Great Britain by
BPCC Hazell Books
Aylesbury, Bucks, England
Member of BPCC Ltd.

In memory of my father,
whose music was always special

Chapter One

"**Y**ou're *not* going to believe this!" I shouted to my best friend, Lisa, who was walking beside me.

"Not so loud, please," she muttered under her breath.

"You don't understand," I continued, lowering my voice a little. "I mean, sure no one is excited to be back at school." I glanced at the walls of Robert Moses High School. They looked the same, except that a little more plaster had fallen off the walls since last semester. The skating rink where I had spent a good part of my intersession seemed much more appealing at the moment.

"But look—just look at this!" I pointed to my schedule. "This has to be a mistake. Maybe it's someone else's."

Lisa glanced at the schedule. "Oh, no!" she said, clutching my arm. She obviously understood how serious the problem was. "Did you choose band as one of your electives?"

"Are you kidding? No way!" I replied.

"Then how did it end up on your schedule?"

"Who knows? Maybe the computer had a bad day when it put together my schedule. I chose theater for my elective, and modern dance was my second choice. There's no way on earth I would choose band, even as my one hundredth choice."

Lisa laughed out loud. "You can't take band, Maddy! You're tone deaf!"

"Thanks a lot," I said. "So much for supportive best friends." But she was right. I'm as tone deaf as they come. "Seriously, Lisa, what am I going to do? I've only had three clarinet lessons, and they were all disasters!"

"I know, I remember." Lisa tapped her chin as she pondered my problem. "It's no big deal, really. I'm sure that when you explain the situation, they'll put you in another class. Don't worry so much, Maddy."

"You don't understand," I said, exasperated. "Electives fill up quickly and I need this eighth class if I want to graduate a semester early."

"What do you want to do that for?"

"So I can take a trip around the world before I go to college," I explained.

"But you can't graduate early!" Lisa wailed.

"Why not?"

"Because we have too many important places to go together when we're seniors. What about the prom? Isn't that supposed to be the most important night of a girl's life?" Lisa asked.

I shook my head. "There's no way I'm sticking around just for the prom!"

"What about the trip we had planned to the dude ranch?" she asked.

"We can still do it," I told Lisa.

"What about the fact that school wouldn't be the same without you?" she demanded.

"Well . . . I'll think about it," I said, grinning at Lisa. For a moment I had forgotten all about my schedule problem, but now we were standing outside the band room and I began to panic. "What should I do?" I cried.

"Just go right in and explain. Mr. Walker is the teacher, and he's a really nice guy. He'll understand."

"This is crazy, Lisa. How did I end up in this situation? It's just not fair!" I started feeling angry. "Band isn't even supposed to be offered as an elective in the spring semester. It's only supposed to be offered in the fall."

"Don't you remember Mr. Poindexter's speech right before Christmas?" Lisa did a great imitation of the principal. "Due to the overwhelming student interest in electives, this year we will offer band, cooking, and metal

3

shop during the spring semester as well as the fall."

"Oh, yeah, now I remember." I groaned. "He thought it was *great* news. Well, I think it stinks!"

"I know. Look, I have to run to class, but let's meet after school at Pino's. A slice of pizza always makes things seem better."

"Okay." I waved good-bye to her, then took a deep breath and opened the door. I walked to the front of the room and stood there, ready to pounce on Mr. Walker as soon as he entered.

Instead, this incredibly handsome guy walked up to me. I had never seen him around school before, which was strange, considering how gorgeous he was. "Are you okay?" he asked me.

"Yeah, sure." I was flabbergasted. "Why do you ask?"

"You looked like you were about to faint."

I did feel a bit faint, but only because I was looking into his eyes. "Really, I'm okay," I assured him. "Thanks."

"Anytime," he said. Then he jumped up the steps to the back of the room and joined his friend.

I looked around at the other students. I noticed two girls who seemed very mismatched as friends. One was dressed like a punk rocker and the other was turned out in a complete sixties look. There was a very pretty girl sitting off to the side, and one guy was sitting away from the crowd pretending to play an instrument. I really felt out of place, and I hate that.

"Here comes the big W.!" shouted the handsome guy who had been so sweet to me. A middle-aged man whose glasses were falling off his nose stumbled into the classroom. He was wearing a french beret, a red and pink plaid shirt, and green pants.

"I like your outfit, Mr. W.!" Handsome shouted. The rest of the class was whispering and giggling. Mr. Walker tripped twice on his way down to the podium, then absently hung his beret on top of the music stand and searched for a place to put his music. Handsome raced to the front of the room, grabbed the teacher's hat, and tossed it onto the hat rack. I couldn't believe how cute he was— thick brown curly hair, enormous brown eyes, a perfect nose, and a wonderfully muscular body. And he was so helpful.

"Thanks, George," Mr. Walker said as Handsome handed him the sheets of music.

"For you, Mr. W., anything. Can I help you get organized?" George asked.

"Sure," Mr. Walker said, and George started separating the piles of papers on the music stand.

"We need some music in this room," George

5

remarked. "What do you think, Mr. Walker? I mean, this *is* band. What if I get my sax? I learned some new show tunes over break. Would you like me to play them?" He was so sweet, and he sounded so enthusiastic.

"Yeah, George, go for it!" shouted one of the guys he had been sitting with earlier. Suddenly there was a chorus of voices in the classroom chanting, "George, George, George!"

Mr. Walker shook his head. "No, thank you, Mr. Held. Maybe another time. Now can we please get on with class?" George returned to his seat, and the teacher turned to me. "Yes? How may I help you?"

You could start by introducing me to George, I thought. I realized that there was no way I was going to drop this class, even if I couldn't distinguish an F-sharp from a C. "I just wanted to make sure this was band," I said quietly. The minute I spoke, I wished I hadn't. What a stupid thing to say. I hoped George hadn't heard me.

But he had. "No, it's home ec!" he called out. "Today, Mr. Walker is going to teach us how to orchestrate a soufflé."

Everyone in the class burst out laughing, and I felt my cheeks turn red.

"Yes, this is band, young lady. Have a seat," Mr. Walker said.

At that moment I wished I was a turtle so I

could hide in my shell. I walked to a chair and sat down.

"It's time to fill out registration cards," Mr. Walker announced, passing them around the room. "I'd also like you to describe, in a few short sentences, why you chose this elective."

Because I have perfect pitch, I wrote in large, bold print. I chuckled to myself. Could anyone in the class possibly tell I was tone deaf? Do tone deaf people have a certain look? If so, was there any way to disguise it, and pretend to be musically talented? I'd have to ask Lisa. Mr. Walker continued to shuffle his papers while the class obediently filled out the cards.

Then he stated, "We also need to appoint 'band babies.' "

"Band babies!" I cried out before I could stop myself. I imagined tiny infants in diapers holding enormous instruments in their hands. "What are they?" I asked the boy sitting next to me.

"Service monitors," he responded. "But George thought that was boring, so he came up with the name 'band babies.' "

I had to give George credit. He was not only cute and charming, but also creative.

"I guess this isn't your first semester in band, then," I said to my neighbor, who appeared to be muttering rhythms under his breath.

7

He shook his head. "Sixth."

I gulped. I was going to be humiliated. "Well, it's my first and I'm terrified," I admitted honestly.

I gazed across the room at George. He was pretending to play the sax while his buddies applauded him.

"Weren't band babies already assigned last semester?" I asked.

"Yes, but Mr. Walker doesn't like a student to do the same thing for more than one semester."

"What's your name?" I asked, turning my attention back to my neighbor.

"Jeff. Jeff Lang."

"What instrument do you play, Jeff?"

"The flute."

"Oh. I like the flute," I told him, nodding. "You must be pretty good."

He shrugged. "I'm okay. What's your name?"

"Madeline Davis. Who's that thin girl with frizzy hair?" I asked.

"That's Cynthia. She and Sonia are inseparable." I figured Sonia was the girl dressed in all-black punk clothes.

"So, how do you like this class?" I asked Jeff.

"I like it a lot. I enjoy playing the flute. I find it very relaxing."

I couldn't imagine how playing an instrument could possibly be relaxing, but I could see how Jeff might think so. He seemed like a natural-born musician to me. I hoped I wouldn't be sitting next to him for very long. He'd probably faint when he heard me play.

"Sonia!" Mr. Walker yelled, looking right at Cynthia.

"I'm Cynthia, Mr. Walker," she informed him politely.

"Oh, yes, Cynthia. I meant you. You can turn the sheet music for the piano during recitals, Miss Bowe."

"Whoa! Take a bow, Bowe!" George teased her.

"Ha ha, very funny," Cynthia snapped.

Mr. Walker continued going through the list of names, distributing assignments. I couldn't keep everyone straight, mostly because I was busy staring at George.

"Miss Costa."

Sonia perked up. "Yes, Mr. Walker?"

"You can clean the instruments every Friday."

"Mr. Walker, that was my job last semester, and I hated it," she complained. "Can't I do something else?"

"I'll help Sonia clean the instruments," George volunteered. "It's a pretty messy job."

"You will? Thanks, George!" Sonia was smiling now, and I prayed she wasn't interested in George, too.

I turned to Jeff. "What instrument does Sonia play?"

"Clarinet."

"What about Cynthia?"

"Clarinet."

Things weren't turning out so badly after all. Now I was absolutely certain that the clarinet would be my instrument. Sonia and Cynthia looked like a lot of fun. Besides, I *had* taken some clarinet lessons.

"Our final job is putting the instruments away." Mr. Walker announced.

To my surprise, I felt my hand fly up in the air.

"Yes?" said Mr. Walker.

"Davis. I mean Madeline. I mean . . . I don't know what I mean."

"Make sure you know your own name the next time you volunteer for something!" George snickered.

George certainly knew who I was now. This was the second stupid, embarrassing thing I had said. A few people giggled, and I felt like everyone in the room was looking at me.

"Enough!" Mr. Walker snapped in a loud voice, and the class quieted immediately. "Miss Davis, are you absolutely certain you can handle this job? There are several heavy instruments—the tuba, the trombone, the sax."

I glanced at George for a second. He was jumping around in the back of the room, pretending to play the guitar, and I bit my bottom lip to keep from laughing out loud. I couldn't figure out why the rest of the class wasn't laughing, but I guessed they were just used to his antics. I wasn't, though; I wanted to go over and laugh and dance alongside him.

I went ahead and agreed to be the instrument monitor.

Chapter Two

"You did what?" I had never seen Lisa's eyes so big before.

"I volunteered to be a 'band baby.'" I sighed.

"I know I may sound ignorant, but what is a band baby?"

"A service monitor. I'm supposed to put the instruments away."

"I can't believe you, Maddy. First you're dying to drop this class. The next minute, you've not only decided to stay in it, but you're a band baby. Now you're trying to learn the keyboard. It just doesn't make sense."

Nothing made sense to me these days. I knew it was insane to stay in the class, that I would fail miserably, but I couldn't help myself. Why couldn't I be levelheaded like Lisa when it came to making decisions?

I stared at the piano. My parents were music lovers, and they had tried desperately to make me and my sister Stacy into concert pianists. Finally my instructor had told my parents to give up; we did not have an ounce of talent between us and they were going to have to accept it.

"Steve is the musical one in the family," I said out loud. "Steve's talented, don't you think?" Steve's my ten-year-old brother. He has an ear for music, though I have no idea where it came from.

"What does that have to do with anything?" Lisa said, laughing. "Sure he's talented, musically, but you're talented in other ways. You're a terrific actress. You were great in last summer's production of 'Arsenic and Old Lace.'."

"Thanks, Lise." I needed to hear that. I was feeling so insecure about band that I had forgotten I could do anything well.

"Now are you ready to start?" Lisa's long and elegant fingers were poised above the keys.

"I guess so," I said.

"Repeat after me," she commanded. "Do."

"Do," I sang.

Lisa winced. "*Listen*, Madeline." She hit each key carefully. "Do, re, mi, fa, so, la, ti, do," she gracefully sang.

"Do, re, mi . . . no, I can't do it," I protested as my voice cracked.

"Then why are you staying in the class?"

"I had no choice," I lied.

"That's ridiculous. People always have choices. What's up?"

I thought for a minute. Should I tell her the truth? Just this past fall Lisa had laughed at me for switching out of three different acting classes. When I'd explained that each teacher was a 'cold fish,' she'd teased me for weeks. I didn't want Lisa to make fun of me for staying in band class just for a guy I didn't know.

"Come on, Mad, tell me," she coaxed. "We don't have any secrets between us. I mean, I always tell you everything."

I thought about the time two years ago when Lisa's dad had lost his job and had been out of work for six months. Lisa had been really embarrassed, but she hadn't hesitated to tell me about it.

"Well . . ." I began.

"Wait, I know!" Lisa grinned broadly. "I'll bet it's a boy. You've got a crush on a boy in band class and you're too embarrassed to tell me!"

I sighed heavily. "You know me too well. So, what should I do?"

"Let's eat now and talk later. We'll definitely work something out."

"Good idea!" I stood up, anxious to forget about music for a while. Lisa and I raced down to the first floor of my family's apartment. We lived on two floors of a brownstone in the Park Slope area of Brooklyn.

"How's music practice, girls?" my mother asked.

"It's okay, Mom, but we've decided to take a break for a while. We're starved," I told her, clutching my stomach dramatically.

"Dinner will be ready soon," she promised.

"Great!" Lisa responded. We went back upstairs and flopped down onto my bed.

"So, what's his name?" Lisa asked.

"George Held," I said, grinning. "And he's gorgeous, funny, polite, incredibly talented . . ."

"So where has he been all these years?" Lisa interrupted. "How come we've never seen him before? Do you think he's a new student?"

"No way." I sat up on the bed, mulling over the possibilities. "He's definitely not a new student. He was in band last semester. Besides, he knows everyone in the class."

"Does he have a nice voice?" Lisa asked.

"Yes." I sighed dreamily.

"I can't believe you never even saw him hanging out at the pizza parlor!"

"Well, George is totally immersed in band," I explained. "There's probably a band hangout where he goes all the time."

"Maybe there is a special hideaway," Lisa said thoughtfully. "But with Lisa Levine and Madeline Davis on the case, the hideaway won't be secret for long!"

"Dinner's ready, girls," my mother called. Lisa and I were at the table ten seconds later.

"I guess you *were* starved," my mother said, winking at me as I took a huge serving of mashed potatoes.

"How was your first day of school?" my father asked us both.

"Fine," we answered in unison.

"How about yours?" my father asked Steve.

"Great, Dad!" Steve said. "I'm going to play soccer this year."

"That's terrific. Soccer's one of my favorite games." My father smiled.

"There's going to be a lecture by Anne Tyler at N.Y.U. next month," my mother announced.

"Really?" my father responded in an excited voice.

I glanced at Lisa and rolled my eyes. I couldn't believe the things my parents got excited over. Both of them were English teachers, and dinner conversations at home could get pretty boring. Sometimes I wished my sister Stacy still lived at home. She always knew how to steer the conversation in an interesting direction.

"Let's reread *The Accidental Tourist* together this evening," my mother suggested.

"That sounds like a wonderful idea, dear."

I could tell Lisa was trying hard not to laugh.

"So, Maddy, I hear you're in band," my father remarked.

"Yes." I looked down at the table. I really didn't feel like talking about it.

"What instrument are you planning on playing?" he persisted.

"I guess the clarinet. That's what I played before."

"Darling, you hated the clarinet," my mother reminded me.

"I'm older now. I'm ready to apply myself musically."

"I don't know," my mom said. "Maybe you should transfer to another class."

"I think she's right," Steve said.

"You're all wrong," Lisa argued. "Madeline has talent. She just needs practice."

Steve snorted. "For about a million years."

My mother glared at Steve. Then she looked at me. "I don't want to discourage you," she began. "But your piano lessons didn't seem to work out—"

"And you had only *three* clarinet lessons before you dropped that too," my father added.

"Enough is enough!" I ran out of the kitchen and up the stairs into my room. I felt bad, especially because part of me knew my parents were right. I imagined myself in one of those old melodramas where the heroine has nothing to do but be miserable, and all because of a man. I threw myself down on my bed and buried my face in a pillow.

Then I heard someone coming up the stairs.

"Are you okay?" Lisa said. "Your parents are kind of worried."

"I'm such a fool!" I cried.

"Maddy, you're just in love." Lisa sat down and started stroking my hair. "Tell me more about him."

I couldn't help smiling. "He plays the saxophone. He's funny, charming, and unbelievably handsome."

"Sounds great."

"You mean, you don't think this is incredibly stupid?"

"Are you kidding? I think it's wonderful!"

I turned around and looked at Lisa. I couldn't believe she understood. But why should I have expected her not to? She knew me better than anyone else. "So what should I do?" I asked her.

"Well, first things first. You need to learn how to read music." Lisa went over to my desk and took out a sheet of paper and a ruler. "You've done that before, right?"

I nodded. "So there's hope?"

"Of course there is!" she said. "Now, let's see . . ."

While Lisa drew some bars of music, I stared at the ceiling and thought about what a good impression I was going to make on George. He'd never see the old, clumsy Maddy Davis again!

Chapter Three

Mr. Walker tumbled into the room, his glasses falling off his nose. He was weighed down by a big black bag.

"Oh, no! It's the killer mouthpiece bag!" George cried. Everyone in the class laughed.

"Yes, George. It's that time of the year again. Time to assign rental instruments."

George Held, I said to myself. *What a nice name.* Madeline and George had a great ring to it, too. In my mind, Lisa's plan played itself over and over again like a broken record. She had told me to be coy and sweet, even a little shy. I *was* sort of shy, but it seemed strange to have to make an effort to be that way.

"What instrument are you planning on playing, Costa?" George called across the room. Mr. Walker didn't seem to mind.

"Clarinet, of course!" Sonia's voice rang out.

"What about you, Cynthia?" George asked.

"Ditto," she said.

"And Davis? What about you?"

I took a deep breath. I didn't want to appear stupid in front of George; I had already stuck my foot in my mouth one time too many. I would play the clarinet. After all, I had already taken three clarinet lessons. Besides, Sonia and Cynthia played the clarinet, and I liked them. But before I had a chance to tell George, Mr. Walker interrupted.

"Okay, George," he said mildly. "It's time to assign instruments. Do you think you can keep quiet for just a few minutes?"

"Sure, I can manage a few minutes." George's eyes were sparkling as he looked at me. Just looking at him made me a thousand times more terrified about trying out my instrument.

"Miss Bowe," Mr. Walker called out, and Cynthia meekly walked up to the front of the room.

"I want to play the clarinet like last semester," she said in a small voice.

Mr. Walker shoved the mouthpiece at her. She struggled to get a sound out of it, and eventually a few squeaks rang out in the air. He assigned her a number and handed her the clarinet case.

While the other students were getting their instruments, I thought about what it would be like to go out with George. Maybe we could go to the beach together. I wondered if he loved the sand and the ocean as much as I did.

Suddenly Ricardo Alexander, one of George's friends, raced up to the front of the room and grabbed a gold mouthpiece off the table.

"This is my trombone," he said, and then he started playing it. I couldn't believe a whole song could be played with just a mouthpiece. George jumped out of his seat to join Ricardo. He scooped up a sax mouthpiece and started keeping time with his friend. It sounded like great music to me, but I couldn't really tell. That's what it's like when you're tone deaf. The class was clapping wildly when still another guy joined the two of them.

Jeff, the guy who sat to my left, looked bored.

"Are you okay?" I asked him.

"Sure," he replied, but he was frowning.

I was surprised. Jeff obviously couldn't appreciate some honest fun. I looked up at Mr. Walker, who was busy shuffling papers once again. The music stopped abruptly and George and his friends were back in their seats.

"Psst!" Someone hissed in my direction. I turned and saw Sonia motioning for me to join her and Cynthia. When Mr. Walker wasn't looking, I got up and hurried across the room.

"Hi!" Sonia said when I sat down next to her. "What do you think of those clowns?"

She had a dazzling smile. She was wearing a large, loose black sweater over black stretch pants, black and white striped socks, and black patent-leather shoes with big satin bows.

"Jonathan's taken," Cynthia announced. I couldn't get over how different she was from Sonia. In her long, loose frilly shirt and a multicolored peasant skirt she was Sonia's complete opposite.

"Is he your boyfriend?" I inquired.

Cynthia grinned. "No, but he will be."

"Whoa, before we talk boyfriends, let's talk names. What's your *first* name, Miss Davis?" Sonia asked me.

"Madeline, but call me Maddy."

"What instrument do you play, Maddy?"

"The clarinet," I said, praying that I wouldn't humiliate myself when Mr. Walker called my name.

"Now that we've covered preliminaries, would you like to go for pizza with us after school sometime?" Sonia continued.

"I'd love to!" I said. Then I felt a twinge of guilt. Spending time together after school was one of my rituals with Lisa. I hoped we could all go together.

"Do you like to dance?" Cynthia asked me.

"Are you asking me on a date?" I quipped.

"No, silly—we'll let George take care of that! I just wanted to get to know you better."

Was I that transparent? Was it so obvious

to my new friends that I was interested in George? I quickly changed the subject.

"What's Ricardo like?" I asked.

"Tall, dark, and handsome, and he doesn't even know I exist." Sonia sighed.

"Hey, instrument monitor!"

I looked up. The love of my life was talking to me.

"Walker's calling you." He grinned quizzically.

"Help!" I whispered under my breath.

Sonia heard me, and gently patted my shoulder. "Knock 'em dead!" she said.

I'm doomed, I thought miserably. What Sonia didn't understand was the impossibility of me knocking anybody dead.

"Miss Davis, please come up to the front of the room," Mr Walker said.

"Uh, I've played the clarinet before," I said, hoping to get out of the mouthpiece test.

"Good. Let's hear you." Mr. Walker handed me a wide-bodied case.

My palms were sweaty as I took it from him.

"Anyone home today?" Ricardo called out.

"Wrong instrument," Mr. Walker said, grabbing the case from me and handing me another. "Try this one out for size."

Slowly I took the instrument out of the case. I put the mouthpiece right up to my lips, and blew as hard as I could. No sound emerged.

To my surprise, George darted up to the front of the room. "Watch my lips," he told me. "Watch the movement." George looked like he was about to burst into laughter any minute. "Can you do this?" He blew into the mouthpiece so loud it sounded like a giant foghorn.

"I'll try," I said, giggling. George winked at me and returned to his seat. I blew into the mouthpiece with all the breath I could muster. Finally a giant squawk came out.

"Bravo!" George shouted with a small smile. I waved at him as I walked back to my seat.

"Please come up to the front of the room, Jeff," Mr. Walker requested.

Jeff ambled to the front. He picked up the flute and placed it to his lips. Mr. Walker picked up the baton and asked Jeff to play Beethoven's Pastorale Symphony *con poco* something. It sounded like *con loco* to me, which didn't make sense. I knew that *loco* meant "crazy" in Spanish.

The music flowed beautifully from the flute. Gradually Mr. Walker picked up the tempo and Jeff kept up with no problem. I thought about the title of the piece. It was very appropriate. I looked around the room and realized I wasn't the only one in the class who was captivated by the soothing music; everyone was. After about fifteen minutes Jeff and Mr. Walker stopped and Jeff gently dismantled the flute and put it back in its case.

"Thanks, Mr. Walker. I hope you had a pleasant holiday break." His voice had a nice ring to it, just like his music.

"Great job, Jeff," George said. What a guy! He even knew how to give compliments.

When I put the instruments away that afternoon, I noticed that George's saxophone was number 23—and my clarinet was number 32. I thought that was a good omen. After all, weren't opposites supposed to attract?

"There he is," I said, pointing. Lisa and I were standing in the hallway outside band class, looking through the glass panel in the door. George was playing a warm-up tune on his saxophone. "What do you think?" I asked.

"He's gorgeous!" Lisa turned to me with a solemn look on her face. "But I'm still not sure if it's a great idea for you to stay in this class. They're bound to find out you're tone deaf."

"Who is?"

"The authorities," Lisa answered with mock seriousness.

"Look at the authority," I told her. Lisa giggled as she looked back into the room and saw Mr. Walker place his hat on top of a music stand. When it fell off, he bent to retrieve it and ended up falling on the floor.

"Stay in band." Lisa nodded.

"Just think," I said with a sigh. "Instead of the great dramatic couple, Spencer Tracy and Katharine Hepburn, George and I will be the great musical couple. Sonny and Cher of the 1990s! . . ."

My friend giggled. "Cut the dramatics, Mad. You'll be George and Maddy, a typical high school couple."

"Never typical, my dear—not with him."

"Oh, okay," Lisa said. "I give up. Let's meet after class at Pino's."

"Sounds fine to me. See you!" I opened the door and strolled into the room. Jeff was the first one to wave at me. I waved back. It was fun to have made new friends in the middle of the school year.

"Where should I sit, Mr. Walker?" I asked.

"The back of the clarinet section," Mr. Walker directed me. I assumed that meant that I was a third clarinet. I knew enough about band to understand that I had been placed in the section for people who can hardly play.

"How did he know to place me here?" I asked Sonia.

"Didn't you tell him you only took a few lessons? Didn't you struggle to get a sound

26

out of the mouthpiece? Aren't you a bad player?"

"I guess I *didn't* play very well," I admitted sadly.

"Well, Cynthia and I have been in band since freshman year and we still can't play. We'll probably always be third clarinet, don't you think, Cynthia?"

"Definitely!" Cynthia agreed.

"I don't think I'll ever learn," I said.

"Can you read music?" Sonia asked, cracking a piece of gum in her mouth.

"Yeah, sort of. Very slowly, though!"

"You'll learn."

"Miss Costa, how do I feel about gum chewing in class?" Mr. Walker shouted.

"You hate it!"

"So what should you do?"

"Spit it out," said Sonia, placing the gum on the tip of her nose, which made George and the rest of the class laugh loudly. I was dying inside. I wanted to be able to play my instrument really well so George would notice me. I took my clarinet out of its case and examined it carefully, wondering if I'd remember a thing from my lessons.

"Now, class, feel your instrument's keys and get to know them," Mr. Walker directed.

"I know mine, and I don't like them," Sonia whispered to Cynthia.

I giggled quietly.

Getting to know my instrument was the last thing on my mind. It was difficult to focus on this thin black stick when George was in my line of vision, directly across the room. George was a natural; I watched his fingers fly over the saxophone's keys. He looked so comfortable and relaxed, wearing a green polo shirt, faded jeans, and new high-top sneakers. He seemed to love the saxophone, the way he inspected it, gazing under every key like there was magic there. And he wasn't always loud; in fact, while his friends Ricardo and Jonathan were talking, George was quietly examining his instrument—while I quietly examined him. At that moment, I wished I was a famous jazz clarinetist, and that George and I were about to do a duet.

I turned to concentrate on my instrument and noticed Jeff. He was studying his flute in a very serious way. He wasn't playful with his music, the way George was. As he held the instrument up to his lips, I felt as if he were a million miles away and absolutely nothing could break his concentration.

It seemed like all the kids were focused on their instruments except me. What *was* I doing in this class? At that moment George looked up and met my gaze. *Hi, Mad*, he mouthed. Then I knew why I was taking band!

"Many of you returning students already know how to play your instruments," Mr.

Walker said loudly. "I'm passing out key instructions for those of you who may be beginners. Practice is the key. Practice, practice, practice!" Mr. Walker fumbled through his papers, and then almost threw them around the room at everyone.

"Mr. Walker, you've given me the instructions for playing the sax," I told him. The rest of the instructions dropped from Mr. Walker's hands. Soon there were papers all over the floor. Jeff quickly helped him pick them up. I had noticed that Mr. Walker seemed to need a lot of help. I wondered if he would possibly be able to teach me to play the clarinet. *Maybe George could give me private lessons*, I mused. In any case, it was clear that it was going to take a miracle for me to make it through the class for one day, never mind the whole term!

After school, Lisa and I met at Pino's.

"How did it go?" Lisa asked eagerly. I watched the cheese drop off her pizza and fall on the plate.

"I don't know, Lisa. Maybe this *was* a big mistake," I said. "I mean, George is as great as ever, but once a tone deaf person, always a tone deaf person."

"You can do it, Mad. I'll help you. Aren't you going to eat your pizza?"

"I'm not hungry today." I suddenly felt very

tired. It was probably all the tension of the day. But if Lisa said I could survive in band, I would do it. Like Mr. Walker said, I'd have to practice, practice, practice.

The next day, I meandered halfheartedly into class, still not convinced I had made the right decision to stick it out in band. George changed my mind during warm-ups. Warm-ups were the first fifteen minutes of every class, where the students simply practiced scales or sometimes played tunes. George popped out of his seat, sax in hand, and started playing spontaneously. The notes were quick and lively. I had seen at least a dozen movies about jazz musicians and George looked like he had stepped out of one of them. His whole body was in motion, as if there was music in his soul.

Cynthia shook her head. "He's unbelievable," she said.

"No question," I agreed. I gazed at him in admiration. George played everything from rock to classical to jazz, and I could barely hit one note correctly.

"Warm-up time is over!" Mr. Walker called, stepping into the room. "It's obvious we have many different levels here," he continued. "I had asked the school for a beginning and intermediate budget, but Mr. Poindexter said the funds just weren't there, so we're all stuck together. Most of you are beginners, though, so I'm not too worried."

I wondered if there was a sub-beginner category. I wondered if there was a category for people who, like myself, were tone deaf, but in love.

"Let's start with scales," Mr. Walker said.

I blew into my clarinet one, two, three times, but nothing came out. It didn't sound like any sounds emerged from Cynthia's or Sonia's either, but Stephanie, the first clarinet, could be heard loud and clear.

"Why don't we spend all of today's period on scales, with apologies to Ricardo, Jonathan, George, Jeff, and Stephanie?" Mr. Walker suggested.

I made the motions of playing while watching George's miraculous concentration. I would practice, day and night, night and day, if it would get us together.

George walked up to me after class. "Anytime you need help, just let me know," he offered, smiling.

"Oh, sure, th-thanks," I stuttered. I could hear my heart pounding as I watched him walk out of the room. Now I was more determined than ever to rise above the beginners level. As I put away my clarinet, I wondered about the possibilities of a talentless person learning how to play. Meanwhile, Jeff Lang was still on the other side of the room, playing his flute.

"Time to put it away," I told him, adding, "you really do like to play the flute, don't you?"

"I do." He blushed. "But there are other things I like, too."

"Why don't you join me in the instrument room?" I asked.

"Sure." Jeff's eyes opened wide as if he were surprised.

I was in a good mood and had lots of talk inside me. "So what other things do you like?"

Jeff handed me the instruments while I stood on the stool, which made my job a lot easier.

"Music. Art. Friendship," he said, his hand on his chin. He looked so completely serious, it made me giggle.

"What's so funny?" he asked, handing me George's sax case. I grabbed for it too quickly, and it almost fell out of my hands.

"You. You were so serious just now," I said.

"Yeah," he said contemplatively. "I can be pretty serious. But I can be funny, too—and fun."

"What do you like to do that's fun?" I asked.

"I like to go to the theater, especially comedies," he answered.

"I love the theater! I live and breathe it," I said excitedly.

"I know," he said with a grin. "I saw you in all of the drama club's productions. You were great in *Kiss Me, Kate!*"

"Gee, thanks." I felt myself blushing.

"Listen, I have to run," he said. "But maybe we can see a Broadway show together sometime."

"I'd love it," I told him honestly.

"See you later. It was nice talking to you." He waved good-bye.

"Same here!" I called out as he shut the door.

It was only one week into the class, and not only had I made progress with George, but I had made good friends in Sonia, Cynthia, and Jeff. Staying in band class had been an excellent decision, not impulsive in the least.

Chapter Four

"How's your practicing going, Madeline?" Sonia asked.

I was still counting notes on the line, and I could kind of read music. I had reached the point where I could barely squeak out 'Three Blind Mice' on the clarinet. But I was practicing, probably more than anyone in the class. "Pretty well," I answered, shrugging.

"I'd rather watch TV than practice—and I usually do," she quipped. "My parents made me take this class." Sonia was talking really loudly. It was warm-up time and I was worried Mr. Walker would get mad. I couldn't afford to get on anyone's bad side. But when I looked up, Mr. Walker was busy conducting a symphony orchestra to an invisible audience.

A month ago, I would have preferred watching *L.A. Law*, *Cheers*, or *Miami Vice* reruns to practicing the clarinet. But now there was no time for television, and hardly any time for studying. I was glad I had decided to take a semester off from drama club. Now my life was the drama, and my new role as a musician was a serious and demanding one.

"I want to do really well in this class," I told Sonia. I gazed at George. His fingers looked like they were dancing across the keys. He'd stare at the music, tap the rhythm against the stand, then test out the notes on his sax. He did all of this without emitting a sound. He played only when he was supposed to, but when he played, the whole room seemed to dance with the rhythm of his beats.

"It's only an elective, so the grade is no big deal. In fact, this is a bozo class," Cynthia said.

"I still want to do well," I said, fumbling to assemble my clarinet.

"I want to do well with *some* people," Sonia said, pointing toward Ricardo.

"Miss Costa, could you possibly manage to be quiet during warm-ups for just one day?" Mr. Walker waved his baton at her.

"Are you kidding, Mr. Walker? When have you ever known Sonia to keep quiet?" George asked playfully.

"George, could *you* possibly manage not to answer for people, and to perhaps not play full pieces during warm-ups? Warm-ups are intended just as an exercise," Mr. Walker reminded him.

"Are you kidding, Mr. Walker?" Sonia laughed, throwing up her arms. "When have you ever known George to mind his own business?"

Several people laughed, including Jeff.

"We're even now, Costa," George cried across the room.

"I've always wanted to say that," Sonia admitted to me and Cynthia. Jeff continued practicing his scales. He winked at me, and I winked back.

"Let's meet after class at Pino's," Cynthia whispered into my ear. "Pass it down."

"Let's meet after class at Pino's," I whispered into Sonia's ear. I was glad my new friends had asked me along on a day Lisa couldn't go. Lisa had told me that she had to stay late after school for the next few weeks to prepare for the school science fair. She was a star science pupil.

"Miss Davis!" Mr. Walker shouted. I jumped out of my seat. "Let's see how well you're reading notes."

I walked up to the front of the room, where various scales had been written on the blackboard. I answered everything correctly. I was able to distinguish whole notes from half notes and quarter notes. Jeff gave me an 'okay' signal.

"Fine, fine," Mr. Walker said, pushing his glasses back up on his nose. "You may go back to your seat."

I strutted back as if I were walking on air.

"Okay, Jeff, do a C scale for us, an F-sharp scale, then a D scale."

"Major or minor?"

"Major."

Jeff made the scales sound like magic.

"He's so talented," Cynthia observed.

"And he's so *quiet*," Sonia added approvingly.

"He's not really *so* quiet," I said, annoyed for some reason. I had to agree that Jeff was talented, but George was talented, too, and they never made as much of a fuss over his abilities.

I counted the minutes until the end of the period, hoping I could hide my complete lack of talent for one more day. I watched as George helped Sonia clean the instruments. Then he walked out of the room without even saying good-bye to me. I wanted to cry.

"Put those instruments away quickly," Sonia told me. "We have a lot of gossiping to do!"

"That's for sure. I'll meet you at Pino's," I said.

"Sounds good." Sonia raced out of the room, her knapsack dangling on her shoulder.

While I put away the instruments I reviewed my options. I needed to find a way to get to know George better. Should I ask him to help me practice or to help me to put away the instruments? Either way, we'd surely become friends.

Finally I placed the last instrument, Jeff's flute, on the shelf. I breathed a sigh of relief. I definitely needed to unwind. I tried to run down Seventh Avenue to Pino's, but my legs wouldn't cooperate—I was too tired. When I arrived at the restaurant, Cynthia and Sonia were already eating and chatting away.

"Welcome, fellow clown!" Sonia said brightly. "This slice is on me," she added, pointing to a piece of pizza piled high with cheese. As always, the smells of Pino's worked their magic on me. The wonderfully sumptuous cheese and fresh tomato sauce smells wafting through the air made me feel warm and welcome.

"So, what do you think of Walker?" Cynthia asked. She took a bite of her slice.

"He's totally lost in space!" I laughed.

Cynthia nodded. "I wouldn't be surprised if one day he walked into the cafeteria, thinking it was band, and started conducting."

"He'd be glad if band was as crowded as lunch," I joked.

Sonia giggled.

I debated whether I should tell them how I felt about George. I decided to mention him briefly and gauge their reaction. "Hey, what do you guys think of George Held?"

"George Held?" Cynthia popped out of her seat, her bobbed hair swaying back and forth.

I couldn't believe it. She seemed like the quietest girl in all of Brooklyn, but here she was, putting on a show in front of everyone at Pino's. She swayed her body in tune with the sax she was pretending to play, batting her eyes repeatedly as she wrinkled her brow in concentration. She did a great George imitation. Sonia and I were laughing so hard our eyes were watering. When she sat down, Cynthia received a round of applause from some of the other customers.

"Does he really bat his eyes like that?" I asked. I had never noticed that before.

Sonia snorted. "Does the sun come up every morning?"

"Then I guess he does," I responded, feeling disappointed. It seemed so phony. I didn't want to think that a guy I liked was phony.

"It's not that he does it in a phony way," Sonia said, as though she were reading my mind. "I think he just gets a little nervous when he plays."

I smiled, relieved, but it still seemed odd that someone who was so talented could get nervous. On the other hand, it made George seem less godlike, which was good. It meant he was approachable.

"You like him, don't you?" Sonia asked me.

I could feel the heat rising in my face, and imagined my cheeks had turned beet red. "Yeah, I guess so."

"It's okay," Cynthia said, patting my back gently. "Join the club." She sipped some cola.

"You too?" I asked, stirring my soda vigorously with my straw.

"No, I have my eye on his friend, Jonathan."

"And you?" I asked Sonia.

"I told you. It's Ricardo for me. You know, the trombone player. Do you guys want to get ices? I know it's the middle of winter, but ices are good anytime." Sonia had read my mind again—my throat was parched!

"Yes, please, a lemon." I opened my purse to get some money.

"Please," she said, "put your money away."

I smiled. "Thanks."

"Listen," Cynthia said, "you don't have much to worry about. George doesn't seem to date very much."

"What about that pretty girl, Stephanie? He always flirts with her in band." I said.

"No problem!" Cynthia said. "She has a boyfriend. He's a freshman at Cornell."

Sonia returned with the ices. I gobbled mine like I hadn't eaten in years. "Then why is she always flirting with George?" I asked after I had licked every last drop off my spoon.

"I don't know. I guess she just likes him," Sonia said.

"What does he think?"

"I guess he likes it," Sonia said matter-of-factly. "But I don't think she's his type."

40

"How do you know?" I inquired.

"Sonia knows *everything*," Cynthia bragged. "And she and I are going to help you with George Held."

"Okay, shoot. Tell me about George. I want specifics. Where does he live? What's his family like? Tell me *everything*!"

"Okay, okay." Sonia pushed her hair back. "He lives on Garfield Place. I think his family owns a brownstone."

"Wow!" I exclaimed.

"I don't know what his parents do for a living, but I know he and his older brother are pretty musical."

Cynthia continued chomping away on her pizza.

"How do you know about his brother?" I asked.

"I saw both of them giving a musical recital at the Brooklyn Academy a few years ago." Sonia made believe the table was a piano keyboard, and her fingers flew up and down.

"Help! He'll never want to go out with me." I groaned.

"Yes he will," Sonia said.

From that day on, my friends started a big campaign to make me even more funny, charming, and lovely than they claimed I already was. Sonia had a book called *The Perfect Woman,* and she started reading important

41

sections from it to me every day at lunch. The three of us were fortunate enough to share the same fourth period lunch, but it was early enough to be breakfast time as far as we were concerned, so we could never eat a bite.

"You should start eating more at lunch-time," Sonia told me seriously one day. "It says on page thirty-six that 'lovely ladies should be the perfect weight, not too thin, not too heavy.' Since you're the perfect weight now, if you stop eating, you'll get too thin."

"Okay, okay." I sighed, picking up my fork. Sonia had been nagging me for days with this book and I was growing tired of it.

"What's okay?" came a voice over my shoulder. I looked up, surprised. It was Jeff.

"Is this the 'third clarinets only' table? Or can anyone sit here?" Jeff asked.

Sonia, Cynthia, and I burst out laughing.

"You're allowed to sit here," Cynthia said. "Some nonclarinet players are welcome."

"Gee, thanks," Jeff said. "Do you girls do everything together these days?"

"Not everything," Sonia replied. "Just most things."

"You have a study group, right?" Jeff asked.

"It's a practice group. We're helping each other to become better musicians," Cynthia said. At least that was our intention, although we ended up just having a gossip session most times we got together.

"I bet you do a lot of yapping during these sessions."

"Who, us?" Sonia pretended to be deeply offended.

"I have a joke for you," Jeff said. "Why should you never gossip in a stable?"

We all shrugged our shoulders.

"Because all horses carry tails."

"That's a great joke, Jeff," Sonia said rolling her eyeballs, while Cynthia and I groaned loudly. "I didn't know you knew any jokes."

"Just a couple." Jeff grinned. "So, Mad, how's the drama stuff going?"

"It's going, going, gone." I sighed. "No time for it with all the music practicing I have to do." I turned to look at my friends. They were busy looking at the latest fashions in *Seventeen*.

"Aw, come on, Mad. No time to even go to the movies?" Jeff coaxed. I realized I had never noticed what a nice green his eyes were.

I shrugged. "Not really. And I *love* the movies."

"Me too!" Jeff said excitedly. "What kind of movies do you like?"

"Anything with Tom Cruise in it!" I exclaimed. "I loved *Rain Man*. Did you see it? Dustin Hoffman was excellent, too."

"I liked it a lot," Jeff said, "but not as much as *Fame*."

I practically choked on my orange juice.

43

"*Fame?* Jeff, do you know how old that movie is?"

"Sure, but it's a musical, and I *love* musicals. Plus, it took place at the High School of Performing Arts, and I almost went there," he explained.

"Did you really? You mean, you got in and all, but decided not to go?"

"Yup."

"Why didn't you?"

"I didn't want to be with only art people. After all, I love science and history, too," he said.

"That was exactly why I decided not to go, too," George said, appearing out of nowhere and taking a seat right next to me. I wanted to act normal, but I knew it was going to be difficult with him sitting so close by.

"You auditioned for Performing Arts, George?" Jeff looked perplexed, which was exactly the way I felt. I couldn't believe George had lunch this period, and that he had overheard the conversation between me and Jeff, and that Sonia and Cynthia were oblivious to all of this!

George nodded. "I auditioned on the piano, though. But I decided that I wanted to be with regular people—not just talented ones, like Jeff," he said.

Jeff didn't even acknowledge the compliment. It didn't seem fair when George was being so nice. "Listen, I have to go," Jeff said abruptly, getting up, tray in hand. He had hardly eaten.

"Oh, before I forget, I'll be playing at Snooky's this Saturday night," George told us. "My brother and I will be doing some jazz together."

"I'll try to make it," Jeff said, but his voice told me that he wouldn't. I wondered what was bothering him.

"Sonia, Cynthia, did you hear?" George called across the table.

"You've told us about Snooky's at least a hundred times, George," Sonia said in an exasperated tone.

"Sorry, I was just so excited," he apologized.

Excited and exciting, I thought. The cafeteria bell rang and we all got up to go to our next classes.

"Well, I'll be there," I told George.

"Thanks." He smiled, and his whole face lit up.

Wherever you go, I'll follow, I added silently.

Chapter Five

"Da, da, da, *da,*" I sang at the top of my lungs, accompanied by Beethoven's Fifth Symphony. I stood in front of my mirror, mouthing the sounds blasting out from my stereo. The music took me miles away. . . . I was playing as first clarinet in the school statewide competition. There were only a few students involved in this special exhibition for talented students, and of course, I was one of them. George was particularly impressed because I had been asked to sing, conduct, *and* play my clarinet. It was spring, and I was wearing my white linen dress.

"Da, da, da, *da,*" I screeched. It was Sunday, and I felt like I could spend my whole day just singing away.

My father walked into the room. "What's going on, Maddy?" There was an unspoken rule in our house that you weren't supposed to enter anyone's room without knocking, like my dad had just done, but I didn't have the energy to argue. I lowered the volume of the stereo. "I'm practicing."

"This is what you call practicing?" He pointed to my bed, where a dozen classical records were strewn around. I had checked out a lot of them from the Brooklyn Public Library; I thought they might help train my ear.

"Well, sort of." I looked up at the ceiling, down at the floor, anywhere but into my father's eyes.

"Since when do you like classical music?"

Since I met George, I said to myself. "Dad, listen, I just want to learn how to play," I said instead.

"Your mother and I have always loved music. We both play, and we've always encouraged you to. What's so confusing is that you were never interested before."

"Yeah, but now I *need* to play," I said, before I could stop myself.

"Why should someone need to play?" my father asked, confused.

I shrugged my shoulders. "Just because." I wished I could come up with a better answer.

My dad is a pretty neat guy. In fact, my whole family is very open and I could talk to them about anything. Still, there was no way on earth he would understand my taking a class just for a guy.

"The only reason I'm concerned is that lately you don't seem to be studying much else. Also, we hardly see Lisa around these days. Is anything wrong between the two of you?"

"No, why?" We *had* been seeing less of each other, but she was busy with her science project, and I was just plain busy.

"I'm just curious. You two used to speak on the phone about ten times a day. And what about your grades?" my father inquired again.

After only a few weeks of band class, my grades were dropping just a little. I had always been a pretty good student without trying very hard, but my luck was running out.

"I know you wanted to get some advanced placement credit as a senior; you'll never be able to at this rate," my father went on.

"Columbia will take me with or without A.P. credit," I hedged.

"Sure, but they won't accept you with marginal grades."

I felt all the wrong keys going off inside me at once, and to make matters worse, my brother Steve charged into the room.

"Do you need help with your instrument?" he asked me.

"Not from you! Besides, you don't know how to play the clarinet." I practically shoved him out the door.

"Maybe so, but I bet I can still play it better

48

than you," Steve retorted. "So could a chimpanzee!"

"Get out!" I cried. "Dad, please make him leave."

"Madeline is tone deaf, nah, nah, nah, nah!" Steve chanted.

"Out!" I screamed.

My father followed Steve out the door and started to reprimand him, but it didn't make any difference to me. Steve was right. I was still hopelessly bad at the clarinet. I started to cry. A few seconds later, my mother was by my side.

"What's wrong, honey?" She stroked my hair. "No class is worth this agony."

"It's not that."

"What is it, then?" she asked gently.

I looked into her large, sympathetic hazel eyes. She was so understanding. I knew that I could tell her about George, but if I did, I also knew she'd ask me about him all the time. This was a pattern we'd established way back in second grade. My mother had helped me get over my first boyfriend. Unfortunately, she felt it was her business to know everything about every boyfriend I had from then on.

"If it's a guy, it's not worth all this grief either, you know. Remember Scott Smith in the second grade? If you could get over him, you can get over anyone," she said.

I didn't know whether to laugh or cry. She was wrong—George *was* worth it. Instead, I stopped my tears and whispered, "I really do want to learn the clarinet, Mom."

"Then we're behind you all the way." She squeezed my shoulders and smiled at me.

"Thanks, Mom."

"Don't worry, everything will work out if you just keep trying."

My mother's a wonderful person, but at the moment I just didn't believe everything would work out fine. I needed to talk to Lisa. I knew she would understand. After my mother left my room I got on the phone and dialed her number.

"Hi Lise, what's up?" I said when she answered.

"Nothing much."

"I haven't spoken to you in such a long time," I said nervously. "How come?"

"I guess we've both been pretty busy," she said, her voice sounding distant.

"Yeah." I took a deep breath. "So, what have you been up to?"

"Well, I'm going on a date," she said.

"Really! With whom?" I tried to sound interested and excited, but I felt really bad. Lisa hadn't even called to tell me she was dating anyone!

"Just a guy from my history class."

"Oh. Does he have a name?" I asked. She

was acting very oddly. "What's going on, Lisa? Why are we talking like we're strangers?" I blurted out.

"I don't know. I hardly hear from you these days," Lisa said.

"I've been practicing."

"Every afternoon and night?"

The truth was, I had been going to Pino's most afternoons with my new friends. And I *was* practicing every night, or trying to. "Listen, you've been busy practically every afternoon, too," I reminded her.

"I know. Oh, Mad, let's not fight. I'll talk to you soon. I have to run and get ready for my date."

"Yeah, sure." I hung up the phone. I felt sick. So much for Lisa understanding! I lay down on my bed and stared at the ceiling. After a while my eyes drifted to my giant black and white photographs of Spencer Tracy, Cary Grant, Greta Garbo, and Katharine Hepburn. I must have stared at them for an hour. When I finally looked at the clock, it was almost four o'clock. I was growing restless. It was too sad to be alone.

I decided to go to Pino's and see if any of the gang was there. When I got there, though, none of my friends were around. I got a soda and sat down anyway, surrounded by the buzzing voices of other people having a great time. I sipped my drink and thought about band. Maybe I should just drop the class. After all, I could get by with taking seven classes. I wouldn't be able to graduate early, but on the other hand, I probably wouldn't be so nervous. My grades would improve, my parents would stop worrying, I'd get along better with my brother, and Lisa and I would probably go back to being best friends.

But what about my new friends? Jeff had promised to take me to a musical on Broadway. I loved gossiping and eating pizza with Sonia and Cynthia. And what about George, who was the reason I was in this mess to begin with? I had never met anyone like him before, and I probably wouldn't ever again. One minute he was friendly, and the next minute he ignored me. I had gone to see him and his brother perform, and he'd acted as if I were a stranger. Was he worth all this aggravation? I rubbed my temples. My brain was killing me from thinking so much!

"How's my favorite musician?"

I looked up. Like magic, George had appeared and was standing next to my chair. I was speechless.

"I was walking down Seventh Avenue and I noticed your beautiful hair. It looked so pretty I just had to come in."

"My hair?" I asked. I had never thought of it as special. It was long, brown, and terribly curly. I used to try to straighten it, but that took at least two hours and I usually gave up before then.

"So, what's up, Maddy?"

I could feel butterflies floating in my stomach. Had he really come into Pino's for me and my hair? "Not much," I managed to say, and then felt like kicking myself. *He's really going to think you're exciting now,* I thought. *Say something else!* But my mind went blank. I could feel a blush creeping across my face as George stared at me.

To my relief, George broke the silence. "Don't you think Walker is a kooky guy?" he asked playfully.

"He sure is!"

"Don't let him make you nervous," he said.

"I won't," I replied. Mr. Walker wasn't the one who made me nervous!

George gestured toward the counter. "Can I join you for a slice? Can I get you anything?"

"I'd love another soda, thanks." I wondered if I should have said *love.* I didn't want him to think I was throwing myself at him.

George returned with my soda, several large slices of pizza, and an ice.

"You can eat all of that?" I was shocked.

"I need to eat all of this. It helps with weight lifting." George showed me his muscle, and then started laughing. "That was pretty tacky, wasn't it?" He swallowed half a slice of pizza in one enormous gulp. I sipped my soda, a

53

drop at a time. I wanted it to last forever. I wanted this moment to last forever. I couldn't believe that I had ever contemplated dropping band!

"So, how do you like the class?" George asked.

"Oh, I love it," I said breezily.

"I can understand why." George grinned after inhaling another slice of pizza. "Walker's a neat guy, and we have a tight group of people and a few very funny guys."

"Who could you possibly be referring to, George?" I found myself growing bolder.

"Oh, no one in particular," he said. "By the way, I forgot to ask you—what did the beaver say to the tree?"

"I have absolutely no idea."

"It's been nice gnawing you!"

"Oh, no!" It was such a corny joke that it was actually funny. I felt a little less nervous. "Do you tell jokes all the time?"

"No. Only most of the time. What do you like to do?"

"Go to the theater, watch movies, dance, ice skate." I tried to come up with things I thought George might enjoy, too.

"Then we share one common interest aside from band." George slurped down the last remains of his ice.

"What's that?" I felt hopeful and expectant.

"I love to dance. Look, it's getting dark," George observed.

I turned around and gazed out the window. A brilliant twilight filled the sky. I couldn't believe how quickly the time had passed.

"Want to get going?" He held out his hand and helped me up from my seat. We walked out of Pino's together.

"Good night," he said softly. "I'm glad I ran into you."

"Me too," I replied. "Good night." Then we walked our separate ways. Only I didn't walk, I glided home. Once again, fate had brought George and me together. I thought our story would make a terrific movie.

The next day when I woke up, I was deliriously happy. I hummed tunes as I got ready for school.

"Are you okay?" my brother asked, peeking into my room before he left.

"I'm fine!" I sang out. He looked at me as if I were crazy. I didn't care. Nothing could upset me. I was in love!

As I walked to school, I thought the world was a wonderful place. It was starting to warm up, spring would be coming soon and best of all, *George liked me.* I was in such bliss, I didn't see where I was going and practically tumbled on top of Lisa, who was sitting on the front steps of Robert Moses High School.

"Hi, how was your date?" I said as casually as I could. I tried to make believe our awkward phone conversation had never happened. If I ignored it, maybe things would be okay.

"It wasn't." She looked pretty gloomy.

"I'm sorry. What happened?" I sat down next to her.

"He rescheduled it for this coming Friday. I'm not sure I trust him now. So, any developments with the guy in band?" she asked, trying to look more cheerful.

I told her the pizza parlor story. I was so excited, I couldn't get the words out fast enough.

"Sounds promising." Lisa smiled. "I'm really happy for you. I bet you can't wait for band class today."

"I'm counting the minutes. Listen, I want you to come to my house this Saturday afternoon. I'd like you to meet my new friends. Then you can tell me all about your date."

"If it happens." She stood up. "I've got to run. Saturday sounds great. I'll see you then." She gave me a friendly pat on the arm and left.

My life had turned around completely in the last twenty-four hours, and I was glad. Not only was the outlook very optimistic with

George, but everything was back to normal with me and Lisa.

I walked into band class expectantly. George was at the far end of the room talking to his friends. I looked over at him, hoping he would see me and wave, but he didn't even stop to acknowledge me. It was almost as if he were ignoring me. I knew that yesterday at Pino's had to mean something, yet . . .

I slumped in my seat, unable to muster any enthusiasm for warm-ups.

"What's wrong?" Sonia asked. My face must have been a dead giveaway. *Why couldn't George be so observant?* I wondered.

"I can't play!" I complained. "I'm pressing the right keys on the clarinet, but horrible noises are coming out!"

"Big deal!"

"What do you mean? It *is* a big deal!" I said angrily.

"Fake it," Cynthia said.

"What's that supposed to mean? I'm faking it already. I'm tone deaf."

"I figured," Sonia said nonchalantly. "You can fool everyone if you just put your fingers on the correct keys and keep up with the rhythm, but just pretend to blow into the mouthpiece."

"You mean I can do that and still not get caught?" I asked.

"Are you kidding? People fake all the time!" Sonia explained.

I spent the next few minutes perfecting my faking technique. While I was busy doing that, Sonia told me that she had a new plan of action for the George situation.

I took my lips off the mouthpiece and breathed a sigh of relief. "My savior! What's the plan?"

"I'll tell you when I come over on Saturday."

When I was packing up the instruments in the storage room at the end of class, I didn't know whether to feel happy or sad. Sonia had a new plan of action, but it seemed as if George had forgotten all about our rendez-vous at Pino's. I hadn't thought I would need a plan after that.

Just then Jeff appeared by my side. "What's up?" he asked. He had an unusual knack for appearing at just the right moment. He was wearing a V-neck sweater that was exactly the same shade of green as his eyes.

"I was just thinking . . ." I stopped. How could I possibly go on? How could I possibly tell Jeff about my crush on George?

"I bet you were thinking about how tough it is learning to play a musical instrument."

"That's *one* of the things I was thinking about." I could tell Jeff knew I wasn't being completely truthful.

"I know it's difficult. Sometimes those notes just don't come out."

"Yeah." I sighed.

"Why don't you let me help you? I know how to play all the wind instruments."

I thought about it. I could sure use help, in more ways than one.

At that moment, George stepped into the room. "Don't forget to practice your dancing—and keep that gorgeous hair down!"

I smiled. "Okay," I said. Then George was gone, as quickly as he had appeared.

I turned to Jeff, who didn't look amused. "Thanks for offering your help, but I think I'll pass," I said.

"Okay," he said, making a fast exit. "See you tomorrow."

I hardly noticed him leaving. I didn't need to work on my clarinet playing, now that George liked me!

Chapter Six

"We're going to 'Madify' you," Sonia said, sweeping my hair up on top of my head. "This means a complete make-over, including dance lessons and an introduction to the art of telling jokes." Sonia, Cynthia, and I were lounging around my room. It was a dreary, rainy Saturday, and we couldn't bring ourselves to practice music.

"We need background music," I noted, turning on the stereo.

The doorbell rang. "Oh, it's Lisa," I told my friends. "I forgot to tell you I invited her over." I raced down the stairs and opened the door. "Come on up," I said, tugging at her arm.

"Don't I even get to take off my coat?" she asked.

"No. How was your date?" I charged up the stairs ahead of her.

"Awful."

"Why?"

"We went out for pizza, and he asked *me* to pay for both of us! Plus, he was incredibly boring and he didn't ask me one single thing about *me*," Lisa said.

"What a loser! How did you manage to keep your eyes open?"

"I hardly did."

I laughed. "He sounds really different from George. Come on." I almost pulled her into my room. "Sonia and Cynthia, meet my best friend, Lisa."

"I've heard so much about you," Sonia exclaimed.

"I've seen you around school, too," Lisa replied quietly.

"We're beautifying Madeline," Cynthia said.

"I think Mad's fine just the way she is." Lisa smiled coolly. I could tell she was upset, but I couldn't figure out what was bothering her.

"We're not just beautifying Maddy," Sonia explained to Lisa. "We're going to give her a new look in terms of clothes. And we're also going to teach her some jokes, since George is a real funny guy."

"Oh." Lisa was eyeing Sonia as if she thought Sonia was very strange.

"Okay, Maddy, listen. You have to start wearing a lot of black and white—no bright colors," Sonia continued. "Black and white are *the* New York colors."

"I suppose you're going to tell me something about my makeup, too," I said, smiling.

"Yup," Sonia said. "You can't wear red lip gloss. You need to wear subtle makeup." Sonia was very dogmatic about everything. Still, I had to trust her. George had asked her out on a date last year, so she must have done something right.

"Oh, I meant to tell you about this. You have to hear this one!" Sonia exclaimed, interrupting herself and jumping up on the bed. Lisa sat down on the floor and took her biology book out of her knapsack.

"If it's coming from the gossip queen, it has to be good," Cynthia said, grinning at me.

"Mr. Walker and Miss Quinn are dating!" Sonia announced.

"You're kidding!" I said. Miss Quinn was our gym teacher, and she was very strange.

"How do you know?" Cynthia asked.

"I just know." Sonia smiled mysteriously.

"They've got to be the most mismatched pair in the universe!" I shrieked.

"Wait. If you think that's bad, you have to hear about an even more unlikely couple," Sonia added. "Would you believe, Ira Reiser and Laura Blumberg?"

Ira played the trumpet. He was Jeff's friend, and a lot like him: he was quiet, serious, and sweet. Laura was the biggest talker in class—besides Sonia, of course—and a drummer in the band.

"Now I've heard everything." Cynthia sighed. "If Laura can land a guy, I certainly can."

"Okay, enough band gossip. It's time for Cynthia and me to make Maddy a comedian," Sonia declared. "Here's the first joke. What are two things you can never have for breakfast?" She held up two fingers in the air.

"Beats me." Cynthia shrugged.

"Lunch and dinner."

I giggled. "That one's so stupid, it's funny."

"Remember, the joke teller never laughs," Sonia said in a serious voice. "Okay, what do you call a cat that drinks lemonade?"

"This one I know," Cynthia said. "A sour puss."

I groaned.

"And finally," Sonia continued, ignoring both of us, "what did the ocean say to the shore?"

Cynthia and I shook our heads.

"Nothing." Sonia raised one hand in the air. "It just waved."

All three of us started laughing uncontrollably. Then I realized that Lisa hadn't said a word for a long time. She was sitting on the floor, completely engrossed in her biology book.

I stopped laughing.

"Do you have an exam?" I asked her.

"No," she responded, not looking up from her book.

"Then why are you studying?"

"I like biology."

Cynthia and Sonia were quiet, listening to the conversation. I desperately wanted Lisa to talk, really talk to me. "Do you like my hair this way?" Cynthia had braided it so that I had one long strand hanging from the top of my head.

Lisa finally looked up. "It's okay," she said indifferently.

I felt horrible. I had no idea what I had done to make her act like this.

"Maybe we could do your hair, too," Cynthia told Lisa.

"That's okay," Lisa said.

The silence was deafening.

"Actually, you two share a lot of interests," I told Lisa and Cynthia, trying to be as enthusiastic as possible.

"Like what?" Cynthia seemed eager to please.

"Well, music," I said animatedly. "You both love music."

"That depends. I like classical," Lisa said dryly.

"I like rock." Cynthia shrugged her shoulders.

"I give up." I sighed. "Let's work on my hair. I'm not wild about this hairdo."

"Let's work on your interests," Sonia suggested. "George is a jazz lover. We're going to have to teach you a lot about jazz." She opened her knapsack and took out a few records.

I picked up an album and looked at the cover. "Winton Marsalis? Who's he?"

Lisa was shocked. "You've never heard of him?"

I shook my head.

"I've never heard of him either," Cynthia admitted.

"Well, I guess Cynthia and I have something in common—jazz ignorance," I said sheepishly.

Lisa smiled and I felt good. The atmosphere was getting better. Then my mom burst into the room with a plate of freshly baked chocolate chip cookies.

"You didn't knock," I reminded her.

"Sorry!" She smiled. "I just wanted to get these to you right away." She held out the plate and we took the cookies, muttering thanks between bites.

"What are you girls so busy with?" my mother asked. She raised her eyebrows when she noticed my hairdo, but didn't comment.

"Just fooling around," Cynthia told her.

"Could this have anything to do with a guy—or band?"

I gulped. Why did my mother seem so clueless one day and so brilliant the next? "No, Mom," I said. "Thanks for the snack." I gave her a meaningful look.

My mother hastily exited the room, carrying the empty plate with her.

"Mothers!" I cried out after she had left.

"I know," Cynthia said.

Lisa opened one of her books again and started reading. I couldn't figure out if she really *did* have a test coming up, or if she was just avoiding me.

"What's happening in school?" I asked her.

"Well," Lisa said, looking up reluctantly, "I have a new lab partner and he's really cute. And smart, too."

It was going to be tough to get Lisa off the topic of biology. "What's his name?" I asked, trying to sound interested.

"Jeff Lang."

"Oh, I know Jeff!" I told Lisa. "He's really sweet, and he's an incredible flute player. But I wouldn't exactly call him cute." I turned to Sonia and Cynthia, who nodded their heads in agreement.

"What's wrong with Jeff's looks?" Lisa asked. There was a biting tone in her voice.

"Oh, his hair is too straight," I declared.

"What else?"

"His eyes are a wishy-washy green." I thought about it some more. "And his nose is slightly crooked."

"You mean he's not perfect?" Lisa snapped.

"That's it. He's not perfect."

"I know George Held is absolutely perfect, though," Lisa said, her voice dripping with sarcasm.

I had had it with Lisa's nasty tone. "What's that supposed to mean?" I demanded.

"You're only interested in *perfect* guys who look like movie stars," Lisa said accusingly.

"That's not true!" I shouted. Of course, I had plenty of movie star fantasies, but the guys I usually dated weren't that glamorous.

Lisa grabbed her coat and yelled, "Oh, grow up, Mad. It's true, and you know it!" She gathered up the rest of her things and left, slamming the door.

Cynthia and Sonia were quiet for a moment. "What was that all about?" Sonia finally asked.

I felt like crying, but I wasn't about to let Lisa ruin my day. She had such an incredible nerve, implying that I was shallow. She didn't understand at all. George was the real thing! I forced myself to shrug my shoulders.

"I have absolutely no idea," I said as lightly as I could. "She's not usually like that." *Not until she met the two of you,* I thought. *Could my best friend be jealous?* It didn't seem possible. Lisa was too mature for that. I felt disappointed. I had looked forward to my band friends meeting Lisa for so long, and when it had happened it had been a complete disaster.

"Come on," Cynthia said, trying to cheer me up, "let's take the bus to Macy's. We have a lot of serious shopping to do!"

"I'm ready," I said, grabbing my jacket.

Chapter Seven

"I like your outfit," George said as I walked past him on the way to my seat.

"Thanks." I could feel my cheeks flush. I was wearing my Macy's special: gray leggings, a long black turtleneck, and black and gray striped socks. Sonia and Cynthia had decided it was a knockout outfit, and now I had to agree.

There was some chaos before warm-ups in class that day. While Mr. Walker was busy sorting out sheet music, we used the opportunity to make the rounds and chat. Just as I was about to tell Cynthia what George had said, Jeff pulled up a chair and sat down next to me.

"Black is a good color on you," he said. "If you could call it a color."

I laughed.

"What's so funny?" he wanted to know.

"You're so literal, questioning whether or not black is a color."

With a serious look, Jeff said, "But black and white aren't really colors, you know."

"I know, I know." I smiled. I thought he might launch into a long scientific lecture about colors, since now I knew science was another of his passions.

"So, how are you managing?" Jeff asked. I wondered what he meant by the word *managing*. Was he talking about my pitiful musical ability, or did he know something about me and George?

"Okay, I guess." I tried to sound cool and confident. "What about yourself?"

"I'm all right. I just wish there was more time to practice music and read. But between work and school, there's not enough time left over."

"You work, too? Doing what?" I was impressed.

"Just delivering newspapers in the morning. It's no big deal." He was about to say more when Mr. Walker recruited him to help sort music. He left at exactly the right moment, because the next minute George was at my side.

"Let's go to Pino's together after class," he said.

I felt my heart leap inside my chest until he added, "I'm asking Sonia and Cynthia, too, because the three of you have the best taste in the class. I figured if we all brainstormed together, we could decide what kind of gift to get Mr. Walker. After all, our first performance is in a few weeks."

Don't remind me, I thought to myself. I didn't want to be faking the clarinet for the big performance. That wasn't the only thing that was making me feel bad, either. My outfit was terrific, and I was wearing just the right amount of makeup, but apparently I still wasn't special enough to go to Pino's with George alone. Still, I had no choice but to go with the gang. It was that or nothing. "Sure, we'll meet after class," I told George.

"Great." He seemed genuinely excited and his brown eyes flashed when he grinned.

Suddenly Mr. Walker shouted, "Warm-up time, everyone!" and George dashed back to his seat.

"We'll start with the theme from *An American Tale*," Mr. Walker announced. "I know you all know this piece by heart since we've played it dozens of times before."

It was actually my favorite piece. It was so beautiful that I wished I really *did* know how to play it. In the middle of the theme, George stood up and began to jazz up the music. Soon he was joined by his best friends.

"Stop it, George!" Mr. Walker cried, looking at Jonathan.

"I'm not George!" Jonathan replied between notes.

Mr. Walker was so upset by Jonathan's answer that he walked over to Ricardo's trombone and started yelling at it.

"Mr. Walker, I'm right here!" George shouted. By now everyone had stopped playing. "I think we're going to have to make a trip to the store this afternoon for a pair of new glasses," he told Mr. Walker affectionately.

Even Mr. Walker had to hold back a smile. He might not have realized how absent-minded he was, but he did know his vision wasn't perfect.

"Leave him alone," Jeff snapped. "Without him, all of you would still be playing scales." I had never heard such an angry tone in his voice.

"I know that, Lang. Don't get so bent out of shape. It was only a joke," George replied.

"Well, it wasn't funny," Jeff retorted.

"Both of you—be quiet!" Mr. Walker ordered. He returned to the podium and tapped his baton against the stand. "Let's get back to the music."

After I had put away the instruments, Cynthia and I headed for Pino's. George and Sonia were meeting us there. I couldn't stop thinking about the scene in class that afternoon. Jeff was right. Mr. Walker was a nice man and he worked very hard for our class. There was too much fooling around going on, and it was almost always at his expense. Yet Mr. Walker didn't seem to mind. Sometimes he teased George and his friends back.

When we arrived, I was still deep in thought. We gave George our orders and he left the table to pick them up. He returned a few minutes later carrying a tray laden with slices of pizza and sodas, deposited the food on the table, and started talking.

"What's Jeff Lang's problem?" he wanted to know.

"He's just a little too serious," Sonia said.

"He sure is," Cynthia commented.

"I mean," Sonia muttered between bites, "you can't even fool around in class with him."

"But it's a *class*, after all. People should take it more seriously," I said, surprising myself with how defensive I sounded. Jeff was my friend. So what if he was a serious person?

"Oh, please!" Sonia cried. "Who's talking about taking *music* seriously?"

"I'm not talking about music, I'm talking about the class and Mr. Walker. Look at how much he's helped all of you," I said.

"But we all *like* Mr. Walker," Sonia insisted. "That's not the point. George adores him, and vice versa."

"That's the truth. I like Mr. Walker a lot. I like Jeff, too. I just think he ought to lighten up a little. Let's drop it, okay?" George seemed irritated.

"Fine." I wanted to end the discussion as well. I was mad that I couldn't be alone with George, but I was also annoyed that everyone seemed to be picking on Jeff. I poked at the crust of my pizza with a straw.

"I hope you're not mad at me, Maddy."

I glanced up at George. He had an anxious look on his face and a drop of sauce on the tip of his nose. I took my napkin and wiped off the sauce. "Why should I be mad at you?"

"I don't know." He shrugged. "I do tend to go overboard sometimes."

I smiled. "As long as you don't sink, I don't care."

"Maybe you can save me if I ever start to," he said.

I laughed. Out of the corner of my eye, I saw smiles on Cynthia's and Sonia's faces. I was glad we were all on the same side again.

"You're having some trouble in band, aren't you?" George asked me.

"A little," I admitted.

"Well, if you need a tutor, let me know. I love teaching people music," he said.

"It might help, Maddy," Sonia said. "A little extra help, especially from such a great musician, never hurt anyone."

I was so thrilled by the idea that I didn't know what to say. Before I could find my voice, George said, "Now, on to crucial decisions. What should we get Mr. Walker?"

"What about some new clothes?" Cynthia suggested. We all burst out laughing. Mr. Walker was a terrible dresser.

"Wait, wait, I have it!" Sonia cried. "What about a pocket watch?"

"That sounds great," George responded, so enthusiastically that I wished it had been my idea. I wanted to impress George with something—anything! "Excellent," he continued. "Let's make a date to shop for it together. From now on, Mr. Walker will get to class on time! You know what, Mad?" he added, turning to me. "We make a great team."

I grinned sheepishly. It hadn't even been my idea, but if he didn't remember, I wasn't going to correct him. I walked home in a daze. Things were finally working out between George and me! I was so excited that I couldn't sleep that night.

But the next day in class, once again George barely seemed to notice my entrance. During warm-ups, he started improvising some jazz dance music, and a group of other students started playing along.

"Enough!" Mr. Walker yelled, but he couldn't make himself heard over the noise. The students who weren't playing started dancing around the room. It looked like a scene out of a movie. I looked over at Jeff, but he was frowning. Sometimes I just couldn't figure him out. You would think that he would enjoy watching these talented people having a good time, especially since he was so talented himself. His reaction reminded me of Lisa. She would hate this scene, too. She was serious, like Jeff. I hadn't heard much from her since the time I'd invited here to meet Sonia and Cynthia. I still couldn't understand what was going on between us.

George danced as he played, and as I watched him I decided I wanted him to be my tutor. I'd tell him after class.

"Time to play!" Mr. Walker shouted, his voice struggling to rise above the volume in the classroom. He hit his hand against the music stand as if it were a baton.

George saw what happened and stopped playing. "Ouch!" he cried. The other students stopped playing one by one.

Mr. Walker shook his fingers and winced. After a moment he said, "Madeline, I'd like to see you after class."

Me? What had I done wrong? I hadn't been involved in the scene at all. I shrugged and began faking the piece we were working on that day with unusual enthusiasm.

"Cynthia, please put away the instruments

today," Mr. Walker said when class was over. "Madeline?"

I crept up to the front. Everyone else was getting their things together and leaving.

"Madeline, I'm aware that you had a few private lessons, but it's different working in a group. I think you need a lot more help with group work," Mr Walker began.

"Really?" I said.

"Yes. So I have taken the liberty of assigning you a tutor."

I smiled inwardly and thought, *And guess who asked to tutor me, just yesterday?* When I hadn't jumped at his offer, George had obviously decided to try another way. "Who will that be?" I asked. *As if I didn't know!*

"Jeff Lang," Mr. Walker said.

"Jeff?" I gasped.

Why hadn't I dropped band on day one, like I had planned?

Chapter Eight

"Play it, Sam."

As Humphrey Bogart spoke, I felt my heart do somersaults. It was Saturday morning, and I was in my room watching *Casablanca* on television. No matter how many times I watched that movie, it still sent chills up my spine, especially when Bogart gazed into Ingrid Bergman's eyes. They were in love, the kind of love George and I could have shared, if Mr. Walker hadn't ruined everything by giving me Jeff as a tutor.

Being tutored by George would have been an opportunity to know him better. But Jeff was a friend, and I didn't need to know him better. He was so serious that I knew the tutoring sessions would be serious as well, and that thought didn't thrill me. The door-bell rang and I heard my brother muttering something as he answered it downstairs.

A minute later, Jeff casually walked into my room. "Wow! *Casablanca!*" he exclaimed. "I love this movie! 'Play it, Sam,' " he said, in a perfect imitation of Humphrey Bogart.

I giggled. "That was great. Do you study voice, too?"

"Sometimes." He shrugged. "Actually, I just love old movies. I've seen this film at least a dozen times."

He took a seat next to me on the floor, and we started acting out segments of the film. I knew the lines a lot better than Jeff, though. The entire time, Jeff's eyes were glued to the screen, as if he were watching the movie for the first time.

"What a great love story," he said at the end of the film.

"Yeah. I love a great love story." I thought about me and George.

"Me too," Jeff said. I was surprised. Jeff didn't seem like the kind of guy who would like romantic things. But I was relieved, too, because I figured tutoring wouldn't be so bad after all. Jeff and I shared a lot of interests.

"Why did you say you wanted to stick it out in the class?" he asked me.

"My whole family is musically talented, aside from me and my sister Stacy. You know what it's like being an outsider?"

"Sure, I know."

"Come on, let's go into the living room." I led him down the stairs and sat on the couch. Jeff sat down next to me. "What do you mean, you know how I feel? I don't understand," I said.

"You know," he said, flushing slightly. "I've always felt a little different—because I like the flute so much. It's not exactly a popular instrument. So sometimes I feel like an outsider, too."

"Oh, that's ridiculous. You shouldn't feel that way," I said. He was different, though. He wasn't part of George's crowd—or *any* crowd, for that matter. I gazed into his intense green eyes.

He looked away. "Come on, let's start," he said. "Take out your clarinet. We have just a month to learn 'Greensleeves' and 'Rhapsody in Blue.' Oh, and a few Sousa marches, too."

Take out my clarinet? I panicked. I was embarrassed by the prospect of Jeff finding out I was tone deaf. But even worse, he would discover that I hadn't been playing all these weeks in class.

Fortunately, my mother managed to save the day. She barged into the living room just as I was taking the clarinet out of its case and cleaning the mouthpiece. "Would you like something to eat?" she asked. "You must be—"

"Mom, meet Jeff Lang. He's my tutor."

"Nice to meet you, Mrs. Davis." Jeff stood

79

up and shook my mother's hand. He was very polite and I was very relieved. I had been afraid that my mom would think Jeff was George. I had finally broken down and told her that I liked a boy in my band class named George. The last thing I had said on the subject was that I thought George was going to tutor me. I hadn't yet told her about the change in plans.

"No thank you, Mrs. Davis. We have a lot of practicing to do," Jeff was saying.

"Well, let me know if you want anything," my mother said.

"We will." He smiled at her.

"Maybe we should go back up to my room and work there," I said, stalling for time. "There'll be too many interruptions in the living room."

But Jeff knew what I was doing. "Enough!" he commanded. "Start playing. Why don't you try starting with 'Rhapsody'?"

I decided to tell him the truth, as humiliating as it was. "Jeff?" I said. "You're not going to believe this, but I don't know the finger movements."

"What have you been doing these past few weeks? Faking it?"

I nodded.

I was so anxious that I was actually clutching the instrument. He gently pried my fingers loose from the clarinet. He went over the finger movements one by one, slowly at first, but then faster each time. After each time, he made me imitate both the timing and the movement of his fingers. We did it so many times that my fingers ached. Within an hour's time, I knew the fingering and pacing for 'Rhapsody.'

"Okay, now let's try it with the wind," he said.

"What?" I looked at him with a puzzled expression.

"Blow into your clarinet *and* use your fingers. In other words, play."

"Oh." I was nervous, but I decided to try my hardest. A squeak emerged, then another. It sounded awful.

"Calm down." Jeff touched my shoulder. "It happens to everyone."

"Does it?" I felt a little better, even though I was sure it had never happened to George.

"Sure. Beginners always squeak."

But beginners aren't always tone deaf, I thought.

"Let's try it again," he suggested.

We played the opening bars to the piece at least a hundred times. Jeff was a great teacher. He was very patient, and my squeaks didn't seem to bother him at all. By the time he left at four o'clock, I was worn out. He was really serious about what he was doing. We had hardly spoken all afternoon, except about the music. If George had been my tutor, I knew we would have had a lot more fun.

"Are you up for this tomorrow?" Jeff asked as I walked him to the front door.

"Not really." I sighed. I was completely exhausted. "But I guess I have no choice."

"You might surprise yourself." He smiled encouragingly. "You might begin to like this."

Or George might begin to like me, so it'll be worth it, I thought. "Maybe," I said. "The world is filled with surprises. See you tomorrow."

"See you."

As soon as Jeff left, I called Lisa. I missed talking to her, and I hoped that if I made the first move, she would forget what had happened last Saturday. I wanted to tell her everything that had happened: the tutoring sessions, my disappointment with George, how serious Jeff was, and how my fingers throbbed from pressing the keys.

"Hello," Lisa said, answering the phone.

"It's me, Mad," I said.

"Oh." Lisa's voice took on a cool tone.

"What's wrong?" I asked.

"Nothing. Everything's okay."

But everything wasn't okay. We had hardly been talking at all since Saturday, and I was determined to get things back to normal between us. The best way to do that was to act as if nothing had happened. "You're not going to believe this," I said.

"What?" Lisa said, sounding bored.

I decided to ignore her mood. "You know

Jeff, your lab partner from biology class? Well, Mr. Walker decided I needed extra tutoring, so he asked Jeff to be my tutor."

"So what?"

"So what? So George is the most talented person in my band class. Why couldn't he tutor me?" I asked. I was beginning to feel a little annoyed at her.

"I don't know." Lisa sounded as if she didn't care, either.

"Actually, I'm worried," I continued. "I've never failed any class before. What if I fail band? I'll never be able to get into a good college. What am I going to do?"

"You got yourself into this mess. Figure it out for yourself," Lisa said impatiently.

"Hey, I thought you were my best friend. Why are you acting like this?" I was hurt.

"I'm really, *really* tired of hearing about band," Lisa replied.

"What should I talk about, then? Biology?" I said snidely.

"I don't know. You figure it out," Lisa retorted.

"Give me some time," I snapped, and then I slammed the phone down. I couldn't help it. I was very upset. I didn't understand what had gone wrong with our friendship, and I had no idea how to fix it.

"Your tutor's here!" my father yelled up the stairs at nine o'clock the next morning.

At that moment I was relieved that Jeff was my tutor. It wouldn't matter how I looked. I slipped on an old pair of jeans and a sweatshirt, quickly laced up my high-tops, and raced down the stairs. The rest of my family was still sleeping. If I had a choice, I would have been sleeping, too, but I had to practice if I didn't want to fail band. It was hard to believe I was spending the whole weekend practicing the clarinet.

Jeff was sitting patiently in the living room.

"Hi." I smiled at him.

"Looks like we're twins." He grinned, taking off his jacket. He was wearing a sweatshirt and jeans, too. I looked over my outfit and his. George would have made more jokes about our identical outfits, but Jeff wasn't George.

"Here." Jeff handed me a paper bag. "Bagels, lox, and cream cheese. You have to have a good breakfast if you're going to put in a day of practice."

"A day?" I had been thinking of calling Sonia and Cynthia and meeting them at Macy's that afternoon.

"You only have three weekends left to practice," Jeff reminded me.

"Okay, you're the boss. Thanks for the bagels."

"You're welcome. I brought an extra clarinet, too."

"You own your own instruments?" Either Jeff was very rich, or very dedicated.

"I own several instruments. I want to be either a professional musician or a scientist, so I work hard at both," he explained.

We ate our breakfast in silence. Whenever I looked up, Jeff was smiling at me. I had to admit he looked pretty cute in his rumpled sweatshirt. Then we went up to my room to start on the routine: warm-ups, scales, and a few short pieces.

"Let's try 'Rhapsody' again," Jeff said.

This time, we played it as a duet. There were less squeaks in my playing than the day before, but the sounds emerging out of Jeff's clarinet were magnificent. When we finished, Jeff remarked, "We play well together."

"You mean *you* play well," I said. "I missed about half of the notes."

"Yeah, but it's only been a day. You're obviously a good pupil."

"That's because you're a good teacher."

"I try." He looked a little embarrassed.

"How long have you been playing?" I asked.

"Eight years."

"Wow!" I gasped. "That's a long time."

"Well, I've been interested in music since I was really young. My family always encouraged me, and I just wanted to play everything I could get my hands on."

"I can see that. You're so good at the clarinet *and* the flute."

"How about you? Why did you take band, anyway?" Jeff asked.

I fumbled for an answer. "Uh, for the challenge," I managed to say. *The challenge of meeting George,* I added to myself.

"Wow." Jeff was impressed.

"Are there any challenges for you, Jeff Lang?" I wanted to change the subject.

"I'm fascinated by the universe—the whole solar system, and especially the stars," he said.

"Really?" He had aroused my curiosity. "What about them?"

"Just the fact that they're such a mystery."

"Do you ever make wishes on stars?" I asked. "I do, all the time."

He smiled and nodded. "What do you wish for?"

George, I thought, but I said, "It's a secret. What about you?"

"My wishes are secret, too. But maybe one day soon I'll tell you. Okay, star," Jeff said with a laugh, "it's back to music time. One day," he added, "I'm going to take you on a star watch. I'll point out all the different stars to you."

"Sounds like fun." *More fun than this,* I thought. "What's next?" I asked.

"John Philip Sousa." Jeff pretended he was playing the trombone.

"Don't tell me you play the trombone, too?"

He seemed embarrassed by my question. "Yeah."

"That's great. I mean, I'm really impressed." I was. He seemed to know so much about so many different things.

"Some people think I'm just a goody two shoes."

"No way. I respect anyone who can play three instruments."

"Anyway, let's get back to the marches," he said, anxious to avoid any more talk about himself. Jeff played, and I tried to play. I couldn't help thinking about George and comparing him to Jeff. If he were teaching me, he'd probably be marching around the room by now. He'd have me in stitches.

Jeff might not have been funny, but he was diligent. Every day after school he came over to my house and helped me learn the pieces for the concert. Sonia became concerned about the attention he was giving me.

"You don't want George to get any ideas," she warned me one day while she was helping me put the instruments away.

"What ideas? Jeff's my tutor, that's all. We've become friends over the past few weeks."

"He's your friend? Mr. Goody Two Shoes? You're not serious, are you?" Sonia asked.

"He's not as boring as you think," I told her. "He's quiet, but he's an interesting guy." I really meant what I said. We had been practicing together for a while now, and I had gotten to know him better. Sometimes, in the middle of practice, Jeff would halt everything and say, "Ice-cream time!" Then we'd race out of the apartment down to the ice-cream stand on Seventh Avenue and order huge chocolate-chocolate chip cones. We took turns paying. Jeff had become someone special in my life, someone I really trusted and someone I had fun with. He wasn't just my tutor anymore.

"He's a great guy, Sonia," I insisted.

"Yeah, right. Hard-working Jeff, with his knowledge of music, science, and the arts. He's a real scream," she said dryly.

"You're not being fair, Sonia. You don't really know him," I reminded her.

Sonia shrugged. "Each to her own, I guess." I hoped she wasn't going to treat me strangely because I was friendly with Jeff. I still wasn't speaking much to Lisa, and I didn't want to lose any more friends.

The next Friday, after school, Jeff and I decided to skip our usual music session and head straight for ice cream. It was a beautiful spring day, much too good to waste staying inside and squeaking.

"We've worked hard. We deserve it," Jeff announced, grinning. "Besides, the concert is this weekend—and you know all the pieces by heart!"

We raced to the ice-cream shop closest to school and breathlessly ordered chocolate ice cream sundaes. "My treat," I told Jeff.

"Why?" he asked.

"For being such a good teacher," I said.

"Well, you're a good student."

I raised an eyebrow and looked at him. "Are you kidding?" I poked at my ice cream with a spoon. "Hey, let's make chocolate soup," I said, mashing my ice cream up and down.

"Great! I haven't done this since I was a kid," Jeff said, grabbing a spoon off the counter and helping me stir the ice cream into a thick stew.

We both started eating greedily, but were interrupted a few minutes later. A familiar voice said, "Can I join you?" I looked up and there was George, looking irresistible, as usual. He was holding a cone in one hand.

"Sure, sit down," Jeff offered, but he didn't sound very friendly.

I suddenly felt very self-conscious. My sundae looked like it belonged to a messy eight-year-old. It was one giant pool of chocolate. I dabbed my mouth with a napkin, and then smiled shyly at George.

"So, I hear you've gotten to be a really good player, Mad," George said.

"I wouldn't say that, but I am better. Thanks to—" I pointed to Jeff with my spoon.

"Jeff's a talented musician," George agreed.

Jeff didn't say anything. George was being so nice to him, and he was acting so rude in return. I glared at him.

"Actually, I've been working pretty hard myself. I've been doing some gigs, trying to save money for college. I'm also doing volunteer work at Kings County Hospital. I play the sax for the old folks once a week." George started to pretend he was playing his sax.

I could only admire George for what he had told me. As busy as he was, to do volunteer work for the pleasure of others! I ignored my "soup" and stared at him as he finished his cone. After it was gone, he fished a kazoo out of his pocket and gaily played an excerpt from a Sousa march.

I clapped. "Bravo, George!"

"I've been practicing hard, too." He flashed me a dazzling smile. "By the way, I hope you haven't forgotten that tomorrow's our date to pick out the watch for Walker. It's now or never, since Sunday's the big day."

"Well, Saturday's a practice day. But I think we're finished, right, Jeff? Like you said, I know how to play all the pieces now."

"Then I guess we're finished," Jeff said quietly. He excused himself to go to the bathroom.

"Call your friends and tell them to meet us," George said.

"What time?"

"Ten o'clock, at the bus stop on Flatbush Avenue."

I nodded. "Sounds good."

We talked for a while about what sort of watch to buy for Mr. Walker. Then I looked at my watch. Ten minutes had gone by since Jeff had gone to the bathroom. I wanted to make sure he was all right. He had looked a little pale when he left. I walked over to the bathroom, intending to call to him through the door, but the door was open. Jeff was nowhere to be seen.

"He probably forgot to tell us that he had to go home," George suggested.

"I guess so," I said, feeling puzzled. It wasn't like Jeff to leave without saying good-bye. Was he mad at me? He and I had been getting along so well. What was his problem?

I shrugged. I would worry about Jeff later. Tomorrow was my date with George, and for the moment, that was my biggest concern.

Chapter Nine

The shopping trip was a success. George paid a lot of attention to me, and treated us all to Chinese food. We found a magnificent pocket watch for Mr. Walker. But now Sunday, performance time, was here, and I didn't feel right. It wasn't just the fact that I was nervous, even though George had assured me that I would knock everyone out with my looks alone. It was Jeff. I hadn't heard from him since Friday, and I was afraid I had done something to upset him. I was so scared about playing and about seeing Jeff again that my hands were shaking.

"You look beautiful, darling. Let's go." My father was pacing back and forth in the hall-way outside my bedroom door. He was acting as if I were about to make my debut at Carnegie Hall.

"*Please* stop pacing, Dad," I said. "I'm nervous enough as it is. *I'm* the one who's performing."

"But you're late. You won't be playing anything if you don't get moving."

Steve darted into my room. "But I have to look beautiful for my dear, darling George!" he cried.

"No one invited you into this room," I snapped.

"Everyone calm down," my mother said. "We're leaving in five minutes, with or without the performer. Now, let's all leave Madeline's room."

I breathed a sigh of relief, and glanced in the mirror one last time. I had braided my hair, and put on the perfect amount of blush and lip gloss, and dressed in a black velvet skirt and a white silk blouse. I looked like a serious musician. "I'm ready!" I called out.

"But do you have the George seal of approval?" Steve teased.

"Don't bother coming, twerp," I said, irritated.

"If the two of you can't get along," my mother said, "then I'll . . ."

"You'll what, Mom?" Steve grinned.

"I don't know what I'll do," she said, admitting defeat. We all laughed. I hugged her, and noticed how intensely my arms were trembling.

When we arrived at Robert Moses High, my parents and Steve wished me good luck and proceeded to find seats in the audience. I walked backstage, behind the closed curtains. As I collected my clarinet from the table and walked to my assigned seat, I felt as if everyone's eyes were on me. George's certainly were; he winked at me. But Jeff had his eyes cast down on the ground.

"Great shirt!" Sonia exclaimed when I took my seat next to her.

"Ssh," Mr. Walker hissed. "Quiet up on stage. Soon you'll be doing warm-ups."

"So, what do you think of the outfit?" I whispered to my fellow third clarinets.

"You look gorgeous," Cynthia said sincerely.

"You look pretty good yourselves, guys," I said. They looked elegantly funky in their identical black suede miniskirts and white washed-silk T-shirts.

"The question is, how do you *feel*?" Cynthia asked.

"As though, if someone blew at me, I'd break into a million tiny pieces."

"Me too!" Cynthia giggled nervously.

"Can you play the pieces, Maddy?" Sonia asked.

"Thanks to Jeff, I can," I said.

"Speaking of Jeff," Sonia remarked, "what's his problem? I mean, he's always quiet, but now he's not even talking to *you*."

"Warm-ups, everyone," Mr. Walker said, interrupting our conversation.

"I don't know." I shrugged and looked over at Jeff. He was quietly practicing his scales. He was such a contrast to George, who sat on the stage as if he were the star. George didn't even warm up. His confidence was contagious. I felt a little like a star, too, until I noticed a tiny rip in my stocking that was turning into a major hole. I was so worried about it that I missed Cynthia presenting Mr. Walker with the pocket watch we had so carefully selected.

Suddenly the curtain went up. It looked like there were a lot of people in the audience. My hands were sweating so much that I thought I would drop the clarinet.

"Ready?" Mr. Walker tapped the baton against the music stand. *As ready as I'll ever be,* I thought.

"He told us to start with 'Greensleeves,' right?" I asked Cynthia as Mr. Walker did his usual "one and two and three" count.

"No, 'Rhapsody,' " Cynthia hissed.

It was too late. Mr. Walker was conducting 'Rhapsody,' but some people were playing 'Greensleeves.'

"Stop!" he suddenly screamed. A few people in the audience laughed.

"Let's make believe that never happened," Mr. Walker announced loudly and nervously. "Everyone, 'Rhapsody in Blue.' " I glanced across the room and caught Jeff smiling at me. That gave me renewed confidence, despite the fact that my palms were wetter than ever.

We started over, and I imagined I was playing with the New York Philharmonic. Mr. Walker's arms moved like a bird dancing in the air. I felt the notes flow out of me, and they sounded wonderful. Then, suddenly, Mr. Walker lost his rhythm and his conducting became impossibly fast.

Sonia paused for an instant. "Has Walker lost his marbles?" she whispered. At that moment the baton flew out of Mr. Walker's hands. He looked so mortified that I felt terrible for him. I felt bad for us, too, because everyone was so nervous and excited that they lost their places.

I was so anxious that I blasted out an F-sharp with too much force. It was the right note, but it came out like a screech. I wanted to die.

At that instant, George raced up to the front of the stage and rescued Mr. Walker's baton from the floor. He gave it back to Mr. Walker and then slipped back to his seat. Mr. Walker seemed to recover a little after that, and began to conduct again, this time keeping the correct rhythm. Soon, the entire band was playing in sync, and the music began to flow properly again. The audience seemed enraptured by the melody. I felt all the tension drain out of me.

That wasn't the end of the magic. When we played the Sousa marches, the music roared throughout the auditorium. John Philip Sousa had never sounded so good to me before. Jeff had a solo, and it was wonderful, as I'd expected it to be, but the big surprise of the evening was when the audience demanded an encore and George stood up and started jamming jazz. Mr. Walker was very relaxed about it and allowed George, Jonathan, and Ricardo to play their jam session. Some of the more sophisticated players joined in. I watched them in awe.

"Look at those guys. Aren't they great?" Sonia asked, squeezing my hand.

"Stunning."

At the end of the performance, we received a standing ovation. Mr. Walker was blushing furiously and looked ecstatic. I was happy we had done so well. It felt good to be part of something so beautiful. Then I remembered the hideous screech that I had produced from my clarinet. Well, at least it was my only major mistake.

My parents were waiting by the doors of the auditorium. "You were great, honey!" they exclaimed as they embraced me. Even my brother gave me a kiss.

"Good job with that F-sharp," he added mischievously.

"Thanks." I punched him affectionately. "Did

you see George?" I asked my family. "He was the one who took over in the encore."

"I guessed that was him," my mother said.

I glanced around the auditorium. "Where's Lisa? Did she leave already?"

"Uh, actually, she didn't come," Steve said.

"What do you mean, she didn't come?" I demanded.

"Maybe she had plans for this evening," my mother said.

"What plans? She knew about this weeks in advance. I can't believe she didn't come." All my excitement left me. I turned around, unable to believe that my best friend had let me down on my big night. I knew we hadn't been getting along lately, and hadn't spoken to each other for a while, but I was sure Lisa would come to the concert. She knew how much it meant to me. I glanced around one last time, hoping this was all some big mistake. I spotted George, looking stunning in his white shirt, black pants, and thin red tie, walking toward me. But tonight, even the sight of George approaching me couldn't stop my tears from flowing.

"Don't cry, Maddy," George whispered when he reached my side. "You weren't that bad."

"It's not that." I sighed. George touched my shoulder tenderly, and that made me feel a little better.

"We were great," George bragged. "All of us."

"I agree," I said.

A good-looking, well-dressed couple was standing close by. George waved them over to us. "Mom, Dad, this is my main girl," he said, introducing me to his parents. "Madeline, the squeaker. I call her Pip for short," he joked.

We smiled and exchanged proper introductions.

"I've heard a lot about you," his mother said.

I felt my heart leap. I was George's pipsqueak, his main girl, and his mother had heard about me, too! This was proof that George really *did* like me, even if it sometimes seemed that he didn't. For a second I forgot about my problems with Lisa. Maybe, finally, George would ask me out on a real date.

We chatted for a few minutes and then George and his parents excused themselves and headed off into the crowd. I glanced across the room and saw Jeff standing with his family. He looked very cute in his black suit and white oxford cloth shirt. He was smiling shyly as his family congratulated him on his performance. I couldn't get over how different he was from George. Eventually Jeff looked up and met my eyes. He was still smiling shyly, and I wanted to hug him, but I couldn't forget the strange way he'd acted on Friday—or the way he'd ignored me early in the evening. He gave me the thumbs-up sign and I motioned him over.

"You were great," I told him, "unlike the way you were at the ice-cream place. It was so nice of you to say good-bye before you left." I couldn't help sounding sarcastic.

Jeff couldn't meet my eyes for a minute. "I'm sorry," he said. "Something really got to me. Maybe one day I'll explain it to you."

"The same day you tell me about the stars?" I teased him.

"Yeah, something like that." He looked up and laughed. "Anyway, you were great."

"Even with the squeak?" I asked.

"Yes, even with the squeak. Come on," he added, "I want you to meet my family."

"Then let me get mine." I dragged my parents and Steve over so they could meet the Langs.

"This is my family," Jeff announced. "My mom, dad, and my two younger brothers, Warren and Aaron."

"Nice to meet all of you," I said. My parents nodded pleasantly.

"This is the Davis family," Jeff said.

"And this must be the wonderful Madeline Davis, your star pupil," his mother said.

I smiled shyly. It was difficult to think of myself as anyone's star pupil. At that moment I understood just how much Jeff had done for me. He had given up every afternoon, just to hear me squeak. It was funny. My squeaking had earned me a nickname, as well as George's attention, and a new friend, Jeff. Band hadn't turned out so badly after all. George and I had gotten to know each other, and it was only a matter of time before we would be a couple.

Chapter Ten

I don't know what I expected George to do in band class on Monday, but I didn't think he would ignore me. When I walked into class, though, that was what he did. It was as if the weekend had never happened, although everyone was still busy thanking and congratulating each other.

"You were especially great, George," I complimented him, but his response was unenthusiastic.

"Thanks," he said, and turned and talked to someone else.

Mr. Walker was much more effusive. "You were all wonderful," he told us. "Everyone responded with both class and grace to the mishaps at the beginning of the performance. Thanks to one and all." For the first time, Mr. Walker's shirt was in place, his socks matched, his shoelaces were tied, and he was wearing new glasses. "And a special thanks to George Held," he said, beaming.

"Bravo," George shouted, lifting his arms victoriously. Then he stood up and bowed gracefully.

Jonathan and Ricardo stood up and bowed, too, while the rest of the class hooted and whistled at them.

"And now for a toast!" Mr. Walker announced.

"With champagne, of course," George joked.

"Champagne-a-cola, that is." Mr. Walker laughed and pulled out a giant bottle of Coke, paper cups, and some boxes of doughnuts from a bag on the floor.

Sonia giggled. "He's so cute."

Everyone went up to the front of the room to grab a donut and a Coke. We toasted everything under the sun, including the music stands and the dust gathering on the floor. It would have been the best band class ever, if George had noticed me.

"Oh, Maddy, I'm so excited. Jonathan just asked me out for Saturday night," Cynthia told me as she helped me put away the instruments that afternoon.

"I'm really happy for you," I said, and I meant it. But I felt bad for myself. I was supposedly George's main girl, but he was too busy bowing to notice me.

Cynthia left soon after that for a dentist appointment, and I was alone. I didn't really feel like talking to anyone anyway.

To my surprise, Jeff was waiting for me outside the instrument room.

"We are going to continue with tutoring, aren't we?" he asked abruptly.

"Of course, but why don't we take a break for a few days?" I said. "I mean, the concert's over."

"All right. But let's get together sometime over the weekend," he persisted.

"Maybe." I shrugged. I wasn't in the mood to make plans. I shuffled down the sidewalk, barely saying good-bye to Jeff. A big spring dance was coming up, and I didn't have a date. And I had been so sure after Sunday that George would ask me! I walked home feeling miserable.

As I wandered up the street, I noticed the colorful Easter displays in the store windows. The displays reminded me that my family's Easter dinner was coming up. My mom is Jewish and my dad is Christian, so we celebrate both Easter and Passover. It was always a big deal, and even Stacy made a point of coming home that weekend. I thought about who I should invite to this year's Easter celebration. I couldn't invite Sonia without asking Cynthia, but then Lisa would feel left out. I realized that I wanted Lisa to be there. I wasn't sure if she would come, but I wasn't ready to give up on our friendship.

I stopped in front of my favorite knickknack store. Inside the window, a giant blue rabbit was smiling from ear to ear. The rabbit filled me with hope. I decided then and there to invite both Jeff and Lisa to my family's dinner.

I felt a little nervous about calling Lisa, but I knew I had to do it. When I got home, I went straight upstairs, closed my bedroom door, and picked up the phone. I wanted to be calm when she answered, and to act as if she hadn't done anything hurtful, but all I could say was, "Why didn't you come to my concert?"

There was silence at the other end of the line.

"Answer me, Lisa," I pleaded.

Instead of words, I heard her crying. "It's just . . . " she began.

"What?"

"You . . . *excluded* me from your life. All you talked about was band . . . the people, the episodes, band, band, band," she sobbed.

"I did?"

"I know everyone in your class . . . Ricardo, Jonathan, Jeff. But you don't have any idea what's going on in my life," she went on. "You never asked what *I* was doing. I thought you didn't care anymore."

She was right. I started crying, too. "I'm so sorry, Lisa. There is no one in this world as important to me as you are. Do you know how much you hurt me by not coming to my performance?"

"I'm sorry, too," Lisa sniffed. "I guess it was pretty nasty. Friends to the end?"

"Friends to the end," I echoed. "Would you come to my family dinner on Easter?"

"You bet. I love your family dinners. Your mom's the greatest cook."

"Great. So what *have* you been doing?" I asked her. After we had spent some time catching up, I called Jeff.

"You're doing what?" Jeff's voice at the other end of the phone sounded startled.

"Inviting you to my family's Easter dinner."

"I can't believe you're calling me and not George," he said.

I was speechless. This was the last thing in the world I expected Jeff to say. "How did you know I liked George?" I managed to say.

"A person would have to be blind not to notice," he said.

"Is it that obvious?" I panicked.

"Just a little." He laughed, but there was a nervous edge to his voice. "So why me?"

"George is a romantic interest, and you're a very good friend. I only want my good friends at the dinner," I explained.

"Then I guess I'll be there," he said, although he didn't sound very thrilled about it.

"Great!"

After I hung up, I went downstairs and told my mother that Jeff and Lisa were coming.

"I can't believe you're not inviting George," she teased me.

"He didn't ask me to go to the dance, so why should I invite him to dinner?" I countered.

"I agree," my mother said, imitating the pout on my face. "You know you're going to have to go shopping with me."

I sighed. "I know."

"What kind of food does your friend Jeff like?"

I thought carefully. "I don't know what kind of food, but I know he loves double chocolate chip ice cream."

My mother wrote that down on her list. "He's a nice boy, that Jeff," she murmured.

"Yeah, he's neat," I agreed. *But he's not George,* I thought a little sadly.

On Easter Sunday, I woke up to the smell of home-baked lasagna and turkey. I stumbled down the stairs and into the kitchen.

"Mom, what are you doing?" I asked, rubbing my eyes.

"Preparing in advance."

"I'm only having two friends, and then it's just the immediate family," I reminded her. "Seven people total."

"People may get very hungry," my mother exclaimed, throwing her hands up in the air.

"People may get very hungry," I repeated as I made my way up the stairs. I called Lisa after I had turned on the television in my room.

"What are you doing?" I asked.

"Watching television."

"Me too," I said. "I'm bored. And my mother thinks she's cooking for the Queen of England."

Lisa laughed. "We need romantic possibilities in our lives."

"I thought I had one, up until now."

"You'll have him," Lisa assured me. "You'll see."

I felt very doubtful about the whole thing, but I tried to put it out of my mind.

"I want you to know," my father told Jeff that evening, "that you saved our daughter's life, and our ears!"

"Thanks." Jeff blushed. "Frankly," he added, trying to overcome his shyness, "your daughter saved me, too. She made me realize all the wonderful ice-cream flavors I was missing."

My father laughed at that, and Stacy smiled at me. Stacy understood how hard it was for me; she was as tone deaf as I was.

"How do you like living on your own, Stace?" Lisa asked.

Stacy smiled. "It's great. But I miss home sometimes."

"Miss it! I can't wait until I'm old enough to leave!" Lisa exclaimed.

"Don't rush things," Jeff interjected. "Just think of all the rent money you can save by living at home."

My father laughed again. He sank down on the couch next to Lisa. "My daughter tells me you're an avid reader. Who's your favorite author?" he asked Jeff.

"Charles Dickens," Jeff replied. My mother popped her head into the room. " 'It was the best of times, it was the worst of times,' " she quoted.

"What is this—the literary circle?" Stacy said, rolling her eyes. Steve and I chuckled.

"Do you read any contemporary novels?" my mother asked Jeff.

"Mostly I read the classics," Jeff responded.

"Me too!" Lisa and my mother exclaimed at the same time.

It was nice to see everyone getting along so well.

The next thing I knew, we were sitting at the table, which was laden with turkey, potato pancakes, rare roast beef, and a lasagna platter, dripping with mozzarella cheese. "Dig in!" Mom commanded us.

Jeff piled his plate high with food.

"I like a man with a healthy appetite," my father said, filling his own plate equally high. I couldn't believe that much food could even fit on a plate.

Steve was already busy shoveling the food

into his mouth. "Are you a Jets fan?" he asked Jeff.

"Sure thing."

"Tell me about band. What's my sister like in band?" Steve asked.

"I don't really feel like talking about band. Not that your sister isn't wonderful in it." Jeff flashed me a smile.

I was relieved. Steve and Jeff resumed their football discussion in between bites.

"Mrs. Davis, this is the best food I've ever eaten in my life," Jeff commented.

"The chef works very hard. Thank you," my mother responded.

"I'd never turn down a meal at the Davises'," Lisa said.

Jeff nodded. "I can understand why!"

When everyone was full, Steve dragged Jeff over to the piano.

"Let's do a duet." Steve started playing "Heart and Soul," and Jeff joined in. Then Steve switched to "Sweet Adeline."

"Sweet Madeline, my Madeline," Jeff sang, winking at me.

"Let's sing holiday songs," Lisa suggested. She immediately began with "In your Easter bonnet, with all the frills upon it . . ."

"You have a good voice, Lisa," Jeff remarked.

"Brooklyn Academy of Music, ten years!" Stacy and I said at the same time.

"Wow!" Jeff was impressed. He was always

110

impressed with everyone but himself. He seemed so unaware of all his talents, unlike George. I sat up. I had almost forgotten about George until that moment. I was having such a good time. Everyone in my family seemed to like Jeff so much, including Stacy, who was extremely difficult to please.

"Aren't you going to play any Passover songs?" my father asked.

"I don't know any," Steve said.

"I do," Jeff said, and he started playing "One Goat." Everyone joined in, including my sister and me.

When the song was finished, my brother dragged Jeff up to his room to show Jeff his stamp collection. Lisa and I helped my mother clear the table.

"Jeff's really sweet, and very funny," Lisa said, balancing a glass on top of a dish.

"Sweet, definitely. Interesting, yes. I'm not sure he's funny," I said, walking into the kitchen with her.

"Oh, he definitely has a sharp sense of humor," Lisa insisted. "It's just subtle."

My mother was still singing while she washed the dishes.

"I'm starting the coffee and bringing out the dessert," Stacy announced.

"Sounds good. Well, Mad, it looks like your brother made a new friend," my father said.

"No, I think he took *away* my friend," I said a little grumpily.

"What do you care?" My mother laughed. "You'd only have to worry if he had stolen your boyfriend."

Everyone laughed, except me.

"Dessert's ready!" Stacy called from the other room. Everyone rushed in to the dining room to get a bite of Stacy's cheesecake.

"Delicious," Jeff said.

"Scrumptious," Steve agreed in a phony English accent.

"You clown." Stacy leaned over and rumpled his hair affectionately.

The dessert seemed to renew everyone's appetite, especially Jeff's and my dad's. "I hate to leave all the fun," Jeff said after we were finished, "but my parents are expecting me home."

"I'm sorry you have to leave," I said. It was already nine o'clock, and I felt sad that the evening was almost over.

"Can I walk you home?" Jeff asked Lisa.

"Sure. Just let me get my coat," she said.

"Thanks for the wonderful dinner. The company was pretty wonderful, too," Jeff told my family.

"Yeah, thanks a lot, Mr. and Mrs. Davis." Lisa kissed everyone good-bye, and Jeff shook everyone's hand.

As soon as they left, I yelled at Steve. "You

creep! You monopolized Jeff the whole evening. 'Jeff, let me show you this. Jeff, play the piano with me.' It was totally and utterly obnoxious."

"What do you care, unless you like him? I think Jeff's a winner. I'd date him if I were you," Steve said smugly.

"It's none of your business who I date," I told him angrily.

"Enough, you two!" my mother warned. "This has been a very pleasant evening. Let's keep it that way."

I thought it had been extremely pleasant—aside from the fact that Steve had bugged Jeff all night. "Fine. I think I'm going to bed. Good night, everyone," I snapped. I ran upstairs into my room and flopped onto my bed. How could I possibly explain to my dumb brother the difference between romance and friendship?

Chapter Eleven

The next Saturday night was the night of the spring dance, and as predicted, I didn't have a date. Sonia was going with Ricardo, Cynthia was going with Jonathan, Lisa had a date with some guy from her French class, Jeff was babysitting for his brother, and I was alone, in my room, watching the standard Saturday night junk on television. Even my brother had a party to go to. George had had all week to ask me, but he obviously wasn't interested. My favorite musical, *Singin' in the Rain,* was on television, but Gene Kelly was so in love with Debbie Reynolds that it depressed me too.

On Monday, I muddled through my day, barely managing to listen to Sonia and Cynthia's enthusiasm over their dates and the dance. At lunch I heard Ricardo described for the millionth time as "a dreamboat, a wild and zany guy, but sensitive, too." Frankly, I had never seen the sensitive side of Ricardo, although Sonia claimed he had one. Jonathan, on the other hand, was sensitive, even quiet. Sometimes he didn't seem to belong to George's crowd. But I was tired of Cynthia talking about him, too. I wasn't in the mood to see any of them, and when I trudged into band I avoided their smiling faces.

But that wasn't the worst of it. When Mr. Walker walked into the room, his face was beet red.

"Who took the sax?" he yelled.

Nobody answered him.

"Someone in this class had to take it. The only people who have access to the instruments are band members."

The room was silent.

"Did you lock the door before the weekend, Miss Davis?" Mr. Walker stared straight at me.

"I'm sure I did," I answered nervously.

Suddenly George leapt out of his seat. There was a look of panic on his face. "You mean my sax is missing?" he asked. His voice was a mixture of rage and anxiety.

"Yes, it's your sax that's missing," Mr. Walker told him solemnly.

Now I felt worse than ever.

"Miss Davis, are you sure you locked up?"

Mr. Walker repeated. "I don't remember you taking the keys."

"Yes, I'm sure," I said, my voice coming out in a squeak. I sounded almost as bad as my clarinet.

George shook his head. "I'm not so sure you did. I can't imagine anyone in this room taking it."

I couldn't believe what was happening. George was accusing me of being negligent! He was saying I was responsible for his instrument being stolen. And he was acting as if his stupid saxophone was more important than me!

"Is George serious?" Cynthia whispered.

"Looks like he is." I gulped, trying to hold back the tears.

"Madeline's a very responsible person," Jeff said, standing up. "I'm certain she locked the door."

I didn't even have it in me to defend myself anymore.

"Well, it's the first day back after the break. Maybe it's just been misplaced. I'll give it one more day before I tell the principal about this. I'm calling off rehearsals today. You can study the sheet music. I'm not sure I can trust you people with the instruments," Mr. Walker said, shaking his head.

Mr. Walker was talking about only one person—me. I didn't know why I had bothered showing up for school that morning. I grabbed my things and ran home, closed the door of my room, and started crying.

"What's wrong?" My mother knocked at the door and then walked in.

"A sax was stolen over the weekend and Mr. Walker accused me of not locking the door. And the worst part is, George supported him!"

"Oh, sweetie." My mother embraced me. "Can I do anything? Should I write a note?"

"Just don't let Steve and Daddy come in here. I don't think I can deal with them right now."

"Sure." She kissed me and left. I lay back on my bed for a few minutes. If I really hadn't locked the door, all of this was my fault. I felt like calling Lisa, but she wouldn't be home from school yet, and anyway I didn't want to bother her with yet another of my problems.

I thought about not going to school the next day, but that was cowardly. Tomorrow was my seventeenth birthday, but I didn't think it was going to be a happy one.

In band the next day, the first thing Mr. Walker said was, "The instrument has still not been found."

"It wasn't Madeline's fault. I know it wasn't," Sonia argued.

"Why do you say that?" George asked. "Come on, we all like Maddy, but she *is* pretty spacey sometimes."

"Madeline. Are you ready to confess?" Mr. Walker inquired.

"Confess to what?" I asked indignantly. I couldn't believe the way George had just described me. *So that's what he really thinks of me,* I said to myself. *Is this the same George I'm in love with?* "I have nothing to confess!" I shouted angrily. Everyone was startled by the volume of my voice.

"I am going to the principal now," Mr. Walker said. "You can all do warm-ups. I'm leaving Jeff Lang in charge."

"You always leave Jeff in charge," George complained.

"Why shouldn't I?" Mr. Walker countered, and left, slamming the door.

I was glad Jeff was in charge. He was on my side, at least. I stared at my clarinet case rebelliously. I had absolutely no desire to take out the instrument and play. I was through with music and musicians—forever!

"What's George's problem?" Cynthia asked.

"Don't ask me, ask him," I said. But when I looked around the room, he was nowhere in sight.

Suddenly, music filled the room and George danced in, *playing his sax!* Jonathan and Ricardo were dancing right behind him, singing "Happy Birthday" at the top of their lungs.

I didn't know whether to be happy or furious. When the music stopped, George shoved the sax case in front of me.

"Open it," he said. He was beaming.

I reluctantly swung the case open. Inside was an enormous clarinet-shaped birthday cake with writing inscribed on it: TO THE GREATEST PIP-SQUEAK IN THE UNIVERSE. A miniature black plastic clarinet was stuck in the middle of the cake, which I took off immediately. I would keep it forever among my special possessions. The real puzzler was the candles— there were only three.

"Why three?" I asked.

"My three wishes for you," George replied, "love, success, and happiness."

I threw my arms around George and kissed his cheek.

Ricardo grabbed the baton. "Okay, everyone now, in unison, one and two and three." He did a great imitation of Mr. Walker. My classmates were all laughing and singing at the same time.

"I'm sorry I put you through all this grief. I knew you'd be worried sick about the sax and all, but it was too good a joke to pass up," George told me.

"It's okay," I said. In fact, it was really funny. I had fallen for the whole thing. "Thank you!" I shouted to everyone. Then I turned to George. "Walker's going to kill you—or me."

"Nah. We'll put the case away immediately

and make believe it was there all the time."
George lifted out the cake and placed his sax lovingly in the case. Then he took paper plates, plastic forks, and a knife out of a bag.

"Let's eat quickly before Mr. W. comes back," George said, cutting slices of cake for everyone.

"You sneak!" I smiled. I glanced at Jeff to see if he was enjoying my birthday party, but he didn't look very happy. I shook my head. Sometimes Jeff really *was* a goody two shoes. I turned my attention to eating the cake, which was a deep, rich chocolate with a luscious strawberry center.

"I hear Mr. W.'s feet coming down the hall!" Ricardo suddenly cried out. George ran around the room with a plastic bag and started collecting all the plates and forks.

I panicked. I wanted to make sure George's saxophone was back in the instrument room by the time Mr. Walker returned, so I grabbed it and dashed around the back of the room. The only problem was, Jack Farrell had left his oboe case lying on the floor behind his chair, and I tripped over it. "Oh, no!" I cried. I cradled the saxophone case in my arms, so it wouldn't get damaged in the fall.

"Maddy, are you all right?" Sonia called in an anxious voice.

Jeff ran over and helped me up, while George took the sax from me. He glanced inside the case and smiled. "It's fine," he said in a relieved tone.

Just then Mr. Walker opened the door. He stared at the instrument case in George's hands.

"Look, Mr. W.—we found it!" George exclaimed. "Safe and sound."

Unfortunately, I wasn't. My ankle was throbbing, and as Jeff helped me limp back to my seat, I couldn't help thinking that George had been more concerned about his saxophone than me.

Chapter Twelve

"Is it broken?" Sonia shouted into the phone, practically breaking my eardrum.

"No, just very badly sprained," I told her. "Listen, I have to go. I need to rest."

"Okay, feel better. I'll speak to you later—with news. Maybe I'll even stop by."

"Sure." I hung up the phone. I wished that I had sounded more enthusiastic, but at that moment I didn't feel like seeing or talking to anyone. I looked and felt like a washed-out dishrag. Steve came into my room with a big bowl of chicken soup my mom had just prepared.

"You're being so sweet," I told him. "What do you want from me?"

"When Jeff comes over, can I show him my baseball cards?"

"I'm not certain he's coming over," I replied.

122

"He definitely is. Later this afternoon. He called."

"He did? Listen, Steve be a sweetheart, get me my blush and lipstick from the top of my bureau."

"Okay." Steve brought back the makeup and watched as I did some quick touch-ups to my face. "You're getting all fancied up for Jeff?" he asked.

"No, silly. Just in case someone special comes." I was pretty sure that George would drop in at some point during the day and I wanted to look my best.

"I'm leaving, Mad. You look gorgeous." Steve winked.

"Thanks." I felt a smile spread across my face. Sometimes he could be cute, even if he was my obnoxious baby brother.

A few minutes later, my mother escorted Lisa into the room. "Here's your best friend and a plate of brownies. Now I'll leave the two of you alone," she said, closing the door behind her.

"How are you doing? How did you manage to be in this lovely state?" Lisa asked.

"I tripped over an oboe case," I admitted.

Lisa laughed so hard she could hardly keep the brownie in her mouth. "I'm sorry for laughing, Mad, but it's so funny. I mean, an oboe case is really small."

"Funny, Lisa. When you were ten, I remember, you tripped over a pebble and got a bloody nose."

"Now that was one enormous pebble," she quipped. "I'd say it was the size of a rock."

We both burst out laughing this time.

"How's your love life, Lisa?" I asked.

"It isn't. And yours?"

"Could be better," I responded. "When I recover, we'll have to start up a new hunt."

"What about George?"

"He's a weirdo!" I sighed. "I mean, I like him a lot, but just when I think the feeling's mutual, he stops talking to me. Remember how I told you he called me his main girl after the performance?"

"Yeah, sure."

"Well, the next day in class he just acted like nothing happened. He didn't ask me to the spring dance, but then he made this big deal over my birthday. I mean, it was a *major* production."

"How strange!" Lisa exclaimed, looking as puzzled as I felt. "How's your tutoring?"

"On hold, temporarily, but I told Jeff we'd get back to it soon."

"How is Jeff?"

"He's a sweetheart, Lisa. When I tripped, he was the one who helped me up, and he practically carried me home." Just then Sonia and Cynthia barged into the room.

"Hi, girls. Remember me?" Lisa said, smiling.

"Hi, Lisa," they replied in unison.

I was glad my best friend had accepted my new friends.

"How's biology?" Cynthia asked.

"Oh, I've gotten over that obsession." Lisa shrugged. "Now I'm on to bigger and better things."

"Like what?" Sonia asked.

"Men."

"Ugh. Don't talk to me about guys," Sonia said disgustedly.

"What?" I couldn't believe my ears. Sonia *always* wanted to talk about guys.

"I just broke up with Ricardo," she said.

"Why?" Lisa asked.

At the same time, I said, "I don't believe it!"

"He thinks he's God's gift to women," Sonia complained.

"So does George," I said, but I added quickly, "but he's nice too. Not to mention great-looking."

"Speak of the devil," Sonia whispered.

"Were you talking about me?" George inquired. He strutted into the room with his two best friends in tow.

"You—and other people, too." Sonia shrugged.

"But *primarily* us," George insisted. We ignored him.

Jonathan gave Cynthia a quick smile, and she smiled back.

"Can I talk to you, Sonia?" Ricardo asked shyly.

"No. We were just about to leave and go to Pino's. Weren't we, girls?"

"Sure thing," they replied, grabbing their jackets.

"I'll walk you to the door," I said, bending over to grab my crutches. "I mean, the doctor said bed rest for the week, but he didn't say I had to be an invalid."

"No, you relax," Lisa said, pushing me back onto the bed. "Bye," she added, and a chorus of good-byes followed as they exited my room.

"What's the matter with your friends? Don't they like my bodyguards?" George asked.

"Oh, they're just hassled by exams, I guess." I knew it was a feeble excuse, especially since it wasn't a major exam time, but I didn't want George to feel disliked now that I had him exactly where I wanted him. The boys sat on the edge of my bed. I felt like a queen resting on her throne.

"Everything okay in there?" my mother asked. "Need any more brownies?"

"No thanks, Mom. Everything is wonderful," I told her.

George grinned at me. "So, how are you feeling, Pip-squeak?"

"A little bit better. It doesn't hurt so much."

126

I couldn't believe George had called me Pip-squeak again; I loved the fact that he had given me a nickname. George started gently rubbing my ankle. It sent tingles up my spine.

"How long did you say you were going to be laid up?" he asked.

"Most of the week."

"Why so long?" George asked, letting go of my ankle.

"Well, I can use crutches and all, but the doctor says since it's such a bad sprain it would be best if I could have as much bed rest as possible." I sighed.

"Then next Saturday night I'm giving a party in honor of your recovery at my house."

"Seriously?" I couldn't believe it!

"See you then, Pip-squeak. And if you need anything, call." He kissed me on the cheek, and handed me a slip of paper with his phone number on it. I already knew his number, because I had looked it up in the phone book and memorized it, but I didn't tell *him* that.

"Thanks. I'll definitely call if I need anything."

"By the way, don't tell your tutor. He's not invited."

"Okay, sure," I agreed without thinking. Then my mother came into the room and told the boys I needed some rest. The moment they left the house, I started shrieking;

it was difficult to contain myself. I would have leapt out of bed if I could.

"What happened?" My mother rushed into the room in a state of panic.

"George is having a party in my honor!" I cried.

"I'm very happy for you, sweetie." My mother gave me a big bear hug.

"More guests!" Steve shouted from downstairs. I knew it had to be Jeff. Sure enough, he entered the room with his friends Ira, Devin, and Abe. Devin and Abe both played the trumpet in band class. Like Jeff, they were quiet, and I was a little surprised and pleased to see them. All the boys were carrying their instruments with them.

"I'm so sorry," Abe said.

I laughed.

"I've been worried sick about you," Jeff said.

"Don't be ridiculous."

"Well, if you thought that was ridiculous, watch my magic tricks." He whipped out a packet of peanut brittle and a bouquet of roses from behind his back.

"Oh, Jeff. This is wonderful. How did you know that I love peanut brittle?"

"ESP." He pointed toward his head. "And now for something really ridiculous."

"Wait. Before you start, you have to do me a favor. Go into my brother's room for just five minutes so you can look at his baseball cards."

"Okay."

I chatted with the other two guys while he was gone. I couldn't help comparing them to George's friends, who were all loud. The thought of George made butterflies flutter in my stomach. I loved the idea of a party in my honor, but I felt uncomfortable with the fact that Jeff wasn't invited.

Jeff came back into the room. "Now, let's start where we left off. Let me introduce Jeff Lang and the Langettes, doing their latest original hit: 'Madeline, She's So Fine, Like an Effervescent Star that Shines!' "

I was stunned. The boys played while Jeff sang. No one had ever written a song for me before! "I can't believe you wrote that for me," I said when they finished.

"Actually, I've written a few other songs," Jeff said modestly.

"Really? Why didn't you tell Mr. Walker? He was looking for writers for the state contest, remember?"

"I don't think my music is that good yet. Maybe soon."

Suddenly I realized that there was a lot I didn't know about Jeff, and the more I learned about him, the more I liked him. Jeff Lang and the Langettes. I liked that. He *was* funny.

"I'm looking forward to seeing you back in school," Jeff said.

"I'm looking forward to being there." *And to Saturday night,* I thought. "Thanks so much, all of you." Before I knew what I was doing, I leaned over and kissed Jeff on the cheek.

He held his hand up to where I had kissed him and whispered, "Thanks."

"You're welcome," I said, blushing. "I'll see you soon."

Chapter Thirteen

"He said this party was in honor of me," I whispered in Sonia's ear. We were standing in the basement of George's house, which had been lavishly decorated for the occasion. The stereo was going full blast, and the room was full of people having a great time—except for me.

"It is for you," Sonia said.

"Then why is he dancing with Stephanie?" I asked.

"You know George."

But I really didn't. I couldn't understand him at all.

"Look." Cynthia grabbed my arm. Walking into the room was a girl from our class dressed as an invalid, limping along, and carrying a cardboard oboe case.

"A toast to our guest of honor!" George's voice reverberated in the room. "There's only one Madeline Davis in this world!" he cried out.

There's only one George Held, I thought. He was looking as stunning as ever in his faded jeans and white T-shirt. Spring was George's season; he was bronzed and beautiful. For a second, I thought about Jeff. It was actually a good thing he hadn't been invited. He wouldn't like loud, overdone parties, and he would definitely hate this one.

"Are you having fun?" Suddenly, I was face to face with George, who appeared out of nowhere.

"Oh, um, yeah," I said.

And then George was off and running again, the way he was always off and running, back to the center of things. "Now in honor of Pip-squeak," he announced, "a cake that speaks for itself." It was an ice-cream cake shaped like an oboe. My name was printed on it in big bold letters.

I turned to Cynthia. "He's unbelievable. This is so clever. This must be love. I mean, this is the *second* special cake he's given me."

"Maybe it is love," Cynthia admitted. "Though last year for Mr. Walker's birthday, he ordered an ice-cream cake in the shape of a huge baton. Oh, by the way, your outfit is great."

Somehow, the idea that Mr. Walker had once received a cake from George made the whole thing less special. And my outfit *was* great—black leggings, a white T-shirt, and a big black and white striped tank top. I wondered why George hadn't noticed it yet.

"Come on, Mad. Let's dance." George grabbed my arm and pulled me out to the middle of the room. "Great party, isn't it?" he shouted over the loud music.

I couldn't dance very well because my ankle was still healing, but I shifted in time to the music. "You always manage to pat yourself on the back, don't you?" I teased him.

"Someone has to," George replied.

I giggled, but somehow it didn't seem funny. Then I moved closer, and the smell of George's cologne brought me back to reality. Here I was, dancing with the most gorgeous guy in school, the one who I had suffered through band for, the one who had given me two wonderful cakes . . .

"Be careful, Madeline!" Sonia shouted. "Remember, you were just laid up in bed for a week."

"She might be right, George. Can you put any slow music on?" I asked.

"Turn on the slow stuff!" George shouted to his disc jockeys, Ricardo and Jonathan. I noticed Cynthia and Sonia standing disinterestedly off to one side. Then George and I danced slowly, romantically, like Fred Astaire and Ginger Rogers. I stared into his gorgeous eyes. "We'll have to do this again sometime soon," I said. I couldn't believe I was being so bold, but the time had come for us to stop playing around.

"Sure. We'll have to get the gang together again. Listen, Madeline, I'm the host so I have to mingle. Since you're the guest of honor, you should mingle, too." He pulled away from me and was off in a flash.

I slowly walked back to my friends, confused. The whole evening seemed strange and bad.

"What's wrong?" Cynthia asked.

"I don't know." I shrugged my shoulders. "This party was supposedly for me, but George is too busy making the rounds."

"That's George for you," Sonia commented.

Suddenly I felt everything burst inside of me. "He's also incredibly vain," I said, fighting back tears. I started thinking more about George and his looks. Everything about him was neat and orderly. There was never a hair out of place. All of his clothes looked freshly pressed. Even his high-top sneakers were always white, as if he polished them every day.

"Do you know he stopped dancing with me

because he said he had to *mingle*?" I asked Sonia.

"Crowd pleasers. That's all they are," she said angrily.

"Who?" Cynthia asked.

"Jonathan, Ricardo, and George."

I knew how disgusted Sonia was with Ricardo, although Cynthia and Jonathan were still going out. It was spring, yet love was certainly not in the air.

"And now," Ricardo announced, standing on a makeshift podium, "it's time for our number one comedian and all-around star, Mr. George Held."

People started hooting and hollering as George took the stage. I still couldn't believe all of this had been planned in my honor.

"I once knew a girl named Madeline," he began. "Cute, nice, long hair, but the talent just wasn't there." A few people laughed at his rhyme. "Now, eight weeks later, she still can't play. She tries, oh how she tries. She fakes it. She gets a tutor. When the tutor can't help her, she fakes it some more. Then she ruins our almost perfect class performance by squeaking away. But we all love her for her perseverance. And we applaud her efforts for tripping on the smallest instrument in history, the oboe." The crowd was cheering, and George smiled. He was eating up the attention. I was the only one who didn't laugh. When the applause subsided, George ran up to me.

"So, did you like my routine?"

"Not really," I began. "I don't—"

"Great," he said, vanishing into the crowd. He hadn't even stuck around to listen to my response.

"I take it you didn't think it was very funny." Cynthia smiled wryly. "He meant it affectionately, you know."

"Maybe he did, but he still wasn't funny."

"I'm sorry," Sonia said seriously.

"Don't worry—I'll get over it."

"I'm sure if you let George know you're upset, he'd apologize," Cynthia said.

"No, it's okay." And it *was* okay, in a way. I didn't want George to apologize for being who he was. He was funny and charming, but definitely wrapped up in himself. He couldn't help being himself. It would be like asking Mr. Walker to apologize for being spacey, or asking Sonia to say she was sorry for being a gossip. People just are who they are. But I also didn't have to like someone who wasn't right for me, and I had just found out how mismatched George and I really were. I decided it was time to leave.

"If he asks where I went, make up an excuse for me," I told Sonia. It was early, and I figured I could catch a cab on the corner. The guest of honor was leaving the party, and the host didn't even notice. It was just like something out of a horrible, depressing movie, like the ones on the late, late show.

I wondered what Jeff was up to, and hoped he was having a better Saturday night than I was.

Chapter Fourteen

"I'm sorry you had to leave the party so early. What happened, did someone grab your ankle?" George laughed. I was sitting in the cafeteria the next Monday, waiting for Cynthia and Sonia. The food was making me sick. After George's party, I didn't have much of an appetite, anyway.

"I didn't feel very well, so I left," I said. I wasn't in the mood for explanations. Besides, I couldn't get serious with George. And he didn't seem very upset that I had left.

"Anytime you want to get together with the gang, just let me know," he said, smiling.

"Thanks." I smiled, but I knew I'd never be joining George's gang again. He looked as handsome as ever, but he just didn't appeal to me anymore. I looked across at him, but he was already gone, off and running to the next table.

"Guys aren't worth the heartache," I told my friends when they arrived.

"Yeah, tell me about it," Sonia complained.

"What about you and Jonathan?" I asked Cynthia. I knew they had had an argument.

"We made up," Cynthia said.

"Good. I'm glad for you," I said.

"Jonathan is more of an individual than the other two," Sonia observed. "Ricardo always has to follow his fearless leader, George."

I thought about the 'group' or 'gang.' It was easy to become anonymous in a group. People tended to lose their identity. Of course, my friends and I hung out in a group, but with them I always felt I could be myself. I wasn't punky, spunky Sonia or sweet, shy Cynthia. I was just Madeline Davis, whatever and whoever that was.

Could George ever manage to come down from center stage? I wondered. Sure, he had a wonderfully sweet side, but it was more important for him to be *everybody's* favorite person. I realized how few people were true individuals, ones who danced to the rhythm of their own music. Jeff Lang was one of them.

"You look much too serious." George had suddenly returned, and he threw himself down in the seat next to me.

"Oh, I was just thinking of someone special."

George smiled. *It's not you*, I thought, but I didn't say anything.

"There's the bell," Sonia complained. "I'll see you guys in band," she said.

"Bye," I said to my friends. I slowly got out of my seat. I had felt as if I were in a trance all day. I had spent so much time trying to date George, and now that I saw him for what he was, I was no longer interested. It was all a big disappointment that left me feeling vaguely disconnected and strange.

When I saw Jeff before band, I grabbed his arm. "I have to speak to you after class."

"Okay, sure." I guessed he had spent his weekend having a lot more fun than I had had. He was tanned and healthy-looking, and his green eyes sparkled when he looked at me. He wasn't exactly handsome, but he was very cute. We walked into the room together, then went to our separate desks. I sat next to Sonia and Cynthia.

Mr. Walker arrived and the rest of the class began warm-ups. I simply sat, staring into space. There was no way I could warm up to *anything*. I looked around the room at my classmates. George was belting out a Michael Jackson tune on his sax. Ricardo was wearing a Walkman and obviously playing the music that was on his tape. And Jeff was sitting serenely, methodically playing his scales. Jeff was so down to earth, I realized. He never put on a show or tried to pretend he was somebody he wasn't.

"Are you okay?" Cynthia whispered. "Why aren't you playing?"

"Don't worry, I'm fine," I stuttered. I didn't want to tell her that I had just realized that I liked, really liked, Jeff Lang. I didn't want my friends to think I was on the rebound. Besides, they'd probably ask me, "What do you see in *him*?" I'd have to answer all their questions, and I didn't really know how it had happened—it just had.

Somehow I survived the class. I was relieved when the bell rang. Jeff was putting his instrument away quickly, which was strange; he was always the last to leave. I hurried over to him. "Let's start our lessons again," I blurted.

"Why?" His voice was distant.

"I need your help."

"You're improving. You really don't need me anymore," he replied.

"But I do," I protested. I needed him so badly that it almost hurt to admit it.

"Well, I'm busy. I have to study for finals."

"Finals are in a month!" I said, frustrated.

"I need to study very hard. I want to ace all of my exams," he said.

I knew Jeff could help me and study, too. He had done it for weeks. What had I done? Why was Jeff dismissing me like this? "Can't we have a few sessions together?" I pleaded. "I need to perfect the songs for the graduation ceremony."

"Can't you take *no* for an answer?" he said, walking away. "Why don't you ask George to help you? Maybe he can fit you in between parties." Jeff stormed out of the room.

Everyone else had already left, so I had no one to turn to. I had to put the instruments away, when all I felt like doing was crying. I was barely able to lift the sax case and put it on the shelf. I had ruined everything. Jeff thought I was still in love with George. My life was a mess. I finished with the instruments and quickly walked out of the building. I was so lost in thought that I didn't even realize Cynthia was walking beside me on the sidewalk.

"What's wrong, sweetie?" she said, throwing her arm around my shoulder.

"I'm depressed," I mumbled. The rain had stopped, but the sky was still overcast and ominous.

"George isn't worth it," she exclaimed, hopping over a puddle.

"It's not George. It's Jeff." I was walking so quickly that Cynthia could hardly keep up with me.

"I don't understand," she said.

"I've realized that I never really liked George, I was just infatuated with him. It's Jeff who I'm in love with." I turned around so I was face to face with Cynthia.

"What?" Her mouth was wide open. She was clearly in a state of shock.

"I've liked him all along as a friend, and just now it dawned on me how much I care for him." A tear trickled down my cheek.

"So, what's the problem?"

"It's too late. I think he might have liked me all along." I sighed. "But I've taken him for granted. He thinks I like George. Did I tell you he wrote a song for me?"

"That's really neat. I'm sorry, Maddy. What are you going to do?"

"Drop band. I can't deal with this," I said glumly.

"You're not serious, are you? It's almost the end of the semester."

I shook my head. "I don't care, Cynthia. There's no music left in me to play."

That night I called Lisa. I knew she would understand.

"Hi, Mad. What's up?" she asked.

"I like Jeff Lang," I said sadly.

"That's wonderful!" she screamed. "Wait. Your voice. You don't sound like *you* think it's wonderful."

"It would be if he liked me, too."

"Oh, Mad, he's liked you right from the beginning," Lisa said.

"Lisa," I said, trying to hold back the tears, "that's the problem. I never realized it. Now I've lost him." I started to cry.

"Don't be ridiculous, Maddy. Just talk to

him tomorrow. Explain everything. He'll understand. He's a nice guy," she replied.

"There will be no tomorrow," I said.

"Don't be an idiot! There's more than a month left until the end of the semester," Lisa said.

"I don't care. I'm dropping the class," I told her stubbornly.

"What?" Lisa cried. "Wait a minute. Can I reason with you? Can we talk about this?"

"I'm talked out, Lise. I'll call you tomorrow night, when this is all over. Thanks for listening." I hung up the phone.

The next day when band class was over, I waited until everyone else had left the room, and then I approached Mr. Walker.

"Hi, can I talk to you?" I asked.

"Yes, Miss Davis. What can I do for you?"

"I would like to drop band class," I said.

"Why?"

"I can't play."

"You most certainly can," he disagreed. "You've made remarkable progress!"

I couldn't believe Walker was actually trying to convince me to stay in his class. "Half the time I fake, and the other half I fumble," I told him, although, thanks to Jeff, that wasn't really true anymore.

"You exaggerate. Besides, why drop out now, so close to the summer?" Mr. Walker asked me.

"I don't know. I just can't take it anymore," I admitted. Then I glanced over my shoulder because I thought I heard someone at the door. I thought I saw Jeff, but realized it must have been my eyes playing tricks on me.

Mr. Walker looked at his arm as if it were a stranger, and placed it uncomfortably on my shoulder. I appreciated his effort; I knew how difficult it was for him to deal with people— especially teary-eyed students.

"Is the boys' teasing getting to you? I can tell them to stop," he volunteered.

"No. It's not that at all," I said, sniffling.

"Well, think about it. I'll sign you out of the class, though I think it's a shame, but I want you to give it one more day," Mr. Walker said.

"Okay, I'll think about it," I said. But my mind was already made up.

Chapter Fifteen

"I hear you're thinking of dropping band," my mother said.

"I *am* dropping band." I peeked out from behind the covers, where I had been hibernating for the last half an hour. "Who told you?"

"Cynthia. She and Sonia just called. They sounded terribly worried. Sonia heard you talking to your teacher. I don't understand, Maddy. You've improved so much and it's so close to the end of the semester. Why drop out now?"

"Oh, Mom, it's so complicated." The words came out slowly at first, and then I couldn't tell her fast enough. When I finished explaining my hopeless situation, my mother hugged me.

"It's not as difficult a problem as you're making it out to be. Jeff's a wonderful young

146

man. To tell you the truth, I prefer him to George. If you just try talking to him, I'm sure he'll listen."

"Mom, it's not so simple. I've *tried* to talk to him," I told her.

"Directly?"

How could I possibly approach him directly? I thought. My approach to everything had been so indirect these past few months. I had taken a class for all the wrong reasons and I played the part of the interested musician. It seemed too late to discard it now. If I told Jeff the truth about everything, he would think I was silly. I couldn't stand a rejection from him. "I can't Mom. Let's just leave it at that."

"Can I get you anything?" she asked.

"No thanks."

About fifteen minutes later, there was a knock at my door.

"Stay out!" I yelled, thinking it was Steve. I saw the door slowly open. "Hey, what's going on?" I demanded as the door opened all the way. Lisa, Sonia, and Cynthia marched in, all carrying cheerleaders' pompons.

"We're here to cheer you up," Lisa announced.

"I'm not in the mood to be cheered," I said stubbornly.

They ignored me and began to chant:

"Madeline's the best,
The best girl in the West,

Her music, it has zest,
She's never been a pest,
And everyone is blessed,
Knowing Madeline, Madeline—
Hip, hip, hooray!"

They kicked up their heels in unison, the silly pompons bouncing with each kick.

I couldn't help smiling. "It's a good thing you guys aren't real cheerleaders," I teased them. "You're pathetic."

"Yeah, well, so are you. Why don't you call Jeff?" Sonia asked.

"Who told you about him?" I demanded.

"Nobody. It was feminine instinct," Sonia assured me. "You *have* to try to talk to him, Mad. You can't just quit band and never see him again."

"Well, I'm quitting," I insisted.

"You can't quit now," Lisa argued. "You'll lose the class credit. You want to be able to travel around the world, remember?"

"Who cares about the rest of the world if I can't have Jeff Lang?" I wailed.

"We can work on you and Jeff the way we worked on you and George," Cynthia suggested.

"It won't work. After all, it didn't work with George. Besides, there are only six more weeks of school left," I said morosely.

"If there are only six more weeks, you may as well stick it out so you don't lose the credit,"

Sonia said. I had to laugh. It was the first time I had ever heard her sound so practical.

When my friends left, I promised them, like I had promised Mr. Walker, that I'd think about staying in band, but I knew I wouldn't be back. I looked outside my window. Spring was definitely here. The trees were abundant with leaves. The phone rang, but I ignored it.

"Honey, pick up the phone!" my mother called from downstairs.

"Who is it?" I muttered under my breath. I really didn't feel like talking to anyone. I reluctantly picked up the phone. "Hello."

"I'd like to . . . to talk to you," Jeff stuttered. "I was wondering if I could come over." At first I was shocked. Then it occurred to me that my mother must have called him and told him I was dropping out of band. I knew she liked Jeff so much that she'd do anything to get us together. As soon as I got off the phone I was going to kill her!

"Uh, sure," I told Jeff. "Come on over." I was tongue tied. Did he want to talk about tutoring me, or did he just want to talk? Either way, we were getting together.

"See you in a while," Jeff said.

"Okay, um, bye," I said. I hung up the phone. "Mom, please come up here," I yelled.

"What?" she asked. She was already at my door.

"Why did you tell him?"

My mother had a blank expression on her face. "Tell him what?"

"Never mind." She clearly wasn't the culprit. Could my friends have told him? That didn't make sense either; they had just left. My mother walked out, just as puzzled as she had been when she walked in.

"Enough worrying," I muttered to myself. I had no time to waste. I jumped out of bed, realizing I had to fix my face, fix my hair, fix everything. As I applied some fresh blush to my face, I could feel my whole body trembling. Was it from fear or excitement? Sweeping my hair back in a barrette, I reflected it was probably a little bit of both, but mostly happiness, because now I had hope. Maybe Jeff and I could work things out after all.

I heard the doorbell ring downstairs. The minute I opened the door and met his eyes, I felt good. I didn't have to fuss about my hair or my makeup after all. With Jeff I could just be myself. "Hi," I said shyly.

He cleared his throat. "Hi," he replied. I escorted him upstairs to my room. He sat in a chair and I sat cross-legged on the rug.

"Please don't drop the class," he said suddenly. I had never realized how beautifully shaped his mouth was before.

"I have to drop it," I said, reaching up for one of the stuffed animals on my bed. It was a kitten, which had served as my security blanket when I was young. Holding Goldie was somehow comforting. Jeff looked at me holding the kitten, and then quickly looked away. "You don't *have* to drop band," he said. "You've made so much progress."

"Not enough," I said, pulling at the gold hoop in my left ear.

Jeff got up and started pacing around the room. "I mean, you can't leave just because you think you can't play."

I'm leaving because of you, I thought. I had spent too many months going after the wrong guy, when Mr. Right was standing right in front of me all along. When I tried to find my voice, and discovered it wasn't there, it didn't matter. I couldn't possibly explain my feelings for him without sounding like an idiot anyway.

Jeff was still pacing the room. "I mean . . ." His voice came out high-pitched, almost like a squeak. We both laughed nervously. "I forgot what I was going to say."

"Oh." I looked down at the floor, disappointed.

"Oh, now I remember," he said, dropping back into the chair. "I saw you crying when you were with Mr. Walker, and I thought, how ridiculous! You've improved so much. And I'll help you learn the graduation marches you need to know for the end of the semester. I was just being immature when I said I wouldn't help you."

151

Immature? Jeff? What was he talking about? But I had to laugh at his earnestness. He was convinced that it was my inability to play that was forcing me to drop the class. I started laughing, but Jeff's expression remained unsmiling.

"You don't understand," I told him. "I'm tone deaf."

He shrugged. "Big deal. I knew that."

"And I only took the class because of George Held," I said recklessly.

"I knew that, too," Jeff said.

"The worst part is, I don't even like him anymore," I blurted out. A tear rolled down my cheek before I could stop it. Jeff got up and came over to sit by me on the rug.

"So, you don't like George," he said. "It doesn't mean you can't continue to take the class."

"I can't . . . not now . . . I've been so stupid . . . I like *you*, not George . . . and now you're mad at me . . . so I've ruined everything—"

"*Me?*" Jeff looked astonished, surprised, and happy, all at the same time.

I nodded.

"But I've liked you all along," he said. "From the minute I laid eyes on you." He blushed.

"The exact minute?" I couldn't believe what I was hearing.

"No. A few seconds after that."

We both started laughing, but could hardly meet each other's eyes.

"I don't know, Jeff. You just grew on me. I mean, you were filled with so many surprises. We had so much fun together, the tutoring, the ice-cream trips, that night you came over for dinner. . . . You just crept under my skin before I even had a chance to realize it."

"I crept on you *andante*, you mean?" He had an impish look on his face.

"Something like that." I smiled.

"The night of the concert, you looked so pretty. I felt so proud of you," Jeff said quietly.

"Please!" I felt myself blush.

"It was then that I realized how much I hated George Held." He sighed. "I knew you had a crush on him, and there was no way I could compete."

"George is too charming to hate, really," I said.

"That's true. I mean, I didn't hate him for very long. But it seems like I've cared about you forever."

"Wow, Jeff, I didn't realize you were so dramatic."

"I'm Mr. Drama himself." He laughed. "I'm right up there with Laurence Olivier."

"And when will your next performance be, sir?" I asked.

"Well, actually, I got us tickets for *Phantom of the Opera*. What I mean is, I bought two tickets and hoped you'd go with me," he said.

"Are you kidding?" I said excitedly, "I've

been dying to see that for ages. Of course I'll go with you." Impulsively, I leaned over and kissed him on the cheek.

He touched the spot where I had kissed him. "This is getting very romantic."

"Just you wait," I said, grabbing my Gershwin album. "Now I'm going to put on the first song you taught me how to play."

" 'Rhapsody in Blue'!" He grinned. I put the album on my turntable and started it. When I sat back down, Jeff and I were only a fraction of an inch away from one another.

"Did I ever tell you about the Gershwin brothers?" Jeff asked. "They were fascinating."

"I know someone more fascinating." I edged closer to him.

"There's not much that could be more fascinating than the Gershwin brothers," Jeff persisted. "You see . . ."

"Would you just forget about them for a minute and kiss me?" I laughed, amazed by my boldness.

Jeff looked surprised for a moment, but quickly recovered. Before I knew it, the notes of 'Rhapsody' were blasting out of my stereo, and I was held tightly in Jeff's arms, his lips on mine. I heard my heart beating wildly, almost in time to the music. Not bad for someone who was tone deaf!

Stephen Bowkett is an English teacher and librarian in a secondary school in Leicestershire. He has enjoyed writing since his early teens and has had many of his stories published in Science Fiction magazines and broadcast on local radio. He lives in Market Harborough with his wife and two troublesome cats.

Also available in Piper are *Spellbinder* and *Gameplayers*.

don't disillusion me –
i've only got record shops left
21:12:89

Stephen Bowkett

DUALISTS

Piper Books

First published in Great Britain 1987 by Victor Gollancz Ltd
This Piper edition published 1988 by Pan Books Ltd
Cavaye Place, London SW10 9PG
9 8 7 6 5 4 3 2 1
© Stephen Bowkett 1987
ISBN 0 330 30807 6

Phototypeset by Input Typesetting Ltd, London
Printed and bound in Great Britain by
Richard Clay, Bungay, Suffolk

Contents

For Sim – we love you.

By something form'd, I nothing am,
Yet ev'ry thing that you can name.
In no place have I ever been,
Yet ev'ry where I may be seen.
In all things false, yet always true,
I'm still the same – but always new.
Lifeless, life's perfect form I wear,
Can show a nose, eye, tongue or ear.
All shapes and features I can boast,
No flesh, no bones, no blood – no ghost.

Sometimes imperial robes I wear,
Anon in beggar's rags appear.
A giant now, and strait an elf,
I'm ev'ryone, but ne'er myself.
Ne'er sad I mourn, ne'er glad rejoice,
I move my lips but want a voice.
I ne'er was born, nor e'er can die,
Then prythee tell me – what am I?

Extracts from a riddle by Jonathan Swift

Storm in a Teacup

I closed my eyes and tried to think of a place where I'd rather be. Somewhere safe and familiar, somewhere warm and quiet, a place where I'd have no worries or problems or fears . . .

A place that wasn't Seabeck.

I closed my eyes and tried – but it was no use. I could still see the flat, empty beach and the great grey bulk of the sea-wall, the drab green waves and bluish sky all filled with rain and cold. Clearer still, the thought of a new school and all the problems *that* brought hung in my mind: getting used to people – if I could – picking up new routines, settling in, learning to live with funny accents, and the salty air and the sharp crying of seagulls that went on and on. It was like a sour dream with no prospect of waking up . . .

'Simon!'

I opened my eyes and squinted into a blur of blown sand. Kathy Smith was running through switches of dune grass towards me. Her feet kicked up sprays of sand that whipped back into nothingness. She was waving, her face bright with the wide grin that sometimes I could take to, but at other times felt like hitting. Such as now.

'What? What do you want?'

In the two weeks since I'd moved here, Kathy had

9

not once been put off by my rudeness. When I'm in a certain kind of mood I try to push her to the limits of patience, try to wipe the grin away. Never done it yet. She's like some kind of adoring sheepdog. If I sat down with her, I swear she'd rest her head on my lap!

'Want? Oh, nothing really. Your mum thought we should all come down to see if you'd got lost . . .'

I noticed then with a jolt in my chest that Louise Williams and her ten-year-old brother, Chris, were following a short way behind, grey shapes in the rain-haze that was gradually thickening with a build-up of cloud.

The Williamses lived about ten doors down from our new house on the main street; Louise's father was once my dad's best friend. Since the move, either John Williams or his wife had been over to help unpack and sort out. And in that time – only a fortnight – Louise had grown inside me from just a pretty girl I liked looking at, to someone I thought about all the time. I wanted that, but I didn't want it: having been ripped away from all my old friends was enough to contend with. Sometimes I wished I was back in Wales. I wish . . .

'Hi,' I said, putting on a watery smile. Chris smiled back, screwing up his eyes against the sand. Louise said nothing, just stood there almost sullenly in her fawn dufflecoat with its hood pulled up, so that only a few strands of her yellow hair were visible. They twisted and flicked about her face, a thin face that hardly ever smiled, especially, for some reason, when Kathy was about.

'You looked as though the wind was going to blow

10

you over, Simon,' Kathy said, laughing. 'You'll have to put stones in your pockets!'

'Ha ha, Kathy. Really funny that. Yeah, good joke.'

I thought that might have got rid of her grin. Wrong again.

'Ah, he was just playing at seagulls,' Chris piped up, another example of his small and pointless humour. I couldn't be too nasty back, though, with Louise around.

'Yeah Chris, careful I don't poop on you.'

He giggled, then downturned his mouth and stared out to sea. His squint came back as his eyes began to water in the late October wind.

'It's going to rain,' he said glumly.

'Not yet, though,' Kathy answered. 'Wind's too strong for it.'

'And how do *you* know?'

We all looked at Louise. Her voice had a certain quality, sometimes a quietness, that cut right into conversations and stopped them dead. Her tone now was just on the point of being hostile, but her blue eyes sparkled.

'Just do. Because I've lived here all my life. Once the wind slackens the mist will come down, and with it the rain.'

'Really?'

'That's right.'

I imagined I could hear the delicate clash of swords and threw Chris a glance. He was oblivious as usual, eyes glassy-grey as the sea, thoughts elsewhere. I had never met anyone quite as vague. Sometimes, when you talked to him, you realized how clever he was behind all that fog, but his ideas could be weird, too.

He read science fiction and grew cacti. Maybe it was the combination that did it.

'Anyway,' I said, 'I don't see why Mum was really so bothered. Apart from knowing my way around quite well after two weeks, I came out by myself because I wanted to *be* by myself. Still, now you're here . . .'

I looked at Louise, but it was Kathy who responded.

'That's right – we can go back along the beach, be in time for lunch!'

'Super,' Louise said flatly, showing a gleam of teeth.

'OK,' I said. 'All right, Chris?'

'Wha'?'

'Kathy says we'll swim across the channel and spend the afternoon at Butlin's . . .'

'Yeah, great.'

Kathy led us off the dunes, through gulleys of loose sand that would have shifted inside a week. The fringes of whippy marram grass hissed like snakes, each blade of it as tough as plastic.

Five minutes later we stepped over a barrier of sagging picket fence and out on to the beach. It was flat, sandy and bleak, a nowhere between two headlands. I'd been practising my local geography: Dunton Point was away to the left, the Knobble to the right in the direction of Seabeck. Straight out, humped like a black whale's back in the haze, was Head Island with its unmanned lighthouse.

Here on the beach the wind was even stronger, a firm persistent pressure to push us back inland. It was actually possible to lean into it and let it support your weight. This we all did, though Chris leaned too

12

far and dirtied up his hands and the kneecaps of his jeans.

'It's brilliant!' Kathy shouted. 'Isn't this brilliant, Simon?'

I had to admit it was. I nodded and grinned at her and watched her short coppery hair flutter about her face, making her blink. Kathy was a lot plumper than Louise, same age but somehow younger inside. She was growing up and sometimes got self-conscious about it. Soon she'd need to watch her diet. It occurred to me in a flash of inspiration that Louise's distance was due to envy; Kathy was playing with the wind and the cold, Louise was shrugged up inside her coat, keeping well out of it, hating it.

'Hey! Hey, what was that?'

Chris's words flew away downwind. He was pointing out to sea.

'The lighthouse working?' Louise wondered.

It came again, a pinkish flash that dazzled the world silently.

'Lightning, sheet lightning!' I'd seen it a few times before, never this spectacular.

'We're in for a storm, a real wild one.' Kathy was still smiling.

'The joys of living on the coast,' Louise said sullenly. Her family had been here two years, since her father had got a job teaching Physics at Rowley Mead school, where I'd be starting after the half-term holiday. They'd come from Leicestershire, 'Where the salt doesn't rot your car and turn your hair into straw'. Louise's turn of phrase: she really detested Seabeck.

'Well we'd better get a move on,' I said. 'Now we're down here, we'd best stick to the beach . . .'

We started walking, but soon broke into a jogging run. The wind kept pushing us diagonally back into the dunes, and the first damp mists of drizzle were now soaking the backs of our legs.

Suddenly it was like night-time: dark and cold. The wind was dropping and the beach was the most desolate place on Earth, the pale sand hard and moist like an alien wilderness, empty of footprints as far ahead as we could see.

By the time we reached the sea-wall steps and Shore Road, rain was pattering against my jacket: Chris's anorak hood was sopping. My house looked like a smudged-out pencil drawing on dirty paper.

'Come on, we're home!'

The first crash of thunder shuddered overhead as I kicked open the front garden gate.

'You want your heads looking at,' Dad said, as we stood there dripping water on the kitchen floor. I shrugged.

'But who'd want to look at *Chris's* head,' I said reasonably.

'Get your wet stuff off and have some coffee.'

Dad put down the two full mugs he'd just made and fetched four more from the cupboard. He flipped the kettle on again.

I took all the wet coats and hung them over a sheet of polythene in the back porch, then got some towels from the airing cupboard. The atmosphere in the kitchen was warm and steamy, all the windows misted up and the world shut out.

The four of us trooped into the lounge. The telly was on, with the sound turned so low it was only a mumble. Weekend football was being played in a sunny place somewhere else in the world.

Mum sat under a splash of light at the table, absorbed in the latest of her crazy hobbies.

'What's it this time, Mum?'

'Quilling, Simon.'

'Sounds fascinating.'

'Enough of your cheek,' she said. Kathy laughed and I didn't know why.

'And you must be taking up origami, Mr Hallam.' Dad had come back in with the coffees and now sat down to refold his *Telegraph*.

'Or are you kite-making?' I added.

'No, origami, son. I was a third Dan at one time.'

'That's karate, Dad.'

'Oh. Well, I used to do that too: club secretary in fact, until I got the chop.'

We all groaned. The others had yet to learn that Dad had lost all his previous friends because of bad puns.

'Origami's just as much fun. Actually I joined the British Origami Association once—'

'Here it comes,' I warned them.

'—until it folded.'

Chris laughed loudly, out of all proportion to the quality of the joke, I thought. There again, he was probably thinking of something else entirely.

The four of us kids sat in front of the fire, sipping coffee. Chris stared at the flames, Kathy watched Mum busy with her work. I watched Louise.

She sat with her feet tucked in under herself, propped up on her right arm. She was gazing at the room, at Dad's Welsh dresser and his collection of pewter (inherited from Grandad), at the pots and

15

bowls he'd made – now he lectured in ceramics at the polytechnic in Reabridge. Whenever her eyes drifted close to me, I looked away, knowing I'd find cold there, but also dreading I'd find warmth.

I felt my stomach slide just thinking about her, but then came a quick reaction of anger. After all, she'd never shown much interest in me; she was only here at all because our sets of parents were friendly, Mr Williams and Dad having met at the same training college. She was like a wall with no gate, a window with the curtains drawn . . . I mean, she was pretty enough, but not much of a figure – skinny like a boy, and her fair hair cut short at the sides. I'd noticed her on the first day when the Williamses came round to help us unpack, and I thought my luck was in with this good-looking girl only a hundred yards away; went to the same school too.

Kathy complicated things. She lived even closer, a few doors up, and from the start she'd put on that moon-eyed look whenever she saw me. It was embarrassing. After three days I was sick of it, and wondered out loud why she didn't sit on the doorstep each morning with the paper in her mouth, wagging her tail. That had stung her. That had gone in hard. Her brown eyes turned shiny and she gasped in disbelief, and turned round and went home without a word. Next day she was back, bright as the summer sun as though nothing had happened. I wondered if she was stupid, or what.

'Simon—'

I jolted, and coffee slopped from my mug on to the hearthrug.

'Damn, Kathy—'

'Sorry. Um, I was thinking. What d'you want to do tomorrow?'

'Worry about starting my new school on Monday!'

'Oh, that won't be so bad . . .How about going out to the cliffs? If there is a storm we can search for salvage.'

'You're joking!'

'No, I'm serious.' It wasn't difficult to tell with Kathy, her smile said everything.

'What if there isn't a storm?'

'There will be. It's raining hard now, but tonight it'll be worse. Then, more than likely, it will all blow south and the sky will clear.'

'Will it rain tomorrow?'

Kathy shook her head. 'Cold but sunny, sky empty as glass . . .'

I thought about it: sounded good, only I wondered if I could persuade Louise to come along too.

'I should be careful if I were you.' Dad's adult presence dropped from above. I was irritated that he'd been listening in. He folded up his paper and rested it by the side of his chair. Then came the long process of cleaning out and refilling his pipe.

'I've heard the rocks can crumble there, especially out towards Blackshales.'

Kathy was nodding, not trying to pitch an argument back as I would have expected.

'It's an odd section of coast. You never know what it'll do next. After a high sea, all sorts of things are washed up.'

'Not including drowned children, I hope.'

'We'll be careful,' Kathy said, convincing Dad and finalizing the arrangement in one go. It occurred to

17

me that if I had said it, or Louise, Dad wouldn't have believed us.

Lunch came and went. Louise phoned home, but walked back into the lounge hard-faced.

'It rang and rang. They're not home yet.'

Mr and Mrs Williams had gone shopping in Westmartin, the largest town in the area. Had its own market, too. I could see that Chris was getting bored watching TV sport. Louise gave nothing away but her anger. Kathy had wandered over to Mum's table and was learning how to quill.

At four o'clock the storm was at its height, the wind hurling rain at the windows, making the heavy curtains stir and shift, making the flames quiver in the grate. I tried to sense the silent, electric moments just before the lightning flared; then came the long grinding of thunder that drummed through the ground.

It was gone six and after tea when we heard a car horn outside and, a moment later, the clatter of feet in the porch.

'Home safe and sound,' Dad said for everyone's benefit. He pushed himself out of his chair and went to answer the door.

The Williamses walked in, windblown. Louise's mum looked exhausted, while Mr Williams had oil smears on his face and fawn corduroy trousers.

'Rain caught you out?' Dad said with his usual lack of perception and tact. John Williams lifted his hands to heaven.

'Water in the carb. Had to get under the bonnet and dry the whole damn thing out!'

Dad nodded, puffed away at his rosewood.

'Beetles are notorious for that.'

'It's a Cortina.'

'Oh yes. Them too.'

'Still, all back in one piece,' Mrs Williams chipped in quietly. Louise had told me she was a supply teacher in the county; not a very good one, I'd decided. She was too quiet, too vague, her smile always nervous and forced. I could imagine kids running rings round her, the worst of them bringing on tears of frustration.

'Oh yes, we must be thankful for that.' Mr Williams's voice was heavy with sarcasm. 'Forget the fact that my cords are ruined—'

'Better safe than—'

'Oh, for goodness' sake, Penny!'

I stared hard at the television while the atmosphere tightened around me. I had the impression this happened often. On the box some kids' programme was playing and a man with a stupid high voice was talking to a glove puppet.

'Well!' Mum stood and proudly held up a card, on which had been stuck an abstract pattern made from bits of string and tight curls of coloured paper. Is that *it*, I wondered.

'Now that Kathy and I have finished, I can make everyone a nice cup of tea. Meanwhile, John, you and Penny clean up. And then, Greg my darling – any suggestions?'

Dad checked his watch, sucked reflectively at his pipe so that the smoke flowers bloomed. He knew that everyone was watching him. Eventually he came to a decision.

'Pub,' he said with finality, and beamed with such obvious pleasure that the black spell was broken.

Louise and Chris were taken home by their father, Kathy hurried the rainbeaten distance to her house, then the adults drove off to The Countryman and left me in peace.

Now the house did not seem cosy any longer: merely quiet. The unfamiliarity of it crept into my head: the draughts that came from unexpected angles, the snap and whisper of the open coal fire (in the old house we'd had gas), the knowledge that I did not yet know every dark corner and hidden place . . .

In the end I spooked myself into leaving all of the downstairs lights on when I went to bed. I snatched the curtains closed, jumped out of jeans and shirt and into pyjamas, then leaped between the sheets.

I read awhile, then my concentration drifted, and I thought about Kathy's devotion to me and the cold distance between myself and Louise. If only I could combine the best of both worlds . . . Louise filled out a little, with a happy smile and warm eyes, just *dying* to show me the quiet rockpools around Blackshales . . .

Whim became a dream. I felt myself sliding towards sleep and let it happen.

Then the lights went out.

I startled awake, a yell caught somewhere on its way up from my lungs. There was no one to call to, of course. Maybe I could hammer on the walls: the neighbours might call back and reassure me . . .

I felt foolish, but comforted, even had the courage to step to the window and pull the curtains open.

The last of the lightning was playing in the sky way over to the left amongst an avalanche of black clouds. Its thunder was a far distant threat. Kathy had been right. The sky was clearing fast and had by this time changed from deep evening blue to night-time black.

Silence fell. The wind dropped, held in like a breath – then suddenly the lightning was back brilliantly with a sound like 'flink' – like the element of a bulb burning out.

Drumrolling thunder, some weak wind-gusts against the house-side.

'Did you *see* that . . . Did you see it . . .' I whispered to myself, for company, pressed my nose against the window and immediately rubbed away at the breath-mist.

The flash had been green. Bright green. And down in the sea near the beach was an emerald smear – now lost in spray and dark and my disbelief.

And then, high up in the west, glimmering like a flare, the brightest star I had ever seen moving fast towards the horizon.

High-Tide Line

I dreamt of green constellations and huge shadowy shapes in the night. But I did not remember climbing back into bed, or falling asleep. Some time late on the power cut must have ended, and after that Mum and Dad arrived home; neither of them said anything to me about the lights being left on.

I woke earlyish, just after six, when the window square behind the curtains was turning grey.

Mum was making a cooked breakfast – her one concession to normal food. I could hear her clattering crockery and laying the table. I decided to get up and make an early start to the day, and swam into a warm downstairs world of bacon smells and Dad's pipesmoke.

'I don't believe it,' Mum said. She was whisking scrambled egg in a pot.

'Don't worry, the boy's sleepwalking. Aren't you, son?'

'Yes Dad. I – am – not – responsible – for – my – actions—' I went to the cooker and pinched a sausage from under the grill.

'Hey,' Dad said, 'that only leaves me with six!'

'They're not good for you. I'm saving you from yourself.'

'Give me strength. You'll be smoking my pipe for me soon.'

I shook my head. 'No, I'll leave that form of suicide to you.'

'Or will the sausages get me first?' Dad wondered.

He grinned, and he was smiling too with his pale blue eyes; I felt a great wave of love for him. It only lasted a moment, and it didn't happen often, but occasionally a second would arrive when I'd see, not just Dad, but his whole life kind of mapped out in front of me. I remembered him younger, the rows and the worries and the good times. And I saw him in the future, an old man, close to the end of things; retired, grey, quiet, not able to make his pots any more. Maybe it would be like standing on the loneliest head-land in the world. I wanted to tell him that I'd be there too, holding his hand before the sea took him away.

'You all right, Simon?' He plonked a mug of tea in front of me at the table.

'Yeah—' I coughed and wiped at my eyes. 'This flamin' sausage of yours went down the wrong way!'

I made Kathy's day by calling round for her, then we went on and picked up Chris and Louise before walking to the beach – as far as we could along the road; when it started sloping up along the cliff-top, we took to the sands.

The day was chilly, and the sky had a white, washed-out look as though it had been bleached and beaten, and hung out to dry. The sun was a chalky smudge behind us, giving no heat. The briefest of Indian summers had come and gone a fortnight before, early on in October (I remember sweating on

23

the day we moved), and in another two weeks we'd be having frosts and the first sleets mixed in with the rain.

Luckily we'd all had the sense to wrap up. I had on two pairs of socks, my heaviest jeans and a green jumper with canvas elbow-patches I'd picked up from the Army and Navy stores. Chris wore his oversized anorak (he looked like a bell tent), Louise her little-girl dufflecoat: Kathy was muffled up in rainbow-coloured polo neck, a scarf, gloves and a pair of Wellingtons. They were the colour of bananas and she called them her yellie wellows.

After twenty minutes we turned and looked back along our path. Four pairs of footprints stretched in meandering lines away towards Seabeck, lost in mist. The beach was deserted, except for the tiny figure of a man with a pinpoint dog on invisible lead out near Dunton Point. Far up on the sands was the high-tide line, straggles of black seaweed and some shells and assorted bits of flotsam

'It's higher than I've ever seen it,' Kathy told us. In places the stuff had been cast up over the pale, car-sized boulders that lay at the foot of the cliffs.

'Must have been wild down here last night. You'd never have thought it though . . .'

Today the morning was calm, tide fully out, the water flat and dead. Head Island bulked starkly so that its name became obvious – the craggy profile of an old man's face, complete with open toothless mouth and squarish beard.

'How much more've we got to walk?'

Here we go, I thought: the first moan of the day.

'Not far, Chris,' Kathy said, more patiently than I would have done. 'See where the rocks stick out from the sea over there? Just past that is Blackshales, that's where you find the best salvage.'

'Salvage?' Louise spoke up suddenly. 'You mean wreckage.'

'Now and then you find something worth claiming. You make your claim, and the shipping line, or whoever lost it, might reward you for the find. Then it's called salvage. *Wreckage* means bits of driftwood, bottles, seaglass – and on the flats you get jellyfish washed too far ashore for the next tide to sweep them back.'

'Big as dinner plates,' I said, 'and the *teeth* on them! Actually, that was just one of my little jokes . . .'

'One of your *very* little jokes.' Louise gave me a frosty glare. I tried to keep my smile pinned on bright like a badge.

'Oh, she's mardy because Mum and Dad have been rowing again.' Chris kicked at a stone. 'She gets like this nowadays—'

'Just shut it, Chris, right!'

'Anyway . . .' Kathy almost waved her arms to calm things down. 'Look out for driftwood. Your mum's into carving it now, or polishing it up as natural sculpture.'

'Oh yeah, eyes peeled. Never mind the gold doub-loons – go for the driftwood, guys!'

We walked on. Louise said, out of the blue, 'What happens if we actually find something valuable?'

I recognized the gleam in her eyes, because I still remembered the tug of gold-fever myself, when I used to go fossil hunting back home, or on those rare occasions when you find someone's purse or wallet in the street and wonder how big the reward's going to be.

'We report it to the Receiver of Wreck, who's also the local customs' officer – Derek Kinsley, lives in Seabeck.'

'He keeps it?' I asked.

'It's in his care until the insurance companies have dealt with it. Precious metals and so on count as treasure-trove, and you get a percentage of its value. 'Course, driftwood you can keep for free.'

'*Very* funny,' I said, but appreciatively: Kathy's humour was as bouncy as a ball.

We reached the point and passed it, and I had my first view of Blackshales.

It reminded me of Gormenghast: sheer slabby black cliffs, slick and shining with their roots in the sand. The sun was way off behind them, lighting the gorse bushes at the tops, and it was difficult to make out what was rock and what shadow – wings of shadow hanging there like huge bats asleep.

'It's amazing, Kathy.' I nearly whispered it.

'Pretty good, eh?' she said.

She looked sideways at me and smiled, a satisfied smile in knowing she had wanted to impress me and had succeeded. Blackshales was one of her show-pieces, I decided, but one of her secret places too. I made a bet with myself that she knew every crevice in the cliffside, where the best rockpools were; the dangers and the excitements of this lonely beach.

'You come up here often, Kath?'

'Usually by myself—'

'Oh?' Louise added, keeping her eyes to the ground, pretending to search for shells.

'It's peaceful. No-one to bother you. I mean, the *freedom*, Simon . . .'

I nodded. 'Yeah, I know . . .'

'Hey! What's this? Come and look at this!' Chris came running over, grabbed Kathy's hand and dragged her across to a flat patch of sand between grey knuckly rocks.

'What is *that*?'

'It's a jellyfish,' Kathy explained. We all stood round and stared down at the thing. It was like a milky lens, about a foot across, glistening in the thin sunlight. Deep inside the mass I could see reddish strands and vaguer structures that seemed to lead nowhere. It was completely still; I couldn't tell whether it was alive or dead.

'It's disgusting!' Louise's lip curled. She was swallowing hard. Kathy prodded at the jellyfish with her foot.

'It's not. It's a living creature, stranded. It'll have dried out by the time the tide comes back. Either that, or the gulls will have picked it to pieces—'

'Hang on—'

My head jerked up and I stared around – at the cliffs, the beach, back the way we'd come. The sky and the land were empty of seagulls. I knew that gangs of them always foraged after a storm, after every high tide in fact. But now I couldn't see a single one.

I mentioned it, and Kathy's eyes flicked towards the wooden breakwaters farther out that angled sharply into the softly slapping water.

'You get lines of them perched there.'

'Not today . . .'

'We go home?' Kathy wondered. She looked uneasy. It gave Louise her chance to sneer.

'Look who knows all about the seashore. You'll never get your Guide badge this way, Kathy . . . Why don't we find out *why* the beach is deserted, eh?'

Agreement was silent. Out of nothing Louise had made the opportunity to take the lead. She struck out first, beckoning us on, over some shingle, more humps of rock that were slick with green algae—

Then she stopped, dead.

We came up and stood beside her and the silence gathered itself around us.

When Kathy spoke at last, it felt like dropping an armful of china. The air rang with it.

'Something's happened here. Something's—'

'Wrong,' I said. 'But what?'

I took a few steps forward and felt small stones grind and sink in the sand under me. Beneath the cool splash of sun the sand looked pink, pebbles almost a translucent blue. There was the silver glint of water in the distance and – and the gleam of something that was not water, clumps of it strewn about.

As soon as I'd noticed one patch of the stuff, it seemed to be everywhere: quivering gently in hollows, smeared like snail-tracks over the ground. A long thin streak of it led towards the waterline.

'More jellyfish?' Louise asked reluctantly. I could almost see the teeth and tentacles looming in her mind.

'Not jellyfish,' Kathy said thoughtfully, 'nor spilled oil. Odd. Can't remember anything like this before . . .'

'It's monsters,' Chris added, talking quickly to keep out the fear. 'It's monsters from the sea.'

It would be easy enough just to turn round and trek back home, I thought; but then Louise would have a field-day, and it would forever by *my* fault that the mystery was never solved.

I took another couple of careful steps on to the sand

28

and approached the nearest mound of the substance as though it was an unexploded bomb.

'Maybe the storm brought it in—'

Kathy's shadow fell across me as I knelt beside the stuff, and I almost jumped backwards with fright.

'Sorry,' She put her hand over her mouth, then went on: 'I mean, it could be from anywhere if the Gulf Stream brought it ashore.'

I nodded absently, picked up a tiny quartz pebble and dropped it in. The stuff rippled viscously, not quite like jelly, not quite like treacle.

'Isn't pollution, is it?' I asked, then turned cold with alarm. 'You don't suppose it's radioactive!'

'Naa. Anyway, if it was we could hand in a glowing report to the newspapers . . .'

'That's sick.' Louise came across and peered over Kathy's shoulder. She was torn between curiosity and distaste. 'What are we going to do?'

'Take some home,' I suggested, before working out the implications. 'I know your dad will be interested, Lou.'

'It's Lou*ise*, OK? And Dad's a physicist, not a biologist.'

'What's that got to do with it? He's a scientist.'

'Well, he's likely to tell you where you can put it . . . But if you want to take some back, go ahead.'

'Yeah,' Chris added with relish, 'pick it up!'

I gave what must have been a sickly grin, stared at three rather unsympathetic faces and tried a clumsy wink.

'Ah well, Super Simon strikes again!'

I knelt down and searched around for something to poke the substance with. There was a razor-shell nearby. I snapped off the end and pushed the sharp edge down into the jelly. It resisted for an instant, like rubber, but then gave way. The shell sliced clean through, though when I pulled it out, the stuff slowly closed up again and left no mark.

I decided to try one quick touch. I put my finger to the surface and found that it was not moist or slimy, but it was cold, as cold a fish, and it had a rubbery feel. I pushed harder and my finger started to sink in . . .

'Simon!' Kathy's voice was fluttery with unease.

'Shh, it's all right.'

I bent close and sniffed: no smell to it, only the faintly salty, seaweedy tang of the surrounding sand.

'OK. This is it . . .'

I slid my fingers under the mass and picked up a cupped handful. It was heavier than I'd expected and cold . . . Cold, dead, colourless junk.

There was no danger here. It was just another small mystery from the strange world of the sea. I held it carefully, though, protecting it with my other hand like I would a hatchling fallen from a nest.

Then I had a thought.

'Hey, wait. This stuff is – it's moving! It's – it's – quick, Louise, catch it!'

I jumped at Louise and pushed my hand towards her. She had no time to plan a reaction, just did what came naturally. She shaped her mouth into a wide O, screwed up her eyes and said, 'AAAAGGGGHHHH!'

The Guess

'I would guess it's effluent, you know, discharge from a chemical plant somewhere up the channel,' I said, frowning over the bucket we'd put the stuff in when we got home. I jabbed at it with a pencil, took a deep sniff and shook my head. 'Weird stuff. It's kind of – nothing, really . . .'

'Now *there's* a comprehensive analysis, Simon!' Kathy laughed, and I swung my arm lazily to cuff her ear.

'What I mean to say is, that it's neither plastic nor rubber, neither slime nor jelly. It's – it's—'

'Slubber,' Chris piped up. He'd been helping himself from the plateful of cakes Mum and Dad had put out, and this bright idea caused a shower of crumbs in our direction.

'Keep your habits to yourself, Chris,' Kathy told him, but the name had struck the right note in my mind.

'That's not bad, Chris. It almost shows intelligence, that: 'slubber' – neither one thing or another; not slime or rubber, a bit of both!'

'So now,' Louise said, a little pinch-faced (either with the cold or because *she* hadn't thought of it), 'do we tell the police, fire brigade, TV people – or the lot of them?'

'There's not much chance of telling anybody late on a Sunday afternoon,' Kathy added. She was busy at the sink, cleaning up the two pieces of driftwood she'd collected for Mum. 'Anyway, if it *is* from a discharge pipe, you don't want to keep it around here. Might not be safe . . .'

'Oh, I'm sure it's safe enough,' Louise said, determined not to lose face. 'In fact I've never seen a more inert substance in all my – hello, that's odd.'

'What's up?'

We all crowded round Louise as she stood peering into the bucket. I contrived to get as close as possible, so close that I was touching her with my arm as I stared in.

At first, I didn't see what all the fuss was about, but then it hit me . . . The bucket was made of blue plastic, and used mostly when Dad washed his car. Now, strangely enough, the slubber was bluish too, either refracting the colour of the plastic, or somehow actually absorbing its blueness directly.

'This,' Kathy said heavily, or maybe it was cautiously, 'is impossible.'

'And look here –' Louise prodded the stuff with a pencil, and this time the slubber resisted and formed a deep pit where the point of the pencil was pressing.

'It's tougher than it was,' I said, remembering the experiment with a razor-shell. 'And it *is* reacting, somehow, but strangely. It's not behaving like anything I've come across in chemistry lessons.'

'What can we do?' Chris wondered. Kathy chuckled.

'Feed it and lock it up in the shed!'

I gave her a thanks-a-lot grimace and cast around for other suggestions. Chris shrugged.

'Lou?'

'*Louise.*' She favoured me with one of her sulphuric-acid glares and her eyes blazed. 'It's Louise.'

'Louise . . .'

She paused significantly, just to let me know that she was really mad, then walked over and shut the kitchen door.

'I'm tempted to fetch my father and ask his advice. But . . .'

'But what?' Kathy asked, sensibly I thought because at least Mr Williams could make an educated guess. Louise only smiled, brushing back her hair in a gesture that made my knees melt.

'But . . . if he finds out about the stuff, then the cat's really out of the bag, right?'

'What are you talking about?'

'Yes,' I added, 'what's going on?' Just like Kathy, my mind was floundering several steps behind what Louise was thinking.

'*You're* the one who's been going on about treasure and salvage, Kathy. Hasn't it occurred to you that this stuff might be valuable, hm? I mean, wherever it's come from, it's not your usual run-of-the-mill flotsam. It could be *worth* something.'

'It could also be dangerous,' I said, but tentatively. Louise was obviously in one of her determined moods and I didn't want to argue – not least because that could ruin any future chance I might have with her.

'You ring my father, then.' she snapped back. 'And we'll all look pretty silly when he tells us it's octopus droppings.'

She stood with hands plonked on hips, looking magnificently and gorgeously irate. Chris sighed as though he was used to all of this. I noticed Kathy's

33

secret little smile of, well, maybe of understanding. And the whole weight of the moment seemed to settle on my shoulders.

'You'd be great at poker,' I told her, and watched the puzzled frown with satisfaction.

'All right, Louise, you win. How about we put this slubber out of the way for a few days – in the garage, maybe – and do some more tests. It'd make a good science project. Hey, we might even cop some merit marks for it!'

'Merit marks!' Louise shook her head and laughed. 'Don't you ever dream?'

She went to the sink and rummaged about in the cupboard underneath, pulling out a mug and a white plastic container; two-litre ones that used to hold ice-cream. Mum saved them habitually, 'just in case'.

'It'd be better all round if we each took some of the slubber, then no single person has the responsibility – or needs to take the whole blame if we're found out.'

She scooped handfuls out of the bucket into each of the containers, handed one to Kathy and one to Chris. Kathy stood Mum's driftwood on the draining board and reached for the towel. Louise went on:

'I suggest we dilute the stuff with water and leave it outside tonight. We haven't smelt any fumes yet, but it could be giving them off at room temperature. And we'll meet again tomorrow, to talk over plans. Right?'

I took the bucket with what was left of the slubber and filled it under the tap. Kathy came over, wiping loose sand grains off her hands.

'So, Mum's got quilling *and* woodcarving to while away the hours . . . I wonder what would happen if I gave her my homework books?'

Stupid comment I thought, even as I said it; it brought back my worries about the new school with a crash. Kathy guessed it and smiled.

'It'll be all right. It's not a bad place.'

'Just a new place,' I said, and noticed Louise staring at me – it's my patch, her eyes were saying, you'll be on my territory tomorrow.

I must have slept, but in fragments, with long spells of lying awake in between. It began raining again. No storm this time, just a determined and endless downpour of drops that smacked on the slabs in the yard.

I watched the window-square turn grey for the second night running, but by seven-thirty the clouds were clearing and the sun was up and shining. I had an empty pit in my stomach, not entirely through hunger, but I went down to attempt to fill it anyway.

'Morning, Simon.' I could see Dad was trying hard not to comment on my unusally smart appearance: black school trousers, maroon blazer, white shirt and maroon tie. I felt like a raspberry ripple ice-cream.

'Mornin', Dad. Any tea left?'

He hefted the pot, nodded.

'Day off?' I wondered, pointing my eyes at his tatty old sweatshirt and jeans. *And* he hadn't shaved.

'Just an afternoon session today. I thought I'd get my workshop ready: haven't thrown a pot for weeks.'

'Vandal,' I muttered, squinting into the steam as I sipped my hot tea. 'Anyway, when do you suppose you'll have the workshop ready?'

Dad raised a suspicious eyebrow. 'Why, are you mad keen to start firing clay?'

I gave him one of my vague shrugs and let the

subject go; but it had started me thinking about slubber. I wondered how much like clay the substance might be — how readily it might be formed into a variety of objects.

After finishing my tea, I pushed myself up from the table and went outside. Horizontal sunlight was pouring across the garden, and all the grass glistened from earlier showers. Against the house wall the old blue bucket was brimful, the surface of the water reflecting the sun-dazzle.

I ran across and stared in. Nothing. Just water.

'Dammit!'

I whipped off my blazer, rolled up my shirtsleeve and stuck my arm in up to the elbow. I thought I might feel the slubber sloshing around sluggishly at the bottom, but there was only the swirl of the numbingly cold water.

In a sudden temper I lifted the bucket and flung the lot at an old stick of a rosebush over by the garage. The bucket bounced wildly and came to rest on the lawn.

So, I thought, after all the fuss and fancy talk there was nothing left, just water. And that was that.

School buses must smell the same all over the country, I told myself, trying to quell the nerves, especially when it's cold and wet outside and hot within. The atmosphere was heavy with damp hair and clothes, the stink of cigarettes from the back row; and waves of stifling cologne from some kid in the seat in front who thought he was a man. And there was the noise, a solid high wall of it that never let up; kids trying to out-shout each other, girls shrieking, boys yelling their laughter as they bellowed jokes into each other's ears . . .

I tried to create a pocket of peace and privacy by leaning close to the window and staring out with all my concentration; by ignoring the madness inside the coach, maybe it would not bother me.

The day was October-dismal. Within an hour the glittering brightness had been taken away by masses of grey-black cloud, and the rain had started once more. It lashed silently outside at the window and dribbled down the glass. The countryside looked washed out, leached of all colour except for the faded brown of oak leaves and a red speckling of hawthorn berries in the hedgerows.

Kathy had told me that the journey to Rowley Mead would take half an hour. The school was on the outskirts of Reabridge, ten miles away, but over half the kids were bussed in from outlying villages. This coach started at Seabeck, but then followed a twisted path to Westcombe, Chantsey and Dellaford before rejoining the main road . . .

I wondered if I could stand this routine for the rest of the third year – and then for the other years before I left school!

With a shudder and a hiss of pneumatic brakes, the coach slowed and angled its bulk down a side road. The hedges closed in and elder branches fluttered only inches away.

We were high up now, on the coast road – the only road – to Dellaford. Fields sloped away into mist: beyond would be worn-down limestone cliffs and miles of shingle beach, then the sea. All invisible today. Nevertheless I strained my eyes to look at this nothing, trying to wish myself out there instead of in here. The coach driver, in desperation or just as an afterthought, turned on the radio to swamp out the noise of teenagers—

And to the accompaniment of fast hard rock I watched the dry-stone walls and fences separating the fields melt away: grass deepened to a rich emerald green: sunlight the colour of polished copper dissolved through the sky and a golden lion emerged from behind a stand of trumpet-like trees as tall as poplars.

I jerked my face away from the window and fell back into the bath of hot stale air and schoolkid noise. What were they smoking on the back seats? I looked round to see if anyone had noticed my shock. They were all oblivious. Kathy had had the common sense not to sit beside me, and was further down the bus trying hard to write neatly as she finished off a late English essay.

I felt myself sweating, but at the same time I shivered.

I pushed my nose back against the window . . . .

The landscape had changed. Now I was in a valley, in a steep V between high slopes of white rock that had a purplish tinge. More of the emerald-coloured stuff grew in cascades down the valley sides. By craning my neck I was able to see a white sky and spiralling silhouettes, diamond shapes wheeling like paper-ash blown up from a bonfire.

The image began to fade behind a thickening fog. Madly I wiped at the glass: the double-thickness unit was sealed, with no way of opening it. I thought about stopping the coach and jumping out. What was I seeing? What was happening?

Outside, behind the rain curtains, a black bat-thing

drifted closer, its one wide wing spread out, its silver pointed beak aiming in my direction.

I pulled back as it rushed up – and the metal ferrule of an umbrella tapped harshly on the window.

John Williams, Louise's father, stood grimacing into the rain. In the silence I could hear him clearly; everyone else had gone.

'Come on, Simon, unless for some strange reason you'd rather be at home. . . .'

'Maybe it was because you didn't get much sleep,' Kathy suggested, keeping her voice carefully neutral. 'Or—'

'Or maybe I've been watching too many space movies, or maybe I just imagined it, right?'

'I didn't say that . . .' She let the conversation drop and poked at her dinner with a fork. The dining hall (also the Assembly hall) at Rowley Mead was a huge echoing room, with one glass wall facing the tennis courts and playing fields beyond. It was all normal, all drab, all reassuring.

'Anyway, it was so *clear*, Kath. I mean, I could sit here for an hour writing down every detail of what I saw. And I'm not that good at making up stories . . .'

'So.' She shrugged. 'I don't know, then, do I? Could've been anything.'

'But what? And what if it happens again?'

'You tell your parents.'

'What are you suggesting?'

When she looked up, her eyes were calm rather than angry, but her cheeks were flushed.

'That they would believe you and want to find out too, and help you. Like I do . . .'

All of a sudden I started to feel firm ground slip

away from under me. The dining table, with just the two of us sitting at it, seemed very exposed.

'Well,' I said, realizing that Kathy had understood perfectly why I'd told *her* and not Louise or anyone else, 'if it happens again I'll tell Dad. He'll know if I'm crazy – he went to pot himself years ago!'

Kathy cocked her head and gave a little too-funny smile. Her mood lightened.

'Anyway, it can't be stranger than what happened to me and my slubber.'

'Why, what went on?'

'It was the stuff I took home in the old cup Louise gave me. It had a green cartoon Frankenstein on it, and a message: "I'm a Li'l Monster".'

'That,' I said, with as much outrage as I could muster, 'used to be my favourite!'

'Yeah, I can see why'

'So the slubber changed into a mini-Frankenstein and tried to strangle you in your sleep . . .'

'Don't be daft. But what *did* happen was that somehow the paint soaked through the cup and coloured the slubber. When I went to the garage this morning to look at it, the stuff wasn't transparent, but kind of pearly white. And in it were strings of blue and red, patches of green, specks of black from the writing . . .'

'Trouble is, Kathy,' I said, 'that cup is *glazed*. It isn't porous. It couldn't let water through, or paint, or slubber. Ask Dad. Hey, maybe Chris sneaked in to play a trick on you, eh?'

'It happened, Simon. I'm telling you what happened. In fact, the cup will still be there this evening. Come round and see—'

Kathy must have seen the shift in my eyes. She nodded, pointing to my plate with her fork.

'Eat your ravioli before it gets cold. Puts hairs on your chest, y'know . . .'

And I pointed back to her plate.

'So is that why you eat it, Kathy?'

The day drifted by with not much happening, except for me trying hard to feel less uncomfortable; a mix of images, a tatty scrapbook page I would never turn to again.

I found myself in Louise's tutor group: that meant we had the register taken and some subjects together. She sat aloof on the other side of the room amongst a clutch of the best-looking girls in the class. The group radiated disdain for everyone else and tried (successfully) to make the form tutor's life a misery. He was Mr Barrett, also my English teacher; a tall lanky man with a big wide grin, a mass of fair curly hair and a great booming voice that never seemed to sound angry. He had a kind of infectious energy and was full of ideas. I liked him from 'go' and decided to use him as my anchor if I started to drift into trouble.

Then there was Dawson, a short, stocky, hard-looking kid whose one concession to school uniform amounted to a ragged red blazer with torn pockets. He'd stuck badges all over the front of the blazer: of swastikas, heavy metal bands, slogans; one that said 'I am 6'. I could well believe it . . .

The only person in the class apart from Mr Barrett to show anything other than mild curiosity towards me was Claire Goodson. She must have been getting on for six feet tall, but instead of stooping self-consciously, she made the most of it.

She wore bright plastic jewellery (and was often in trouble for it, I found out), hair ribbons of the same colour, and showed a friendliness to match her size.

During afternoon tutorial, when everybody just gathered in groups and talked, Claire came over, whisked my roughwork book away and flourished her autograph across the front cover.

'And three big kisses—'

'Simon.'

'Simon. There!' She bent down and ruffled my hair. I thought I was going to burn up.

'Hey, you come and sit on my lap anytime, Simon, OK'

'If I could climb that high, Claire . . .'

She laughed. And across the room Louise glared death and destruction from the centre of her kingdom.

'So, how did it go?'

'It went,' I said. Mum finished the washing-up that I normally do (a treat because it was my first day at the new school), and put the kettle on. Dad was still out at the poly; the house was quiet. I could have fallen asleep.

'Any problems?'

I thought about that a while, but not long enough for Mum to ask me again. I shook my head heavily.

'No, not really. I'm still settling in.'

'Enough of a problem in itself,' she agreed. 'How are your teachers?'

I told her about Mr Barrett. 'But Louise's dad, you know, is totally different at school. Sort of sarcastic and hostile. He hardly acknowledged I was there.'

'Defence mechanism,' Mum said, 'to preserve his authority. Or maybe he just didn't want to single you out as someone special. You know how kids can be . . . Make any friends?'

I mentioned Claire. 'Really friendly. And she has the most amazing pair' – Mum's eyebrows rose – 'of earrings. Bright yellow. Clashed with her blazer something wicked.'

Mum chuckled, then passed me some coffee. Her mood became wistful, almost serious.

'Simon, we're sorry to put you through this, your dad and I. But when this job came up – well, we couldn't let it pass.'

'I understand, Mum . . .'

'It's not so much the rise in salary. What's money matter anyway, right? But we've both always wanted to live by the sea. And now Greg's organizing his workshop and he can afford to save up for his own kiln.'

'You don't have to explain, Mum,' I said. The talk was getting too heavy for me. 'I don't mind.'

'I want to explain, Simon, for you to know that although this is what we've wanted out of life, we're not doing it selfishly. We've thought about you too. I mean, this place is better than the city, hm? All that beach to play on—'

'To *play* on!'

'You know what I'm trying to say . . . We'll be happy here. This is where we want to stay, quietly, among new friends, with some freedom at last. This is where.'

Mum sipped at her tea quickly, her eyes twinkling, her tone a fine mixture of sadness and happiness. I understood. This was where they wanted to grow old together; this was where they wanted to rest. I understood.

'I think,' I said, 'I'll go for a breath of air. I'm worn out.'

Mum let me go, knowing she'd said enough.

The wind was cool but not chilly yet. Once again the rain had been swept away, and the sky and sea were deep blue, reflecting each other's mirrors. The beach lay like a slice of white paper far below; the roofs of the lower houses came like steps up towards me.

Our garden consisted of three terraces. The bottom one was a mess, tilted bean-canes and the wreckage of a lettuce patch gone to seed. One terrace up, a soaked square of lawn bordered by terracotta pots full of rain-smashed geraniums. The top terrace had been slabbed over to make a patio. It was bounded by a wall of coloured brick, three bricks high, and four steps led down to the lawn.

Beside the house was our garage, pebbledashed, with a trellis sagging off the wall supporting a wilted clematis. It was all dead for the winter, except – my eyes snapped open – except for a rose bush that I had never seen before blowing gently in the breeze. Its leaves were emerald green, its heavy blossoms the deepest scarlet I had ever come across.

Tall Stories

'Well, *I* didn't plant it,' Mum said, almost defensively, as though Dad were accusing her of something wicked. She cupped one of the roses in her hands and inhaled its scent, deeply, like she might quench a thirst.

'And it's not plastic!' she chuckled. 'These are beautiful . . .'

'There *was* a rosebush on this spot,' Dad said, remembering, 'but the previous owner of the house had pruned it back to nothing.'

'Anyway,' I added, 'even if it had been growing here – which it couldn't have done overnight – the rain and wind would've destroyed these flowers. As it is, they're perfect.'

'That's right, not a spot of blight or a single aphid.' Dad twisted one of the blooms off its branch.

'Greg!'

'No point leaving them, my love. However they got here – and I wouldn't put it past John Williams to play a joke like this – they'll be ruined by tomorrow. Best pick them now and enjoy them inside.' He laughed. 'You know, if I could find the horse that manured these, I'd make a fortune—'

It was then I remembered the slubber, how I'd thrown the water containing it over the pruned rose-stick that morning. Even as I thought it, I knew it must be the right explanation; no kick-back of disbelief, I just *knew*. But I said nothing, even though the idea was huge enough to make my head spin.

It took as much courage as I could muster next day to walk up to Louise in the playground. Her gang of friends hung around, all in a circle like a bastion of female superiority. Two of them stared with such obvious distaste that a lesser man would have turned tail and run for it. I decided on the cool approach.

'Hi, Louise . . . girls . . . How're things?'

'*What* things?' the girl closest to me said. She was tall and immaculately dressed, with long black hair held in place by slides. She looked sixteen or seventeen, but I knew she was three years younger. I could feel that heat coming to my face.

'This is Maureen,' Louise told me, showing no mercy by not rescuing me.

'Hi there, Maureen.' I shrugged. 'Your things, if you like.' That made me blush even more, but two of the girls giggled, which took the poison out of whatever Maureen had planned to say.

'Um, anyway, Louise, can we talk?' She opened her hands. 'I mean, like in private . . .'

She gave the others a neutral look, hesitated, then followed me as I walked away.

'Do you like being with them, or something?'

'Don't I suit them?'

'To tell the truth, I don't know which would insult you more, a yes or a no. Aren't they pleasant to *any*body?'

Quite unexpectedly Louise smiled.

'Not really. They can get what they want without having to crawl.'

'It's not quite the same as just being nice to people . . . But that's the game is it, getting what you want?'

Wrong move, I thought: the sun was clouding over in Louise's eyes.

'Look, I didn't mean it like that. To be honest, you've got more going for you than the others. I could feel Maureen's barbed wire cutting me six feet away.'

'She's got reasons,' Louise said, super-seriously. 'She's been hurt before.'

Suddenly I felt I was treading water that was far too deep for me; I was still the new boy and didn't know the cross-currents yet. One toe at a time, I told myself.

I steered Louise towards the tuck shop and treated us to chocolate, then we went to the French area which was quiet and warm, and always poorly patrolled by prefects.

'So,' Louise said, sitting beside me on a double desk, 'what's the problem?'

'Slubber . . .' I told her the story. 'And I wondered if anything similar had happened to you?'

'Not yet, though that sounds weird – but great too.'

'Why?'

'Well the link's obvious. You threw water containing slubber over the rosebush – the bush grew. Maybe the same kind of growing power made so much of it appear on the beach at Blackshales.'

Maybe, I thought unsurely: I was recalling the look of the storm, that world-washing flash of green lightning.

'That doesn't really help us,' I said. 'I mean, we still don't know what it is or where it's come from.'

Louise crumpled up her chocolate wrapper and

threw it over her shoulder. She smiled sweetly when she saw my look of disapproval, then shrugged.

'The answers will come. Maybe Chris will have something to tell us tonight.'

'Chris?'

'He took some down to the greenhouse. Dad went through a phase of gardening – just another little fad to relieve his boredom, you understand. Well, it didn't even outlast the summer. He never goes down the greenhouse now. In fact, he gave Chris some extra pocket money this week 'to set himself up', when Chris said *he* wanted to grow things, apart from his usual cacti.'

Louise laughed lightly.

'The place has got the lot: electric undersoil heating, plenty of peat and stuff, about ten million flowerpots . . .'

'It only takes your mum to wander down with a cup of tea . . .'

'Stop worrying about it. Mum wouldn't know a sweet pea from a sequoia.'

'I'm not sure I would! But you think Chris will find something out?'

'It's likely. He's been feeding slubber to his plants, trying to grow other things in it, putting stuff in a tankful of pond water . . . Before long he'll be mixing up slubber cocktails for himself.' She smiled beautifully. 'If you see a big hairy monster shambling around Seabeck, it's *bound* to be Chris.'

Louise's smile vanished, like the sun going out.

'So don't worry about him, Simon. We want to find out about slubber, don't we?'

'Yes, but—'

'But what? Who dares wins and all that.'

48

'He might be in danger.'

'He won't poison himself. And he's happy. It's the best thing that's ever happened to him. No problem, Simon, OK?'

'OK.'

Louise pushed herself away from the desk, took a step and faced me, standing very close. She wore scent, or scented shampoo, and smelt sweet.

'Come over if you like, and see how he's getting on . . .'

'Your parents won't mind?'

'What's it got to do with them?' Louise's temper flared like electric sparks. '*I'm* inviting you. They don't tell me who my friends are.'

'All right, calm down. I'll come round—'

'Tonight,' she said, 'after tea. OK?' She tilted her head sideways and smiled. Soft blonde hair fell across one eye and she brushed it back; still stood there in a silence she knew I couldn't outlast.

'Well, yes. Fine—'

She turned immediately and walked towards the swing-doors to the outside.

'And thanks for your help, Louise!'

'Oh, Simon,' she called over her shoulder, 'you can buy me chocolate anytime.'

I'd just reached the back porch after finishing tea, when a shape appeared behind the frosted glass of the outside door and set up an excited hammering.

'Who is that, Simon?' Mum said from the kitchen.

'Hang on, I'll find out.'

It was Kathy, face flushed and out of breath. Her brown eyes were wide and brilliant as we stood on the doorstep to talk.

'Look at this, Simon. Just *look*, will you!'

She stuck something up under my nose and couldn't stop chuckling. She was almost dancing with excitement.

'A couple of old mugs, so what?'

'No! *One* old mug – the one I took the slubber home in. And look, a brand-new one!'

I took the mugs from her and examined them. My old favourite I recognized at once. It had a chip on the drinking side, which meant I'd had to hold it in my left hand until I got fed up with that and stuffed the thing away in a cupboard.

The other mug was identical, except, as Kathy had said, it was new, minus chipped edge – perfect.

'It's very good of you to buy me another one, Kathy, really I—'

'No, no,' she said, shouting it, 'you don't understand. There was only one mug when I left home this morning. I'd put it in the garage – I rememberd what Louise had said about fumes. Tonight when I got home – two mugs.'

'And no slubber,' I guessed, feeling my heart start to speed up.

'That's right. Not a trace of it. How did you know?'

'A rose by any other name,' I said. 'Hang on a minute.'

I left her frowning in the kitchen.

'Dad. Have a look at this.'

I held the mug out between him and his newspaper, guessing that he was in the right sort of mood not to get angry. He looked at it languidly for a second, then his gaze swung back to the headlines.

'It's a mug, son.'

He started to smile.

'Is it?' I asked, with no humour in my voice at all.

Dad put the paper down and took the mug in both hands. His big squarish fingers, craftsman's fingers, ran along the curves and contours of the thing, probed inside, traced the slightly raised shape of the Li'l Frankenstein and the writing. I could see interest beginning to come into his eyes.

'Well?'

'It *is* a mug, a pottery mug,' he said carefully, 'but for something that's mass-produced it's been beautifully made.' He ting-ed the rim with his nail. 'Good quality clay, the best glaze, lovely crisp colours in the design . . . Perfect. Ah, not quite perfect.'

He'd been turning the thing over and round, and now held it up for me to see the underside. He chuckled, but my smile was a little flat. Written in a circle in embossed black letters were the words: MAD IN ENGLAND.

Kathy came with me to Louise's house. I knew it wouldn't make Louise too happy, and I wasn't exactly pleased, but I told myself that we were all in this thing together, and besides, it wasn't as though I'd be seeing Louise by herself.

Mr Williams answered the door, gave me a rather mean and suspicious look, merely acknowledged Kathy, and told us 'the kids' were down in the greenhouse. All of a sudden, in the space of a day, he had become a teacher and I a pupil; now he was more than one of Dad's old friends, but something less than a neighbour.

He led us through the house. It resembled what Mum would call a 'show-piece home': ornaments beautifully and perfectly aligned on mantelpiece and side-table, not a speck of dust anywhere; and the place smelt strongly of lavender with a kind of undercurrent of furniture polish. A black cat was sitting silently on the back window-sill of the lounge – just to give the place a cosy touch, I thought acidly, as Mr Williams took us through his pine kitchen and pointed the way down the garden.

'I'll bet "the kids" were never naughty,' I said to Kathy, without smiling, looking back to see Mr Williams watching us from the kitchen window.

'But just wait from now on,' Kathy chuckled, and I could guess what she was thinking.

The greenhouse was blazing like a jewel from the hard light of a bare neon tube fixed along the apex of the roof. I could see Louise and Chris inside, blurred behind a screen of moisture on the glass. I tapped, then pulled the sliding door aside.

'Hi Simon – oh, and Kathy.' Louise's smile faded, but she turned away before it disappeared entirely.

'Have a look at this,' Chris said, oblivious of the cross-currents between us older ones. He was busy with his 'experiments', set up on a bench along one side-wall of the greenhouse. The air had a clean, loamy smell to it, and was warm as new bread. I could almost feel the plants growing around me.

'Right,' he said, standing up and sounding very businesslike. 'Here's what I've done. In *this* tank, some pondweed, snails, a fish from Mum's aquarium—'

'They're neon tetras,' Kathy said, bending to see them more clearly. The fish were about an inch long and glittered like rainbow fragments as they flicked about in the water.

'And there're two of them.'

'Yesterday,' Chris said quietly, with a huge excitement contained, 'there was only one.'

'You're kidding!' Kathy looked at him, wide-eyed, but not disbelievingly. 'Just like my mug,' I heard her whisper.

'And,' he went on, 'there's more pondweed than I put in, and I could swear there are more snails too.'

'How much slubber did you dissolve in the water?' I asked.

'Third of a cup. I used the rest in these pots.'

'They've got cacti in—'

'This morning they had cactus *seed* in,' Chris said, 'and if you know *anything* about cacti, you'll know they take years to grow from seed.'

'And these grew in a day . . .' Kathy shook her head slowly. 'It's amazing.' She picked up a pot and stared at it.

'These are like stones.'

'Lithops,' Chris told her, 'the pebble plant. And this other one is a pin-cushion cactus.' He showed us a plant that was spherical and the size of a king marble. It was covered with a white fuzz of fine spines, and half a dozen tiny red and yellow flowers were sprouting from its surface.

'Grown from seed too?' I wondered.

'In one day. And normally it only flowers in the summer.'

'How about this pot?' Kathy said. 'Just soil in here . . .'

'That one only has slubber planted in it.' Louise came across and took the pot away. I could tell she was controlling her mood carefully, not letting her anger show in front of Kathy and Chris. Maybe I'd be in for the brunt of it later, but I was quietly pleased that she would have preferred us to be alone.

'So, we know that slubber can make things grow, and under unusual circumstances,' I said, collecting up the scraps of evidence, 'like our rosebush blooming out of season . . .'

'And everything shoots up at super speed,' Chris added, eyes sparkling.

'That's right. And it would be interesting to see just *how* extreme the conditions need to be before the slubber stops working – how hot or cold, how humid, whether it's affected by weedkillers . . . Whether slubber-grown fruit is edible.'

I had sudden visions of deserts blooming overnight, of famine eliminated forever, of rare species saved from extinction. Slubber could be the fertilizer of the Earth-Garden.

It was Kathy who spoke up to break the thought.

'It all sounds a bit too easy to me.'

'What do you mean?' Louise said sourly, finding the opening she wanted to be hostile. 'Why can't it just be a miracle?'

'I'm not saying it can't,' Kathy went on reasonably, 'but we have to consider the possible dangers.'

'Like what?'

'Like the fact that there could be harmful chemicals in the stuff. For all we know, it might be industrial waste, or some top secret material that's leaked from a ship. It could be—'

'It could be a secret government experiment to turn harmless little girls like you into pains-in-the-neck who won't quit nagging!'

'That's enough,' I said, holding up my hands – but

54

tentatively, as though I was approaching a red-hot fire.

Kathy just folded her arms calmly, but Louise seemed filled with agitation. There was a flush of colour in her cheeks and her blue eyes blazed. She whirled on me.

'She won't stop me, Simon! I'm going to make the most of this break. Besides, if it *was* some top-secret project, don't you think the coast would be swarming with soldiers by now? No, wherever it's come from, we're the only ones who know about it.'

'Doesn't that worry you?' Kathy wondered, more curious now than anything. 'We might not be able to handle the responsibility. We ought to tell someone. What do you think, Simon?'

I kept my mouth closed and assumed an air of deep contemplation. Actually, I agreed with Kathy; apart from the unknown dangers there might be in the slubber, how could a group of kids hope to work out how best the stuff should be used?

On the other hand, if I took Kathy's side against Louise, then my chances with Louise would be finished.

'Um,' I said. Louise put her hand on my arm.

'I think you're all forgetting,' she said quietly, 'that once word of this leaks out, *we* won't get a look-in. If the authorities hear about slubber, they'll move so fast you won't even see them coming.'

'So what's wrong with—' Kathy began.

'They'll cordon off the beach,' Louise went on relentlessly, 'forbid entry, build a dirty great wall around that slubber and keep it for themselves. What will *we* get? A pat on the back and a half-column in the *Westmartin Gazette*!'

'Maybe they've done it already,' I said, realizing that none of us had been back to Blackshales since the day after the storm. Kathy was shaking her head.

'Unlikely. No reason for anybody to go down there. You won't find tourists about in this weather, and there's no road nearby – no passing motorists will spot anything unusual. As for locals, well, the place is too far out for people to take their dogs for a walk . . . The chances are that Blackshales is still undisturbed. Though for how long . . .'

'Yeah,' I said, 'come the weekend we ought to go back and check, if only to stock up on the stuff for you to carry on with your vital research, eh Chris?'

Kathy laughed, 'I just hope these cacti you're growing aren't man-eaters!'

'In the meantime,' Louise broke in, 'I vote we tell no one. Play it down with the parents, keep it quiet at school—'

'But this is so *important*!' I said, building up for an argument; Louise's smile was cool and reasonable.

'Exactly, and the responsibility's ours to make sure that slubber isn't misused.'

She took one of Chris's flowerpots and held it before her eyes.

'I mean, look what's been done with atomic power. OK, so we've got electricity, but we also have enough bombs to blow up the world a hundred times. And do you think ordinary people had a say in that, when the first bomb was about to be built?'

'Circumstances were different then,' I said.

'Yes, Simon, they were. It was hi-tech, top-secret then; but we hold slubber in our *hands*: we are the only ones. For once the ordinary people can say, this is how *we* want the world to be!'

'Or how *you* want the world to be,' Kathy challenged her quietly. Louise cocked her head coyly.

'Don't you wish for food enough for everyone: the seas bulging with fish, the continents filled with animals and trees? Don't you dream?'

It sounded sensible, even logical, and I gave Kathy a look and backed down, changing sides just a little guiltily. It wasn't as though Louise was wrong; and anyway, I thought again that if I crossed her now it would be the last time she'd bother with me.

'OK,' I said, 'we keep it quiet for now.'

I stepped up to Chris's fish tank.

'Any of you touched the slubber for a length of time?' I asked the others 'I mean, the raw stuff?'

'Used rubber gloves,' Chris said. 'Just in case . . .'

'Either of you two?' The girls shook their heads.

'OK.' Gently I lowered my hands into the warmish water, gave them a good soak and then let them dry naturally. Kathy's grin was more amused than it was inquisitive.

'What are you doing?'

'Only another experiment,' I told her.

Next day was brilliantly clear, not too cold, and the journey to school didn't seem as bad. On the Dellaford road I looked out for my golden lion and the tall club-like trees, but saw only ragged fields, some sheep grazing and the dull, beaten-lead shine of the sea.

The morning went well until third lesson: Physics with John Williams. Because I'd been A-banded for general science at my last school, I was in the top set at Rowley Mead. Physics and Maths had always been my weakest subjects (English was my best); but sitting here with the cream of the crop, having arrived at the school mid-term, I felt really lost among atomic numbers and electron shells.

And Williams wasn't making things any easier for me. Whenever the chance came, he threw a question my way and then used it to make me feel small. He'd get a laugh out of the class, but not much of one because I reckoned he was not the most popular of teachers.

It didn't seem to trouble him as he sat behind the demo bench, spitting out technical terms, references to past lessons, the occasional weak joke. We were expected to take notes (homework, write them up by Friday) and some people were scribbling away madly, but I just doodled on my roughwork book, thinking about Claire Goodson's cheerfulness and the three big kisses she'd crossed over the cover . . .

Someone coughed and broke the daydream. I gazed around, suddenly feeling bored, stared through the window—

The playground wasn't there any more. Beyond the window stood bottle-green hills and tall plants like blue feathers. Off to one side I saw a flat sheet of purplish water, rippled by expanding circles as though something had just dived under. The sky was paper-white, but here and there the copper-coloured sunlight was soaking through in vivid patches.

Suddenly a shadow appeared on top of the closest hill; appeared and came towards me, a sleek four-legged animal that padded like a cat.

'Simon Hallam! Pay attention, boy . . .'

Williams's voice come through to me, faint and faraway. I tried to look round, but the world had gone and I was standing in some other land.

'Hallam. Hallam! Are you listening to me?'

I tried. I tried to listen, I tried to talk and tell him what was happening. But the air was filled with the scent of far places, and the golden lion had reached me and I was lost and hopelessly swimming in its eyes.

The Chance

I sat in the medical room with a bucket propped between my legs feeling pretty stupid. This was the standard treatment if a kid left a classroom because he was ill; not that I had been, or was, but John Williams had insisted I report sick at the main office and have the secretary, who was qualified in first aid, to check me over: 'Just to be on the safe side.'

I explained to her that I was fine, wasn't going to throw up or pass out. She smiled in a secretarial way, told me to loosen my tie and gave me the sick bucket to hold.

'Just to be on the safe side?' I wondered.

'Exactly.'

By the time the end of the lesson came I was thoroughly bored, almost looking forward to seeing someone pass by the always-open door at the end of the corridor. The Headmaster had been along, a tall, striding flamingo of a man with cotton-wool tufts of white hair stuck around the sides of an otherwise bald head; then some tough looking kid who put the V-signs up when he saw me staring at him; and two girls passed, ambling slowly, on their way to the loo. They wandered back ten minutes later, still gabbling, in time for the dinner bell.

After that the corridor was jam-packed with people

going to eat. The noise came swelling up and I felt quite lucky to have an open space of my own where I could simply sit and watch everybody else getting irritable.

Mr Williams appeared from the crowd, swung himself round out of the crush and loomed over me, taking a cautious look into the bucket at the same time.

'All right, Hallam?'

Simon, I thought, that's my name; it's Simon.

'Yes, sir. Sorry.'

'What happened?'

'I, uh, must have come over a bit faint or something. Too much sea air, sir.'

He smiled then, mostly with relief I think, and in that smile I saw Louise's good looks mirrored. John Williams must have been a real charmer, I thought, at one time. Now he was looking his forty years: black hair thinning with streaks of grey, wrinkle-lines around his eyes . . . And there was a kind of tiredness about him, as though he had been climbing the same slope for a long time. As though life was a habit.

'Well,' he said, 'take it easy. You didn't half give me a scare. I was shouting, and you just weren't with it.'

'Yeah,' I said quietly, determined to avoid another 'sir'.

'Anyway, get the notes from someone else in the group – written up by Friday, remember.'

'Fine,' I said to the back of his head as he left, and thought, You sod.

'Hi!'

Claire Goodson sat by me at dinner, and that cheered me up no end. She sort of breezed in with her tray of salad and a jacket potato, and plonked herself down beside me as if she didn't care a pin about people gossiping or spreading rumours.

'Claire . . .'

She slipped her blazer off and her plastic gypsy jewellery clacked on her wrists. Today the bangles and beads and earrings were bright pink.

'What happened to you in Physics? Felt faint?'

'I'm as healthy as they come,' I said.

'Not for much longer, eating that garbage.' Claire cast a disapproving glance at my fishcake and chips, then attacked her baked potato.

'You can talk,' I said. 'How do you survive on those bits of leaf and nuts?'

'I manage,' she told me, mouth full of lettuce.

'Yeah, you're in pretty good shape . . .'

I expected a silence then, the self-conscious quietness that would normally descend once a conversation drifts into double meanings. Instead Claire straightened up with exaggerated pride.

'Tall, slim. Not bad, eh?'

'Not bad for a head.' I quipped, avoiding her friendly back-hander and laughing. She laughed too, carefree and languid, and I thought how uncomplicated she seemed, how open her friendship was. Not like Louise, where every meeting was a tangle, and words like stones tossed into a minefield.

A shame, I concluded, that Claire didn't make my pulse beat in quite the same way. . . .

When Louise collared me a little later, I knew at once that something was wrong, but decided that I wasn't going to be made to feel guilty or ashamed or embarrassed because I'd talked to Claire.

I'd been wandering about by myself for twenty minutes, finding my way around, working out which places I ought to avoid in the school. Certain areas, I'd been told, were notorious for trouble, or where the smokers congregated, or where the courting couples helped each other with their homework . . .

Besides, I had not yet attached myself to any of the lads in the tutor group. None of them lived at Seabeck, and although Mrs Brown, the Deputy Headmistress, had put a boy 'in charge' of me because I was new, this kid had gone off with his usual circle after the second day, and I hadn't spoken a word to him since.

'Hello Louise. How are you?' Nice and cool and innocent, I thought, that's the way to play it.

'I'm pretty fed up, actually!'

'Well now, look—'

'I mean, why does Kathy Smith keep hanging *around* these days?'

'Kathy?'

Louise nodded, her face flushing with anger.

'She's turning out to be a real pain. I don't know what it is. But because we were both involved with the slubber, she thinks I'm her friend or something; just comes along and joins the group . . . Starts talking with Maureen about make-up and hair colour. Well, Maureen thinks she's a real wimp. Trots after us like a damn puppy . . .

I let Louise's temper play itself out, all the while feeling bad because I'd thought the same of Kathy before now. She was pleasant and friendly and all that, but did tend to cling. Mum thought she was great; Dad hadn't complained about 'girls all around the house', which was a definite sign of approval too: I'm not sure if he thought we were going together or something. But to me she had a cousin-ish air, she sort of fitted in, only becoming a nuisance when you wanted to go off and do something without her.

'Maybe she's lonely,' I said. It sounded weak, but I meant it. Louise tutted.

'So she's got problems . . .'

Stone wall again. 'Well,' I said pointlessly, 'haven't we all?'

And Louise's blue-eyed gaze came and washed over me, fathomlessly.

We walked once round the outside of the school, got yelled at by a duty-teacher for crossing the fore-court (ultra forbidden except at either end of the day), then drifted back to the playground where crowds of kids had gathered after dinner.

I began to feel nervous, for no good reason I could yet identify – except perhaps that Louise was walking close beside me, our arms touching, and people were beginning to swing their eyes across to us and away again, pretending not to notice.

'How's, um – how's Chris coming on with his experiments?' I asked to break the tension, although Louise seemed quite at ease.

'OK, I think. He checked on them this morning and none of the cacti had grown teeth. Anyway, come round why don't you – this evening – and ask him yourself.'

By now she'd led me to the centre of the metalled playground that, being surrounded on three-and-a-bit sides by school buildings, formed an echoing quad-rangle; shouting and laughter came battering back from all the walls and windows.

'Well, yes . . . great.'

People began staring openly, and for a terrible

second it occurred to me that Louise might have engineered things this way. She stopped walking, turned to face me and held my arm, just enough to stop me.

'See you then, Simon.' She smiled warmly. 'Oh, and I heard you'd been around with Claire Goodson. Take advice from a friend – just be careful, and don't get a reputation. She goes out with anybody, understand me?'

On an impulse I went over to the science block after my final lesson, hoping to find Sid Machin, the Bio. teacher, before my bus left. It was all very well, I'd been thinking, to 'experiment' with the slubber, but the stuff was an *unknown*, and in the deepest sense of the word. Not one of us had a blind clue what it was or what it could do. And to be honest, Louise's throwaway remark about cacti with teeth had sent a shiver up my neck . . .

The labs and corridors were deserted and end-of-day dust hung in the air. I hated empty schools; they seemed less than just empty, like a vacuum.

When I reached the prep room, I saw that the door stood slightly open. I thought for a second that everyone had gone home, but I tapped gently anyway and a voice said, 'Yep?'

'Mr Machin . . .'

I pushed the door open further and noticed a man bent forward over his desk, marking books. Two other piles stood ready by his left hand. As he marked, ticking quickly and casually down the pages, he kept a cigarette held loosely between his lips and had to squint through the rising feathers of smoke to see properly. He had slick, black and very greasy hair, a little beard that was not neat enough to be a goatee, and he looked bored and short-tempered.

'Mr Machin?'

'That's me, son, what d'you want?' He threw down his red ballpoint, took a deep drag on his cigarette and looked up.

As soon as he asked, my mind knotted up; firstly because I wasn't really sure what I wanted to know, but also because I knew I couldn't give anything away.

'It's, er, about some stuff, sir . . .'

'Some stuff.' Machin nodded and looked at the ceiling as though contemplating deeply. 'Ah, I never cease to be amazed at the power of the comprehensive system to train up the world leaders of tomorrow. Here is a boy who might one day be Prime Minister or – dare I even imagine – on the board of directors for Woolworth's. And why? Because he has an inquiring mind that wishes to probe into the mysteries of the universe. He *wants* to *know* about some *stuff*!'

I stood there feeling stupid on the surface but angry inside. Kathy had given me a rundown of Rowley Mead's teachers and had mentioned Machin's perpetual air of sarcasm. Here it was in full flower: I thought the man must have spent too long in smoky prep rooms marking books. All of the deep curiosity he was poking fun at had long ago leached out of his mind, every drop of it.

'I want to know if an organic polymer can, in its natural state, be completely inert – but when introduced to another substance, act as a catalyst?'

Machin lifted his eyebrows (a sign, I learned later, of great respect), and some of the tiredness left his face.

'Well, thank goodness for that. You're not entirely stupid, lad – and you were not referring to anything illegal, immoral or fattening, which makes a change these days.' He smiled a yellowy showing of teeth.

'Is this substance alive?' he wondered. 'I ask because I'm a biologist rather than a chemist, right? And my interest ceases after something's died, decomposed or been fossilized . . .'

'Well, I think I want to know if stuff like this *could* be alive, if it existed . . .'

'There are certain polymers that can speed up chemical reactions, not necessarily because they're polymers. Does that answer you?'

He looked at me hard, and as he stubbed out his cigarette he never took his eyes off me. Now the smoke had dissipated, I noticed how clear and penetrating his gaze could be. Play ignorant, Simon? I asked myself. It would certainly be the easiest way.

'I don't know.'

'Well, you'll need to tell me more then – or be more precise in the questions you ask. I mean, are you thinking of a chemical that causes change or growth? Some systemic fertilizers have remarkable effects—'

'No.' I shook my head. 'I think I'm talking about change *and* growth. Is there a stuff that can alter patterns of molecules so that . . .Or maybe I'm wondering if this material alters its *own* molecules into new patterns.'

'What stuff?' Machin asked quietly, and I felt the thin ice creaking underfoot.

'No stuff in particular, sir . . .'

He chuckled, not trusting me an inch, I thought.

'This, em, hypothetical material: is it natural or manufactured?'

'It would – given its existence – be natural. I think;'

'You're not talking about camouflage here, or a simple chemical change like litmus paper in acid?'

'No, sir, nothing like that.' I could be sure of *that*, at least. 'So, could it exist?'

There was a silence then, one that was neither empty nor pointless. Machin gazed at me thoughtfully for long seconds, then turned to tap another cigarette out of the already-opened packet on his desk.

'No,' he said at last, and rather sadly. 'It couldn't exist. Not on this planet anyway.'

'And if it did?'

'Then it wouldn't be this planet for long. Now is that it?' he asked, not looking my way again.

' 'S, sir.'

'OK. Clear off then.'

I hadn't seen Kathy all that day, and didn't work hard to make the opportunity to catch her up. Louise had given me a priceless second chance and I didn't want Kathy spoiling it. I noticed her sitting ahead of me on the coach home, but when she got off she didn't wait around and was already indoors when I passed the house.

The trouble was, I thought, that while Kathy was, well, *nice* in a way that Louise wasn't (and perhaps could never be), she was not as exciting. The fact that Kathy chased after me made me ignore her all the more, while Louise's aloofness caused *me* to chase ever harder.

At the same time, I realized that there was something dark and not very pleasant in Louise – right at the heart of her. The way she used people was cold, and several degrees more dangerous than the way she used herself, which was merely skilful. The more I thought about the rumours she'd spread about Claire Goodson, the more clearly I saw that it was true. Louise Williams was out to please herself; but despite all of that, I was hooked on her. Kathy with her warm smile, Claire with her bright sense of fun – they just didn't come close . . .

Mum and Dad were both home when I got in. Dad had his Wednesday afternoons free and taught on a Saturday morning instead. It always sounded like a great life to me, until Saturday came along of course!

I walked into the lounge and found that he'd dozed off in front of the fire, a newspaper spread like a thin and inadequate blanket over his chest. His mouth hung open and a soft purring snore was coming out.

Mum was busy painting matt varnish on to the driftwood Kathy had brought for her. She had cleaned and sanded the bleached and twisted shape, and was now dibbing a fine brush into its thin crevices. She blew upwards to clear a strand of hair from her eyes, then noticed me and laid the brush down.

'Well, is it that time already? I've been at this for most of the afternoon . . .'

'It's looking good, Mum.'

She smiled at me, half suspiciously because I didn't usually admire her craftwork without sarcasm, but decided I was on the level. Her smile warmed and softened.

'It's what I like to do.' She held the thing up by its base, tilting it so that the sunlight from the lounge back window caught the faint shades of the washed-out wood. As she moved it, I found my opinion and perception swinging, first one way, then another; for a second the driftwood was beautiful, sea-smoothed and elegant; suddenly the next moment made it seem wrenched and distorted like a twisted bone. My viewpoint changed back and forth like surges of nausea and relief, and some part of me watched this happening and marvelled that people could be so unsure or so fickle.

'Hm,' Mum said, a satisfied sound, gently placing the ornament back on the table. 'It'll need another coat. The wood soaks up varnish like a sponge. Anyway, Simon, how did your day go? Come and tell me in the kitchen . . .'

I followed her through, and put the kettle on to make tea while Mum prepared salad at the sink. I sighed, tempted to go through all the old not-salad-this-time-of-year arguments I used every year when the weather turned colder. Mum wouldn't have listened. She was going through an extended eat-healthy phase that had lasted all summer, leaving Dad and me up to our ears in nuts and pulses and terrible wind. That was one reason why I indulged myself at school with fishcakes and chips and hamburgers – anything to get some *substance* inside me.

Well, it was Mum's way – like the clothes she was wearing. I called them her Love and Peace gear, real ethnic stuff: a white cotton blouse with sleeves like lily-flowers, sweeping dark-green skirt that came nearly to her ankles, wrought-silver jewellery (from India), or sometimes stuff made out of shells. In the hall would be hanging her fawn quilted jacket with a Smiley badge and CND pin on the lapels. And on a really bad day she might wear a cotton headband and sit for an hour in the Lotus position.

The truth was, I thought, that Mum lived a memory of summers in the early 'sixties, when she and Dad met and fell in love at college. She had been beautiful, Dad had been cheeky and charming, they had both been carefree. Mum had told me about 'the early days' dozens of times, and I guessed they must have been brilliant times; long gone, but recollected in the wistful smiles Mum and Dad gave each other, and in the scrapbook photos they sometimes hauled out of the dresser.

Well, if Mum wanted to take the whole thing one stage further, fair enough I decided. People would think she was weird, but she had her nice house by the sea, her life all sorted out and tidy, her memories and hopes held in pale forms of wood hurled up by the evening tide.

'It'll be stewed.'

I jumped, and the dream I was having fell apart.

'Sorry, Mum.' I became businesslike with the cups and remembered to use a strainer when I poured. Not even Mum had been able to talk Dad out of sugar, but she had reduced him to a half-spoonful of unrefined grains, which she watched me stir in to make sure I was not over generous.

I took the tea through and woke Dad, gently shaking him and trying not to laugh at the various grunts and snorts he produced as he climbed up out of sleep. His bleary eyes focused.

'Oh, son. I was asleep. Cup of tea. Thanks,' he said, and something inside me melted.

Mum followed a minute later and plonked the plates of salad down on the little circular table that just fitted into our dining area.

'I hope this isn't *all*,' Dad muttered, not unpleasantly, but he tended to my view that food ought to fill you.

'Of course not. You need something hot and substantial in this weather . . .'

Dad and I perked up.

Mum brought in a stoneware pot held carefully with oven-gloves, placed it on a wicker mat (that she had made herself at evening classes last year), and lifted the lid above the gouts of steam.

'Ratatouille crumble,' she announced proudly.

That, I thought, is the *limit*.

Before going to see Louise I visited Beck's Store on the corner and bought myself a pork pie, which I wolfed down and finished by the time I reached the Williams' front door.

Thankfully Louise answered. I wasn't in the mood for any more of her father.

'Come in.' She held the door wider, and I stepped through into the lavender smell that hung perpetually everywhere in the house.

Louise led me through to the lounge, which was dominated by a hearth made of rustic brick. A Flame Glow gas fire sat in the middle: it had a planished copper front, and lumps of red-, yellow- and orange-coloured glass below the radiants which refracted a false firelight on to the ceiling.

'So tasteful, don't you think?' Louise asked sweetly, catching my expression. She walked over and moved two of the mantelpiece ornaments out of their perfect alignment.

'Give Mother something to do in her leisure time.'

I wasn't really ready for cynicism. The warmth of our own house lingered inside me and I wanted to keep it there. So I sort of laughed non-committally and tried not to look as though I was being critical.

'Coffee?' Louise asked. I nodded, following her with my eyes as she went into the kitchen. She had chosen to wear a skirt rather then her usual jeans, a pale pink skirt and a baggy but fashionable sweat-top tucked in. She had half-rolled the sleeves up and managed to look casual, but at the same time poised and carefully presented. She'd dressed to be attractive and grown-up but, I thought, young and innocent also; girlish. It was a strong mixture.

I sat on the couch and when Louise came back, she sat beside me.

'Parents out?'

'They always go to the pub on Wednesdays, part of their little ritual . . . Well, Mum gets bored at home if there's no supply work on, and Dad likes to break up the week. It gives him something to look forward to, a stepping-stone between weekends. How about yours?'

'Dad makes his own wine when he has time.' I grimaced. 'Sometimes it tastes like paraffin—'

'That's awful!'

'But the really bad stuff you can't drink at all.'

She smiled, politely. Her face did not light up with it.

'Yeah, Dad likes a pint,' I said, 'and Mum drinks Perrier water, but it makes her burp something wicked . . .'

I realized the humour was not going down too well, and I began to feel clumsy. This was Louise's home ground, even more her territory than Rowley Mead. She was playing games there, I suspected, but those I could probably dodge. Here I was kind of locked into the couch by formality and convention; couldn't just get up and wander off. I wondered where Chris was, and asked.

'Oh, in his greenhouse, of course. I reckon the villagers are going to storm the place with blazing torches and hayforks before long.'

'What's been happening then?' I asked.

'Yes, there's no one around,' Louise said ignoring my question. That unnerving quietness was in her voice, and she was staring at me levelly. I felt hollow and my heart was hammering away like anything. She looked great. When she put her hands down in her lap, her skirt-hem went up above her knees. I could hear her breathing, waiting.

I wanted to say something to smash the moment wide open. The quietness was suffocating. This was the chance, she was here, but it was not the way I wanted the chance to be. She had built this second up on a tower and I felt unsafe with it swaying beneath me –

Louise's hair was soft and shiny, her mouth was a little bit open.

I did nothing.

'Come on,' she said at last, not giving anything away, 'let's go and find Chris.'

The air outside was chilly enough to make me shiver as soon as I stepped from the house. Street lights had come on in the early dark and were burning white across the village, while beyond the sea a red sun had melted out along the horizon. Stars and a big bright dot of a planet shone crisply in the purple sky.

In the gloom – and because I was gazing straight upwards – I almost tripped over Louise's cat, fell forward and cracked my head. Louise's aborted giggle turned into a moan of concern, not for me I might add.

'Oh, Tweedle my baby! Big nasty Simon nearly squashed you flat, then . . .'

'Tweedle!' I put as much scorn as I could into the word and wondered why people always seemed to talk to cats in stupid baby-voices. Also, I exaggerated a limping walk and screwed up my face in mock agony.

'Tweedledum,' Louise told me, 'mainly becase he's dumb.'

'You're not kidding.'

'Shall Mummy give you a little kiss-kiss then?'

'Mm, please,' I said chirpily, never for an instant expecting Louise to comply. Instead, she cuddled the animal over her shoulder and walked ahead of me towards the green blaze of the greenhouse.

I followed obediently, forgetting about the limping ploy, and tried to outstare the clear rounds of the cat's green eyes. People say that you can always do that to a cat – that it will always look away first. Not this one. Its glare seemed one of pure hatred towards me, coupled with a haughty smugness that, through being a cat, it had managed to secure a free ride down the garden *and* some love from Louise. Tough luck kid, I heard its furry thoughts whisper in my mind, you're just a loser.

Outside the greenhouse Louise placed Tweedle down with immense care and much fuss, then tapped on the glass for Chris to let us in.

Inside, the heating had been turned up full, making the air humid and thick; you could almost chew the wholesome, peaty smell.

'Look at all this – just look at it!' Chris spread his arms wide when we went in, his eyes sparkling excitedly, as though he owned the most magical kingdom in the world. He was a short kid, plumper than Louise, with a smooth face and a straight, little-boy haircut. I thought he was probably mothered excessively at home and teased at school. This green-house, and his SF books, were his way of escaping.

'OK Einstein, what have you been up to now?'

Actually it was obvious. The surge of growth induced by the slubber had continued, so that Chris had been forced to transfer some of his fish-tank stock to glass coffee jars and an old goldfish bowl. Now, I saw, there were four neon tetras in all, dozens of small black water snails, masses of weed . . .

'I just wonder,' Chris said in his high voice, 'when all the growing will stop!' He was filled with wonder – brimming with it. All of this was something straight out of the stories he read.

'When the slubber is used up—' I started to say, and then it hit me. The slubber was not exactly causing things to grow. It was *copying* things, forming its neutral self into patterns – of leaves, cells shell, stone . . . I should have realized it when the stuff in the plastic washbucket began to turn blue. And Kathy's two Li'l Monster mugs were a giveaway. The second one hadn't *grown*, but had been duplicated from the blueprint of the first.

The answer came complete and with a rush into my head, and I almost blurted it out. But it occurred to me, that neither Louise nor Chris had guessed any of this; Kathy's passing reference to the mugs had gone unnoticed. They were still convinced that slubber was only a kind of super-nutrient, and not something a thousand times more incredible.

But what about the slubber that had no blueprint

to work on? Hey Chris,' I asked, 'where's the stuff you planted by itself?'

'I was leaving it till last,' he said, and brought out a pot from under some polythene. He handed it over with pride.

Out of the loose, light soil grew tiny stands of trumpet-like trees amidst spots of emerald brilliance. Against a coppery sky they would look complete and at home.

I stood and said nothing, holding far places reverently in my hands.

The Superman Connection

Kathy came round the following night, uninvited and not entirely welcome. The day had been a vague drift of hours, lessons dragging one into the other, and nothing else happening to landmark it in my memory. I got home tired – the first week at the new school was really wearing me out – my mind churning sluggishly with mixed thoughts of slubber and Louise, Claire, Mum and Dad, Chris and his pinbright wonder and a plastic flowerpot full of magic.

I actually dozed on the bed and must have slept solidly for an hour before Mum woke me with a gentle knock at the door.

'Uh . . .?' I swam up through dark water into glaring late afternoon sunlight, for an instant dreams and reality mingling like two colour slides laid one on top of the other.

'Simon . . . Sorry to wake you. Kathy's here.'

Being disturbed had made me irritable. I tutted.

'Yeah, all right. I'll come down in—'

'Go on in,' Mum said, and then I realized that Kathy was standing behind her, hidden by the door.

'Thanks, Mrs Hallam.'

And Mum smiled, a sickening isn't-she-a-*nice*-girl smile that stoked my temper up even more.

'I'll make some tea. Sugar, Kath?'

'No thanks. Trying to lose weight.'

Mum left us alone. Kathy stepped through into the room, and stood looking around at my shelves of books and the few rocks and fossils I'd collected from down on the beach.

'I can show you the best places to find those,' she said, reaching up to look at one more closely.

'It's an ammonite.' I still felt drugged by sleep. I sat on the edge of the bed and rubbed at my eyes until yellow flower-stars burst inside them.

'I know, but I can also get you gryphaea, belemnites . . . I found a shark's tooth at Dunton Point last year.'

'You did?' I began to take interest. The moment when Mum had shown her in had been embarrassing, kind of brittle, but now things were smoothing out and I felt more comfortable – also guilty that Kathy was doing all the work. I thought I had better try.

'Do you collect fossils?'

'Only if I see a good one. I mean, one that's interesting to look at; not any particular sort.'

'I just go for variety. In Wales, where we used to live, there was a slag-heap. It must have been three hundred feet high, like a huge black pyramid with patches of yellow grass growing on it. Dad remembers the time when the mine was open and trains used to pull wagonloads of waste up the side of the valley, and then up the steeper slope of the tip to pour it over.

'Anyway,' I went on, deep in the story, 'when the coal was worked out and the pit shut down, kids went up the tip, to play, or go scavenging. And there were some great ponds nearby where you could get newts as long as your hand. But I used to go up for fossils.

Some of them were really fragile, rotted away, and they'd crumble to nothing in your hands. Sometimes though, you could find a slab of slate as big as a newspaper. I'd always take a bag with a hammer and fine chisel. You held the slate between your knees, tapped into the edge with the chisel – and the slate would open up like a book. Inside, as though from a flower press, would be the impressions of ferns and grass, or tree-bark. I've got a big boxful. It's in the garage, haven't unpacked it yet . . .'

'Sounds brilliant.'

'Nothing happening in the valleys now. Glad I moved, really.'

And as I said it I realized that was true. For the first time in three weeks the house and the village and the countryside felt comfortable around me.

I realized, too, that Kathy had sat on the bed and was listening to me intently, smiling with her eyes as Dad did. She was wearing blue denim jeans, new ones that she probably found uncomfortable, and a grey sweatshirt with one of those loose hoods down her back.

'Well . . . anyway . . . I'll show you my collection when I get round to unpacking it. If you like?'

My gaze touched her again. She nodded. I noticed she'd put some make-up on, nothing heavy, but obvious on her because I hadn't seen her wearing any before. Her eyes were dark with eyeshadow, and she had used some pinkish lipstick that didn't really go with the colour of her hair. There was a hint of red on her cheeks, but I couldn't decide if that was real or applied.

She must have seen me looking, because her flush deepened and she stared down at her hands.

'Got some tips off Maureen – Louise's friend.'

'Ah,' I said, wanting to laugh and sneer – not at Kathy. And accompanying that came another pang of guilt and almost shame that Kathy was doing this for me, though I was doing nothing in return.

The truth of it was that Kathy's attempt looked amateurish, like a painted doll. Maureen out of uniform could pass for nineteen, and she knew it. She had looks and poise . . .but with it a cold haughtiness that made her stare down her nose at people like me as though I was nothing. In a few years she'd be going out with accountants or executives, maybe even a pop star if she could hook one.

'So,' I said, mildly curious, 'Maureen gave you some advice, did she?'

'Well . . . I just saw what *she* was using. The group wasn't really bothered. But she did recommend the lipstick.'

Oh Kathy, I thought: Kathy, the world's going to swallow you up.

'Makes you look different,' I said, the words coming out like sharp splinters. I didn't want to lie, or to hurt. She smiled self-consciously.

'What's your favourite fossil?' she asked, breaking the mood.

'My dad. What's yours?'

'It's an ammonite – this big—' She made a saucer-sized round with all her fingers. 'And it's made of iron pyrites, you know, fool's gold. I got my father to slice it in half and polish the sections. It's great.'

'What does he do, then?'

'Stonemason. Gets a lot of work from Carter's, the funeral director in Reabridge.'

I swallowed back the stupid joke I was going to crack and kept my face straight.

'You found this ammonite locally?'

'Mm, at The Knobble. Lot of rockfalls there, like at Lyme Regis, especially after rough weather. It'll be good this winter, to go rock hunting.'

I heard in my mind the word 'together' tacked to the end of the sentence. Kathy had implied it by her tone. I felt the deeper water swirling up around my neck again, and kept quiet.

'Why have you been avoiding me, Simon?' she said out of a silence. The water rose up over my head.

'Oh, come on Kathy, that's not fair . . .' Actually it was fair, but I felt bad because it was true. 'I mean, well, I've been busy. You know, settling in and everything. And I've had these damn Physics notes to write up for Williams.'

I spat the excuses out like orange pips, glad to be rid of them. If Kathy didn't believe me, she was kind enough not to say so. She was looking at her hands again, head lowered, her fringe of coppery hair hanging to hide her eyes.

'I know . . .' She stopped, tried again. 'I know you fancy Louise and all that—'

'Kathy!'

'—but there's no need to ignore me because of it. I don't mind if you prefer her. We can still stay friends.'

'Kathy,' I said again, not sharply in outrage now, but more softly with understanding. She glanced up and her eyes were big and wet with hurt.

'OK. And, um, well yes. Let's go to the beach – not rock hunting, but to see how the slubber is getting on.'

'I thought you'd planned that with—'

'I'm inviting *you*, all right? I decide who I'll go with. We're both mixed up in this . . . And maybe the stuff isn't there any more. Best to be sure. Oh yes,' I added: that had reminded me. 'I've got your mug here.'

I opened up my wardrobe and took both the mugs down off a shelf, where I'd hidden them under a shirt.

'Have your parents become suspicious at all?'

'No. I think, in the end, Dad put the rosebush down to the good soil. I didn't tell him your mug had been made out of slubber.'

'Had made *itself*,' Kathy corrected. 'And it's yours really.'

'Why?'

'The original was yours.'

'No.' I frowned, handed her the copy and, as an afterthought, glanced at the underside of mine.

MADE IN ENGLAND . . .

Friday was much more highly coloured then the Thursday had been. First, I felt good about Kathy. There was agreement between us, we knew where the lines were drawn. When she boarded the coach that morning, she still sat at the front, but our smiles linked us and made me feel that we were sitting close.

On the way back from Assembly I almost got my face slapped. In the crush, among the crowds, I walked along with a new jauntiness. People didn't stare at 'the new boy' any more, and being anonymous was better than being strange. Also the boredom of the day had not started to bite, despite the Headmaster's latest instalment of *The One Who Listens*, this being a story in at least a hundred parts, heavy with metaphors and morals, about a place where people went to pour out their souls to The One Who Listens. This 'thing' was hidden behind a curtain, and the interest of the story was supposed to lie in wondering just what was there. I knew it was going to be a mirror, or God or Jesus – worked it out several days ago. Today's episode was about a man who was dying, and regretting that he hadn't made more of his life, and so on and so on. My classmate Dawson tried to hide a yawn and turned his face into a grimacing mask. At that I almost exploded with laughter, but managed to turn it into a realistic-sounding cough.

Up ahead, as I followed people I knew towards the form room in the English block, I saw Claire chatting away to some friends. This time her jewellery was green, and I was still trying to think of a suitable comment as I drew up level with her.

One of her friends pinched her lips together as she noticed me, but I thought nothing of it.

'Hi, Claire.' I touched her elbow to slow her down. 'You know, I much prefer pink with that maroon blazer . . .'

She turned and looked down and I knew something was wrong. Her whole expression changed in an instant. Mild alarm turned to puzzlement, then shock as she grabbed my lapels and slammed me against the wall. Kids flowed around us, but then started to gather and clog up the corridor. A few started to bray and yell.

'Wha' – wha'—'

'You keep your filthy perverted comments to yourself, Hallam. Just – stay away – from me!' She punctuated her words with extra slams against the corridor wall. The back of my head kept bumping the bottom of a picture frame. I put one hand behind to rub the pain, while with the other I tried to disentangle myself from her grip. Claire was strong, and stronger because she was angry; I stood no chance. Desperately I looked for help and saw Sid Machin pushing a path up the corridor.

'Look, I – what's going on? What's wrong?'

Suddenly the rage flamed away and brightness came into her eyes. She leaned close, so that I could smell her perfume and her mass of curly hair brushed my forehead.

'I'm not a whore, I don't go with anyone. And I was only trying to make you feel welcome—'

She released me, pushing me back hard one final time.

Kids were laughing now, tempted to stay and watch the finale, but most moving away as Machin reached us. His teacher's eyes assessed the situation and he let Claire go without a word. Then he cuffed my ear with no real force.

'On your way, lad. And leave the girls alone – until playtime anyway.'

Morning break. I still felt confused and stung by what had happened. Claire had got hold of some tangled-up story and my name was caught in it. I wondered who had been spreading the rumours and telling the tales; what was worse, I thought I knew.

When the bell signalled the end of second lesson I slid off by myself, not wanting to walk around with anybody, least of all with either Kathy or Louise. I knew I would feel embarrassed and ashamed with them, but somewhere behind it there was a backlash of anger. I would not be pleasant company.

After visiting the tuck shop I struck out towards the far end of the football fields. The school and its barrage of noises faded into a chilly whitish haze. I smelt dark autumn in the air. It was on its way, with the crisp ice of winter not far behind.

Three minutes' walking in a straight line brought me to the field perimeter, a tough diamond-link fence that sagged in places where kids had clambered over after lost footballs. Beyond the fence was grass-ragged wasteground that stretched for fifty yards and ended at the sheer grey wall of a factory unit. Through the dull fog, which was like straining to see into four thicknesses of tracing paper, I could make out the shape and hear the engine whine of a yellow forklift truck moving loaded pallets. The sight of it pulled thoughts and feelings from deep inside me. It was a nothing-job, hardly a way of life, as tedious as the mist and, like the mist, having no end to it.

Where will *I* be, I wondered, in ten years' time? Fifteen and twenty years? By then Rowley Mead will be a memory all faded and gone; maybe I'll have left Seabeck, be somewhere else in the world. Mum and Dad, getting on by then . . . Dad making his pots and bowls, Mum still seeing meaning in bits of twisted wood. Kathy? Louise? Kathy married no doubt, with a kid or two as plump and bonny as their mum. Louise would be different. She was after grander things; she would not let life wash her away and cast her up on some flat and ordinary beach. Her wanting was too tight for her to let herself go and be free; she was clenching in a greedy, almost frightened way. No-one ever saw an open-handed Louise . . . And the sweet smell of her gold hair, hands in her lap, mouth open a little bit . . . All part of her weaponry

What do I want, I thought. Where am I in all this? At times I wanted to *dare*, to pull aside the curtains and see just why I had been put on this planet. And at other times . . . The man in the forklift was so solid and safe in his boredom, his life measured out and counting down in stacks of pallets.

Suddenly the clammy fog was inside me. I shivered, turned around and walked back to the school.

My earlier lightness of mood had gone. I felt not so much depressed as confused, a bit aimless. I also thought that nothing more was going to happen that day . . .

I'd strayed off my line of approach to the school and found myself coming along the side of the bike sheds: open frameworks of rust-spotted iron with a corrugated roof that kids threw stones on to make it clatter. Cigarette ends were lying about, and I could smell cigarette smoke in the still, hanging air. People were only shapes around me, splotches of maroon, their voices quiet.

I reached the corner, turned it, and a boy pushed his splayed hand into my chest. The hand wore a black leather glove.

'Wha'd you say then?' The words were mean and menacing, blunt instruments. My spirits dropped again, like a sigh.

'What? Nothing. I was only walking along.'

The kid jabbed me, twice, and hard. In my mind I saw black trouble rushing up to meet me.

'Wha' did you call me?'

'Nothing, I didn't say anything.' I realized my voice had taken on the high, whining tone I recognized when cowards are confronted by bullies. I was going to start pleading with this slob, I knew it. And I felt weak, made out of straws and paper. Maybe this kid was hard, or maybe not, but he was confident: he was used to bullying, used to making boys' noses bleed. I bet he liked to watch them cry, blubbering through their blood and snot, begging not to have more. The way he wore his black gloves (kept polished and shining and new) told me he enjoyed that.

'I heard you, cretin. Are you calling me a liar?'

A question, barbed like wire, to catch me out whichever way I turned. I began to shake my head and saw another crowed gathering, the second one of the day: pretty girls' faces waiting for the humiliation, boys with slick, hungry smiles. And this lout who was going to give them a show at my expense.

'Yes,' I said. My lips felt numb and there was a throbbing at the back of my eyes. 'You're a liar.'

Everything held still for a second, like people posing for a photograph. I nearly giggled at it, except that I would have cried instead. Out of the stillness I saw the boy's eyes shift: a pike's eyes at the bottom of a dim pond.

I twisted my head aside. He was not going to make *my* nose bleed – but his blow caught the top of my cheekbone, and the crowd and fog and black knobbed shape of fist sparkled into confusion. I fell back against someone's bike, caught the base of my spine on a handlebar or lamp-holder; I was nearly sick with the agony and my head felt buried in snow.

The kid grabbed hold of my blazer and hauled me up. He's watched too many cop films, I thought, and nearly giggled again, pointlessly.

His second punch hit my shoulder and made it ache deep down, like a toothache. I knew that once he started, got into his stride like the wheels of a steam train, there would be no way I could stop him.

I flipped out a weak and semi-open hand to fight back, but I had no trust in myself. I cut his lip, but did him no damage.He swore again foully, smeared blood on to the sleek leather of his glove and grinned redly as he came in to finish me.

I shrank back, cringing at him – here you are girls, here's where I get my face kicked in—

I was going to curl up and take it until a teacher came along, until anyone came along, to rescue me.

And someone did, and I could hardly believe it.

As the kid lifted his fist once more, picking his target, a blur ran up and crashed into the boy and knocked him over. He staggered, went down on one knee, then started to rise. His eyes were wide with astonishment and bright with violence. He stood up.

His attacker let him stand. It was Dawson, blazer all ragged, badges glinting, his square head looked like a pale lump of bone with a bristle haircut. He wore a gold stud-earring in one ear.

'Dawson. You bastard. You're dead—'

I leaned against the bike stands like a sack of sawdust, almost sobbing with relief. Dawson was at least a head shorter than his opponent, but the kid's threat had rung hollow: the bully bullied.

. He swung out his gloved right hand, but Dawson knocked it expertly aside and moved in.

It didn't last long. A few cheers and yells started up in the crowd and died away quickly. This was serious, vicious fighting and not a demonstration bout. Dawson had one ambition and went for it, his face quite expressionless. He aimed all his blows at the kid's head and one, I saw with a perverse kind of

89

pleasure, hammered his nose and splashed blood spectacularly across his face. A final underswung punch
to the boy's stomach doubled him up and put him on
his knees. The machine of Dawson's body stopped
working, and he stood there and waited.

The kid's eyes were fixed on Dawson, harsh at first
but then softening with acquiescence. He began to
cry, pausing to vomit up his breakfast.

Mr Barrett came running like an inadequate
Seventh Cavalry, shouting to clear people away.
Dawson didn't move, and neither did I; I wasn't going
to chicken out of the consequences.

'What's going on here – oh dear, oh dear me – what
has happened?'

Neither of us explained. Mr Barrett would not have
understood. It was too long ago since he was young.

We spent twenty minutes, just after break, in Mr
Davies's office. The Headmaster sat in his swivel
chair, with his long thin legs stretched out and crossed
at the ankles. He looked uncomfortable, like a stick
propped against a wall. Mr Barrett as 'the only
reliable witness' sat in the corner chair with his hands
together, fingers touching his lips as though saying a
prayer. Neither of them spoke a word as Dawson and
then I told our story.

'Well,' Mr Davies said at last, after we had finished.
He let the word hang, trying to make the air feel full
of heavy decisions about to be taken. 'You realize how
serious all of this is?'

'Sir,' I said. Dawson stayed silent.

'We simply cannot have this kind of violence
running unchecked through the school. What we are
trying to do here is to show you children that *caring*

and *co-operation* make the basis of a civilized society. Hitting somebody solves nothing – Birtles is now in the medical room with the secretary. I hope you understand what you've done!'

I nodded again, but smiled a hidden smile inside myself to think of Birtles staring into the sick bucket, wads of wet cotton wool pressed to the bridge of his nose.

'The trouble is, people only care about themselves!'

Mr Davies was letting his anger come out now, but still controlling it, like a tap being slowly turned on.

'It's all what's-in-it-for-me, how-much-can-I-grab, let's-stop-the-other-fellow-getting-there-first . . . People don't *talk* to each other any more; people don't *listen!*'

I thought for one terrible moment we were going to get a preview of the Head's other ninety-five episodes of *The One Who Listens*. And I wanted to interrupt, to stop his silly gabbling. Didn't he realize that what Dawson had done was not for the sake of it? He had seen someone weaker being bullied and had put a stop to it. He had nothing to gain by it, no profit involved, and he hadn't enjoyed smashing Birtles . . .

' . . .am tempted to take a very dim view of it!'

Mr Davies was flushed now, he'd worked himself up like a speaker on a soapbox, reaching the stage where no arguments would sway him.

'Mr Davies.' I opened my mouth and said it, in the same way I had agreed with Birtles that he was a liar. The Headmaster stopped talking.

'I know that what's happened is unpleasant, sir, but nothing would have stopped Birtles from hitting me. I was a new kid and he wanted to try me out.

He could have hurt me badly, sir, but Dawson stopped him. That's all. Birtles was bullying me and Dawson stopped him.'

I shut up again and there was a pause. I thought that the glitter in Mr Davies's eyes was one of surprise, because I was not trying to avoid blame or trying to disagree with him. Dawson stared straight ahead, hard and silent as rock; Mr Barrett slowly lowered his hands and gave me the slightest of nods.

'Hm. Well . . .' Mr Davies pursed up his lips and cast around on his desk for a pen and scrap of paper. He scribbled a few words down, then stuck his beaky face towards us again.

'Well, I'm not going to suggest otherwise, ah, Hallam. Although Dawson here has been in some trouble of the same kind before, Mr Barrett has confirmed that Clive Birtles is a bit of a, um, bully. Let's just hear no more of it, right? And, of course, I'll have to make a note in your records. . . .'

Outside the office everywhere was quiet, a pre-lunch-time lull. I let out a great trembling sigh and felt suddenly weak. Dawson checked his watch, one of those that can convert into a robot. It made me smile, then killed the smile because it was strapped to the same arm that had pounded so expertly into Birtles' face.

'If I take a long pee *and* wash my hands, I can miss the rest of RE—'

'Dawson,' I said: he had started walking off towards the loos.

'Yeah?' He didn't stop walking.

'Why did you bother? It only got you into trouble.'

'You got me out of it—'

'I know, but I mean . . .' I ran up level with him. He shrugged.

' 'Cause I hate it when people tread on anybody, OK? When I was in the Juniors' people picked on me. Sometimes I just sat and cried, sometimes I ran to tell teacher. In the end I sorted it out for myself. Nobody bothers me now.'

'But what Mr Davies said about hitting people and solving nothing . . .'

'Tell it to Birtles. Tell it to the kid next year who's just like Birtles. The world is the world, OK?'

And you have what you make, I added in my mind, and Superman doesn't exist.

We had reached the swing door of the boys' toilets. Dawson pushed it half open and from inside came the noise of running water squeezing in jets from a pipe above the urinals: it sounded like piglets squealing.

'Well, Dawson. Just thanks. If I can give you anything, you know?'

'Well, fifty quid will cover it,' he said, and grinned. One of his side teeth on the left was missing.

The end of afternoon lessons felt like about six layers of blankets lifting off me. There was a certain excitement in the air, because the weekend lay ahead, perhaps because November the fifth was just four days away. The air had a snap to it, autumn clean, and smelt of cool metal.

Of course I had to go through the whole interview routine again with Mum and Dad, who noticed the taut blue bruise on my cheek straight away. Mum was her worrying self, Dad took it all philosophically.

'Bullies exist, my love. Simon hasn't come to any

harm . . .' There was something in that which told me Dad had once suffered it too.

'But what if this boy picks on him again?'

Bribe Birtles; kick his face in; get Dawson to smash him; kneel and beg; run for teacher . . .

'I'll just stay out of his way, Mum,' I said, as convincingly as I could.

I ate a quick tea and went over to Kathy's, surprising myself that I did not feel embarrassed about it.

Her place was small and ordinary, with an ornamental brick wall surrounding a pocket-handkerchief of a garden. There was a wrought-iron front gate, painted blue. Down the drive was a garage, and also a carport that had been built along the house-side. Its roof of plastic sheeting had split in a few places, and was black-green with dirt and flourishing algae.

I knocked at the door. Kathy's father answered. He was a short, fat bald man who looked a lot older than my dad. He had a bristly iron-grey moustache and wore a blue sleeveless cardigan that bulged at his belly. His smile was open, warm and friendly.

'Come in, Simon, come on through.'

I'd never met him before, so Kathy must have told him my name. And what else, I wondered.

I waited in the lounge. It was warm and cosy there. A table lamp melted a yellow cone of light in the corner, and the telly was on. The air smelt rich and savoury, of gravy and cooked dinners.

I thought this was a lovely snug den of a house, where the world was kept locked out, where these people who fitted it so perfectly would outlast all their winters.

Kathy came down five minutes later. She had been

changing into what my mum, and probably all mums, call 'sensible' clothes: heavy cord trousers, plenty of jumpers gloves, scarf and – in Kathy's case – her yellie wellows. She also had a canvas bag slung over her shoulder.

'You look like you're off skiing!' I laughed.

'Cold enough for it.' Kathy's mum came through from the kitchen, looking like a female duplicate of Kathy's dad . . .

'See you both. We won't be back late.'

'Just take care, the two of you.'

We left the house, stepping into the cold air. It felt like the first moment after waking, when you throw the blankets aside on a December morning. A tingling shiver made me shrug up my shoulders.

Kathy said nothing as we walked to the end of Main Street and turned down towards the beach. Then she looked up and lifted her hand, as if to touch my face.

'I heard about what happened, Simon. I'm sorry you got hurt.'

'It isn't so bad. Good job Dawson was around, though, otherwise the story would be different.'

'Not many people like him, I think. Always in trouble, you know, fighting.'

'Well he's got one friend.' I told her. Somehow I didn't mind telling Kathy about the fight; in front of Louise I would have been embarrassed and ashamed, male pride dented and all that. I thought Kathy might have said more, but instead she nodded and stayed silent.

I looked at the sky. 'There'll just be time to reach Blackshales, take a quick look and get back before dark,' I said, speaking as though I'd had years of experience of the outdoors. Kathy smiled up at me, and didn't argue.

We passed a gang of kids hanging around outside the chip shop, then walked past a row of whitewashed cottages that were now holiday homes belonging to people from the city, and along the beach road as far as we could before it slanted uphill to the cliff tops.

We had walked hard, almost jogging at times, and I was whacked.

'Breather,' I said, sitting down on the sea-wall. Kathy sat beside me.

We were looking west, across the channel that must have been fifteen miles wide at this point. The sea was choppy, like dull rippled silver scored with bright new scratches where the whitecaps broke. The sky went through all shades of blue, deepening upwards, and the sun was a huge crimson smear stretched out across the skyline. Below, on the opposite coast, a few lights twinkled like tiny snowflakes on the point of melting. It was beautiful.

'Hey, Simon . . .' Kathy said, irritating me by bursting into the peace and privacy of my moment. She held out a package, something wrapped up in newspaper.

'These chips'll be cold,' I told her, quipping my way out of being annoyed. But the seriousness in her gaze shut me up.

Whatever it was, it was heavy. I hefted it once, twice in my hand, then tore off the paper. I knew what she'd given me before I saw it.

'Because we're friends,' she said gently, and so quietly I almost didn't hear.

An ammonite, sliced through, as big as a saucer and marvellously detailed. It had the rich gleam of the yellow metal it was made from. I held it, turning it in one hand, and my eyes felt prickly-hot.

'But your dad won't—'

'It's mine to give,' Kathy answered. 'And I've got the other half.'

She was not looking at the ammonite, but at me, and her eyes were warm in the same way that her house was warm. For some reason I felt small and mean.

'It'll be the best in my collection,' I told her, every word of it true.

She nodded. 'That's good.' I'd said enough.

We clambered down off the sea-wall and walked the final leg to Blackshales. When the shingle gave way to slabs of weed-slick rock, I held Kathy's hand to help her over (though she saved my dignity at least as many times).

The evening had darkened when we arrived, and the wind from the east was bringing piled masses of cloud to cover the sky's violet. The cliffs hung there like black curtains, blacker even than the clouds or the nearing night.

Incoming tide water swished and slapped. No gulls cried.

We pulled ourselves up over the final hump of rock and looked at the beach. For a second, in the gloom, my eyes would not make sense of things. Then it all came at me in a rush, in a flood. The picture hit me so hard I almost fell backwards.

'It's wonderful,' Kathy whispered, whispered until her words were lost out to sea.

'God, God,' I said, 'I don't believe it. I don't . . .'

We had not come three miles. We had come light-years.

The Gift

The beach below Blackshales is made of terraces of dark rock that break up into boulders and smaller stones, then shingle that finally gives way to a thin strip of flat sand you can see only at low tide. Now, mixed with the smell of salt and ozone, rose the strange and subtle scent of elsewhere . . . Smell apple and you think of orchards and pies, smell roses and you think of gardens and long summer afternoons – but this new smell brought nothing, yet it was tantalizing and almost familiar. It might have been grass, or flowers, but it was neither of these.

And the slubber had grown. Out of streaks and puddles of glassy jelly had come tall club-like trees, and thick mats and blankets of spreading vegetation that even in the fading light jumped out at my eyes with a vivid emerald green. Mixed in with the tall tree-things and the green sweep of stuff were other colourful growths that littered the beach: clumps like sea-anemones but as large as pillarboxes (some of them were bright red, too, while others glowed brilliant yellow or royal blue, violet, turquoise, orange . . .).

'What's happened here? Why has it grown like this?' Kathy had lain stomach-down on the flat top of the rock and had her chin propped in her hands.

She was filled up with wonder: I was reminded of a little girl lying entranced in front of the TV with just the same expression on her face.

'It had no pattern to copy,' I said, guessing it all – but the guesses felt good. 'Oh, maybe there are some more crabs and limpets in the rockpools, perhaps some extra bladderwrack lying about; but most of the slubber was spare. It had to fall back on the only memory it contained, of the place it came from . . .'

It hit me then, hard, that the place it came from was another world. Slubber had nothing to do with Earth at all. It was extraterrestrial, and when I bent down and touched it, held it still and silent in my hands, it gave me a picture of its home: the first picture from a new world.

'It's marvellous . . . It's beautiful.'

It occurred to me that I was starting to feel strange, sort of vague and dreamy. That was the last self-conscious thought I had . . .

From between the skinny motionless trees and the pillarbox growths, the lion padded out like a silky ooze of honey. It came right up to me and stood beside me like a faithful watchdog. I lost Kathy in its presence.

So, this is where you come from . . . How far away is it? And how did you get here? And why? Earth can be a real dump, right – so is that why you're here, to do something about it, to make us a garden again?

There came no answers, but my body and mind were suddenly filled with a huge and glowing sense of *promise*; everything seemed right, if only we used our intelligence for once and put our trust in the truth of the golden lion's eyes.

We can make slubber into what we want, but you

will guide us into what it *should* be; you brought it with you, you show us what it can do . . .

Mum and Dad stood there in the otherworld land, smiling more happily than I'd ever seen them smile. And close beside them was Louise, and beside her Kathy . . . Further back stood other people I loved, dwindling away to a green horizon. And around and among them bloomed a blaze of flowers.

Kathy sat up, turned her back on it all and began to cry.

'Hey, come on. Don't you think it's beautiful too?'

She nodded, sniffling. 'It's not that. It's,well – the world isn't ordinary now. Something more wonderful than I could ever have imagined has happened. I'm *happy* about it, Simon, I'm not sad. Think about what it could mean . . .'

No need for the would to go hungry now, or poor: no need for someone to have more than anyone else. All men could be equal.

'Let's take some more home,' I suggested. The excitement was tight inside me now, as though Christmas had come and was going to last forever.

'Let's see what else it can do!'

Kathy produced a couple of plastic carriers from her canvas bag, and together we shovelled each half-full with our bare hands. Under sugar-like crusts of anemone, some raw slubber was still to be found, unformed and purposeless. The stuff was heavy and cold, like thick wallpaper paste left out overnight. But as I held it, I lost the sense of its weight and deadness, seeing instead a vast potential, like a brilliant light.

Later, going back, Kathy walked with stars in her eyes. The lion shadowed us, a slow amber drift as silent as a dream.

Next day was Saturday. I lay-in until ten-thirty, enjoying one of those warm satisfying sleeps where, from time to time, you can rise to wakefulness like a dolphin nosing the surface of the ocean, take a look around and choose to return into blue sunlit waters.

In the end Mum came and bribed me awake with a plate of buttered toast and a mug of tea.

'Kathy rang,' she said, with a motherly smile of approval. 'She says, go straight round to her garage when you're up . . . Whatever that means.'

'Hm. Strange for a girl to be so interested in banger racing,' I muttered through a mouthful of toast.

Mum's smile disappeared.

I finished breakfast, washed and dressed in a hurry, then ran round to Kathy's corner house, going down the side with its shadowy umbrella of a carport to the garage.

Kathy was in shirtsleeves, and sweating even then as a two-kilowatt fan heater blew a swathe of hot air across the workbench.

'Converting to a sauna, eh?'

'Morning, Simon. I've been busy.'

'So I see . . .'

And she had, arranging pots, jars, bowls and saucers of slubber along the bench.

'Been up since six – and look!'

Kathy had duplicated Chris's experiment of slubber in raw peat, and it had sprouted just the same in a miniature of the landscape we had seen at Blackshales.

'It's empty of ideas,' I said, more to myself. 'It has nothing to copy.'

Kathy held up more pots, wherein a variety of garden plants were shooting up healthily.

'This is an oak tree,' she told me, sticking a seedling under my nose. 'And this is a horse chestnut . . .'

'I'm not a total dimwit,' I pointed out. 'Grown in slubber—'

'No.' She shook her head and grinned sort of mischievously. 'Not grown – copied. That's the mistake Louise and Chris have been making. And that's what I thought at first. But I dug down into the soil of this oak, and I found the original acorn beside a *second* acorn, the one that had germinated.'

'So the slubber only makes *itself* grow super-fast, not the object from which the blueprint was taken!'

'Seems that way,' Kathy said. 'And I've done more . . .'

I had sudden amusing and alarming visions of two garden sheds outside, or a whole gang of dustbins taking shape quietly in a corner—

'Here.'

She handed me an apple, held one herself which was identical.

'Guess which is the slubberized one.'

I stared hard at them both. 'Can't.'

'Bite them, then.'

I tried the first. It was one of those deep, deep-red apples with hard, crisp flesh that flooded my mouth with sweetness when I crunched it.

'Delicious,' I said, spraying juice. Then I took a bite at the second: the same, except that, for an instant, I imagined a whirlpool of colour and a faraway impression of white hills and green plains and gold warmth running in the breeze. I sensed two lion eyes watching me invisibly.

I held the second apple up. 'This one.'

'That's right.' Kathy took it from me and finished

it, wide-eyed. Meanwhile I examined the other things she'd tried to copy in slubber.

A silver dog-chain hung down into a jam-jar of the stuff, and in the half-transparent matrix more thick chromium links were forming. Next to it in a saucer lay a gaudy piece of costume jewellery, a brooch made of brass and flashing *diamanté* crystal; already beside it I saw the outline of a replica.

A third bowl sparked my interest even more. In this one Kathy had placed a ring, obviously gold, with the band worn thin over the years. In its minute claws were held a central blue sapphire and circlet of tiny diamonds.

'Mum's engagement ring,' Kathy said, coming up behind me. She sounded guilty. 'She's terrified of losing it. Now, if she does, I can pretend I've found it. She'd be heartbroken if it went,' she added, as though she had to say more.

'How did you manage to borrow it?'

'She keeps it in a box by her bedside when she has housework to do.' Kathy lifted the bowl closer. 'It'll be perfect. An exact copy . . .'

Perfect? I wondered. I kept seeing my Li'l Monster mug. And the apple – that had not been perfect; the flash of the slubber's homeplace had been trapped in the substance of the fruit – making it *more* than an ordinary apple. But that was not a perfect apple . . .

'Do you suppose,' Kathy was saying dreamily, 'that you could take a copy and make a copy of that, then a copy of *that*, and so on down the line?'

'I don't think so. It'd be like tape-to-tape copying, where each generation loses some of the quality of the original. No,' I decided, 'I think you'd need fresh, new slubber each time. Anyway, why've you got this heater blasting out? You're not trying to lose weight by sweating, are you?'

Kathy's eyebrows drew together.

'I don't *need* to lose weight, do I?'

I saw a cliff-edge and suicide looming ahead and tried to laugh cheerfully: I sounded weak and frightened, as though I was standing in front of a Mafia boss.

'No, no, no . . . no. I was just being, well, you know me . . . funny . . .'

'Funny, exactly.' She took her hands off her hips, and with that the danger passed. 'I've noticed that slubber works faster in the heat, like most chemical processes, in fact.'

'That's why things came on so well in Chris's greenhouse.'

'And why those slubber-anemone things were only finished on the outside. The chilly weather has made it sluggish.'

'Well it's not chilly in here. In fact I'm dying of thirst!'

Kathy laughed. 'Know what you mean. I'll fetch drinks.'

She went to the door, then paused with it half open and looked back at me.

'Do you realize, Simon, that a person could do *anything* with slubber? It's like magic. Diamonds, gold, money – everything like that would be worthless. You could even copy a million *Mona Lisas* . . . But I wonder if they'd be worthless too?'

'Da Vinci painted the *first* one,' I pointed out. Kathy thought for a moment then shrugged.

'What's the difference between the original and a perfect copy?' she wondered. I shrugged, then said,

'About one week after the secret of slubber escaped, the world would be a totally different place . . .'

'Escaped? I thought we were going to let the secret go?'

'Well,' I said, 'we'll see.' Then I had a thought. 'Hey, I could copy that ammonite you gave me. Then you wouldn't have to part with it . . .'

Kathy's face darkened, through fleeting disappointment to prickly heat.

'Wouldn't be the same,' she said, making me smile. 'I gave you the *first* one.'

Left alone, I glanced at the rest of Kathy's experiments. Really they were more of the same, simply testing the range of things that slubber would copy. Tucked away under the bench in a plastic washing-up bowl lay what remained of the slubber we'd carried home from Blackshales; a two-inch depth of the raw stuff that had not been given any ideas yet, although it was tainted vaguely the colour of the bowl's plastic.

I slid the bowl into the open and the bottom gritted harshly on the concrete floor. This slubber had not had the warmth of the fan heater playing over it, so was cold and stiff and hardly moved when I tapped the bowl with my shoe.

You look so innocent, I thought, and so harmless. But you're probably more dangerous than bullets or bombs, because people won't have to *make* bullets and bombs any more, just drop them in a vat of slubber and stand back. Does that mean we won't try to make *new* things? Might everyone lose the will to make an effort now? Instead of working to earn money for something, you can get it for free from slubber . . . Will governments control slubber to stop that? Will one or a few governments claim slubber for themselves and prevent its use elsewhere? Whoever has slubber could rule the world . . . What are you? Where have you come from? Are you an invasion, a weapon, or a gift . . .?

I had a partial answer to one of those questions. I had seen the world where slubber had come from, its homeplace. It looked beautiful, like a paradise, calm and unpolluted and fruitful, a garden. And I wanted to see it again.

I knelt down and pushed my hands into the slubber, closed my eyes and waited. For a few seconds I felt the cool heaviness of the jelly on my skin, but then it faded just as the warmth of bath-water fades when you lie still. I waited. My hands began to warm the slubber. The slubber gave me pictures.

Slowly they came together out of blur and mist, clearing, assuming colour and depth . . . Then they were sharper than the crispest TV pictures, and I was moving among them this time, not just watching from a distance; I walked through the bright green moss-like grasses that gave the sensation of splashing in water on the seashore. I smelt the succulence of alien flowers; and these flowers, I knew, would not die in the autumn, they would last forever (I had a ghost vision of Mum's red rose still perfect in her bedroom). The sky was a clear lake with a jewel in its bed – the coppery star around which this planet moved. Far away lay hills and white cliffs; living coloured kites drifted in the sky . . . From a stand of tall trees-that-were-not-trees honey melted into view and my golden lion trotted towards me. It was huge, bigger than any earthly cat. In its body was comfort, and in its eyes was peace.

'Oh, I wanted so much to *be* there, by the sea that

had no tides or storms and where lives were not washed so carelessly away; out of my cold world with its sharpness and hardness, its violence and cruelty. I wanted to be where there was no pain or loss, where me and Mum and Dad and – Louise – (Kathy?) – and all those I loved could be safe . . . Please, let me have that.

The lion moved close now, almost touching. I was overwinged by its presence.

Yes, yes I can give you those things,

I said, or did he?

I don't want Mum and Dad to die, not ever.

Yes, don't fear for them.

And, you know, I think Kathy's great. Really, inside me I do.

She will be safe.

I don't worry about myself—

You will be safe.

But old Dawson, he has a rough time . . .

Here all are at peace.

You can do anything, I know, and make the Earth what we want it to be . . . But why not make it like your place, like wherever you come from? It's already started in Blackshales. Everyone could have sunny weather, sunny weather forever!

Sunny weather.

Yes.

The lion smiled.

And in the reddish sunlight of the other place I caught the half-hidden glint of its beautiful white teeth.

My eyes snapped open and I nearly passed out with the faintness and shock. I was back in Kathy's garage with its oilspill on the floor and its cobwebs hung in corners, where spiders ate flies, where butterflies cocooned against the winter.

I looked down. My hands were numb.

'No! There's not enough for that. And – and it's not right!'

I pulled my hands away and fell backwards, staggering and banging my head against the workbench. That sobered me, my mind cleared, while in the bowl the shadows of bones faded, and the blush of skin gave up its promise and the slubber returned to whatever-might-be . . .

When Kathy came back, I said nothing. Instead I drank my tea quickly and went home.

Mum and Dad were having one of their rare rows. In fact, 'row' would be too strong a word to describe it. They were engaged in a 'discussion' that involved some 'decision making'. I made a coffee for us all (I was still thirsty after the garage's dry heat), and sat and listened.

I felt hung in a cool web. It was good. I could make sense of it.

'Well, it's not that I don't want you to have it, Greg, you know that. But we've talked about some carpeting for upstairs – the stuff the Millingtons left isn't really to our taste. And it's worn. Besides, Christmas is pretty expensive anyway these days, and—'

Mum paused. She was sitting at her usual small table by the back window, carefully applying more varnish to her driftwood. She had reached a tricky bit and needed to stop talking while her tongue stuck out a little in concentration.

Dad looked my way, and gave me a Mum's-in-full-swing smile with lifted eyebrows.

'I don't – I don't want this stuff to run. And if you overapply, the cracks and crannies look all *gummy* . . .'

'And we definitely don't want gummy crannies,' I muttered into my cup.

'I might consider putting in some overtime,' Dad suggested, rolling the idea in his mind. 'The ceramics course is fully subscribed for the next two terms and I could easily manage a few extra classes. There, problem solved . . .'

'But then,' Mum said reasonably, 'I would never *see* you, Greg – just as I'd never see you if you went ahead and bought this automatic wheel of yours . . .'

'It isn't mine, Jenny, that's what this fuss is *about*!'

Dad went into his pipe-stoking routine, cleaning out the bowl viciously, stuffing tobacco from his leather envelope-pouch with petulant jabs of his finger.

'Oh, Greg . . .' Whenever Mum said that, she made it sound as though it could have half a dozen different meanings. She glanced up, paintbrush poised, smiling brightly, maybe to soothe Dad – or perhaps in victory at making him cross.

'What do you think Simon?'

'Well. You're lucky, Mum, because you can do your crafts and hobbies while Dad's here. And you get the stuff free, like the driftwood – or it doesn't cost very much, like your quilting paper.'

'Quilling, dear.'

'Yeah. Well you only *walk* on carpet, don't you? And why *should* Christmas be expensive? Let Dad buy his potter's wheel and set up his workshop. Then he can make pots for presents and it won't cost you a cent. There,' I added, imitating Dad's gruff voice, 'problem solved.'

Mum stared at me in surprise, Dad in agreement and beaming cameraderie – sort of 'that's my boy' shining in his eyes.

'I didn't realize you had such a highly developed sense of values, Simon,' Mum said.

'Don't forget logic, Mum, and sheer common sense.'

'Yes, and modesty. Don't you agree, Greg, that thirteen is such an *irritating* age?'

'Mmm,' Dad said, deadpan. '*And* twenty-one; but it'll be your birthday again soon, dear.'

I grinned openly; Mum searched Dad's face for sarcasm, found none and came across to give him a hug.

'Oh you say the nicest things. OK, I suppose I can do without new carpets. You have your automatic potter's wheel—'

'And some new glazes. And maybe I can put a deposit down for my own kiln—'

Mum began to react, so Dad hooked his fingers into her ribs and started to tickle. She shrieked, then went on the attack. I decided that the problem *had* been solved and that the conversation was at an end.

'Right, I'll go and make myself something to eat, then. Or maybe I'll just sit around being bored. Or perhaps I'll invent something . . .'

'Wait, Simon—' Dad caught me at the door. By now his shirtfront was open and his hair in disarray.

'We've been invited to a bonfire party up at the Williamses.'

'When?'

'Well on Bonfire Night of course. That's Tuesday.

110

Just letting you know so that you can be up to date with your homework and have time to spare . . .'

Yes, I thought, unless John Williams piles on some more just for spite.

'Fine,' I said quietly, and with no enthusiasm at all. 'I'll try to fit it in to my busy schedule.'

'You do that.' Dad chuckled in a way that made me think he might have understood. 'So what other momentous plans do you have?'

I lifted my hands in despair and shook my head.

'Well, Sunday is just *so* packed, I don't know how I'll begin to cope . . .'

Actually, nothing ever happened on Sundays; I'd learned that through years of experience. They were grey and dull, the big trough in the graphline of the week.

I turned into bed late on the Saturday night (watched a vampire film) hoping for a lie-in, but slept badly. I dreamed of standing at a cave entrance overlooking a lovely peaceful valley and yearning so much to be there that it was almost painful. But then the cave shifted and rumblings from the depths of the ground became a huge roaring – and the cave was a set of jaws and I had a second to dive in or dive out—

I woke up in a sweat as the roof met the floor.

I dozed fitfully until nine, then decided to visit Louise and Kathy in that order.

The day was the colour of weathered lead, and cold; a sort of heavy day that gave me a dull headache that wouldn't go away.

Instead of ringing the front door bell at the Williams' house, I went straight down the garden to the greenhouse, knowing that Chris would be there –

111

and hoping I might find Louise also. I smiled, for the first time that day, to see both their shapes beyond the pearly vagueness of the glass.

Within a minute of stepping inside, I needed to take off my coat, and then my jumper. The max-min thermometer above the door registered eighty degrees-plus.

'You must be costing you parents a fortune!' I said it loud and clear so that Louise might look at me: both she and Chris had heads down, peering intently into a jar.

'Hmm . . . Hi, Simon. How are you?'

Chris didn't look up, but waved his hand vaguely by way of greeting.

Then another thought struck me.

'Hey, you don't suppose your dad will get suspicious – I mean, you spending so much time down here and all?'

Louise straightened up, faced me. She was flushed and her hair had fallen forward with bending. I felt my pulse start to go. She looked distracted, maybe annoyed.

'Don't worry. Daddy won't mind forking out a few extra pounds to keep us out of the way. Especially today; they're entertaining, you see.'

She affected a plum-in-the-mouth accent and a snooty pose, then smiled at me tiredly. 'Don't worry,' she added, more sincerely. 'Look at this.'

She took my cool and tentative hand in hers (it was hot, insistent), and led me to the end bench where Chris was still engrossed.

'Well – don't you thing that's incredible?'

I found myself looking into a big pickling jar, like a sweet jar. It must have been a foot high and had a plastic screw top that was a handspan wide. Inside it were two hamsters and a ghost.

'God,' I whispered. 'God Almighty. You're *making* them!'

It was true, and the fact of it hit me like a stone. These were not such distant things as snails and fish; these animals had eyes that seemed to look at you, and warm blood, and they were creatures you could love . . .

The original hamster was curled into a tight ball, foetally, its tiny hooked paws covering the black seeds of its eyes. Both eyes were open, and the thing was looking at me; immersed deep in the slubber, it was still alive.

Beside it, hanging there in the thick, faintly milky jelly, was its duplicate: dun-coloured fur a little matted to its sides, delicate ribcage pulsing in-out-in-out with its short nervous breaths. And its eyes . . . not black this time, but green, as though the replica was not quite perfect or as though it was not looking out from the same kind of brain.

And deeper in the jar, close to the bottom, a second duplicate animal was beginning to take shape. This was no more than an ill-defined veil of mist within which its needle-boned skeleton was only a thickening of the light. Internal organs were just shadows; eyes merely a distant glimmer of emeralds.

This – I thought with a jolt, remembering recent Bio. lessons – this was not test-tube life. It was something different that had nothing to do with science. It was too easy. It was alien.

'What – what will you do once they've formed?'

'Keep them!' Louise laughed as though I was some kind of freak. 'Keep them as pets.'

Chris was already unscrewing the jar and delving inside with his hands grasping. Slubber oozed over the jar-lip and clung to the outside as it slid slowly down.

'What're you doing – oh, stop that!'

Before I could do anything he'd pulled out the original animal and its copy – held them both out for me to inspect. The 'real' one trembled, terrified, in Chris's jellied hands. Close beside it the other looked about curiously, cocked its perfect head at me, and stared.

'Hey! He likes you, Simon.'

Louise stroked the tiny head, but the eyes and the whiskers and the pink nose kept working. They took everything in, they learned: they soaked up the world. It made me feel sick.

'Well . . . I only dropped by to see how you were doing, just to tell Kathy, like.'

'Doing great. Tell Kathy that from me.'

'Yeah,' I muttered, suddenly fascinated by the ghost of the hamster in the jar as it dissolved away to nothing, like a bad dream, deprived of its original pattern.

Later, when I saw Kathy, I mentioned the party but kept quiet about what had gone on in the greenhouse.

'I'll fix an invite for you with Louise,' I said weakly.

We spent a couple of hours continuing with Kathy's experiments, and at one point I mentioned fireworks.

'I'll buy some tomorrow and we'll duplicate them, take loads along with us . . . Ah, but money . . .'

We dug in our pockets and brought out a few pound coins and some silver. I looked at the cash, looked at the slubber bowl, and smiled.

By teatime my pocket bulged with over twenty pounds, grown in under two hours.

Monday morning was overcast and cold. Drizzle came down drearily and would be in for the day, I knew; it was as fine as mist, and I reflected that the seaside in rain is probably the most dismal place on Earth.

We had no Assembly; we spent our tutorial time listening to a lecture by Mr Barrett on the Firework Code, then we each designed a poster to illustrate one of his points. Dawson drew something obscene involving a Roman candle and two Catherine wheels, and was given a hundred lines for it.

'Will it go in the school magazine, sir?' he wondered, at his Monday-morning best.

Another fifty lines for that crack.

At break, the wet day routine was in operation. This meant that all the kids could stay indoors while most of the staff escaped from their teaching rooms into the staff room and left us to it.

I hung around the English block, which was separate from the main school and so tended to be a little quieter. That's where Louise found me.

She was with her retinue – I'd begun to call them the Harpies in my own mind. Louise and the Harpies. Sounded like a rock group. But she looked great, slim and attractive in her uniform, hair worn loose today. She was cool and confident and used her beauty easily – it was too grown-up to be called prettiness. And she was intelligent. She had it all.

'We're giving a party, at my place.'

'My dad mentioned it.'

'I mean, parents will be there and all that stuff.' A

bright and stunning flash of a smile. 'But that's no reason for us kiddies to be put off, is it?'

I shook my head and tried to seem casual, but I could feel it strongly in me and all around me – the glass edges of her words, the knots of intention tightening. Her friends were there like carbon copies of herself, like reinforcements to pump up the emotional power of what Louise was saying.

'Can you make it?' She pushed a hand through her hair and waited. She loved the waiting, the kestrel-eyed watching of the mouse in the field.

'Yeah. But, um . . .'I could hear my heartbeat banging in my ears and felt the blood coming to my face, though no way could I stop now.

'But I'd like to bring Kathy along too.'

There was a second's silence, like a vacuum, and I'd expected it. The reaction I was not so sure about.

Maureen laughed over-loudly behind her hand. One or two of the others smirked. Louise covered up the slight shock that had been stamped across her face and smiled with her lips.

'You're sort of *with* Kathy, now?'

'Sort of.'

'Hmm . . .' Louise reached out and touched the fading bruise on my cheek, and her fingers poured electricity into my head.

'Nearly gone,' she said. 'I heard all about it. Good old Dawson. It's nice to have someone around to help you out of things.'

Then the hand was gone and she was distant once more, across a great gulf. Her skin had been smooth, her touch so delicate.

'Well, drag Kathy along then. And it's bring-a-bottle too, tell your parents. Oh, and best wear jeans

116

for warmth: we'll be outside for fireworks. Yes, tell Kathy to wear jeans.'

I watched them as they walked away, Louise and the Harpies, heads together gossiping. Then I used the rest of my break to sneak out of school to the newsagent's over the road. I bought Dawson a *Superman* comic and stuffed it away into his bag.

'Hell, it looks like the Gunpowder Plot in here!'

Kathy chuckled, pleased at my reaction to her efforts. Her father's garage had been turned into a storeroom for things made out of slubber. She had moved on from jewellery and acorns, to car parts, various liquids (paints, oil, petrol, whisky) . . . more money than I was able to count – pound coins stacked in neat rouleaux of ten on the benchtop – foodstuffs, electrical components, and fireworks, piles of them.

'People are going to get pretty suspicious if we turn up with this lot!'

'Who'll know?' Kathy said, shrugging. 'My parents aren't coming, your mum and dad will think *I've* brought them all – and Louise and Chris know all about it anyway.'

So I shrugged too, but not with Kathy's lightness. I just stared about the place in wonderment and worry, running my fingers over boxes and packages, bottles and bowls.

'Louise is into living things – animals, I mean.' I told her about the hamsters. 'But I think, where will it end?'

'It doesn't *have* to end,' Kathy said with a cool and deadly seriousness. 'I've been thinking, and it seems to me that slubber is like a universal building material – but a material that can understand what it is to be

117

made into. It's like clay being able to imagine the pot it's to form, and then make itself into that pot . . .'

'Sounds weird.'

'What other explanation is there? I've been trying to follow some leads at the library, and I came across a thing called a Von Neumann device. It's named after the scientist who thought of it, and *he* says that the best way for mankind to explore the universe is to build a machine that can use the rocks and stuff on other planets to make replicas of itself. The first Von Neumann machine will land, mine the ore, work the metal, build the components and assemble them – so that in the end *two* machines will take off again, each able to construct others of its kind . . .'

'You're beginning to sound like Chris,' I said: 'my condolences. But slubber isn't like that. It's making things that *we* want, not what *it* wants.'

Kathy lifted her eyebrows. 'Oh yeah? Come on, I've got something to show you.'

She took me up to the house, to the small lounge that was nuzzled into its own quietness.

'Where're your parents?'

'Church. Now look, I've got a video here that I copied with slubber—'

' 'Gainst the law.'

'What law? I'll bet there's no law to cover *this* kind of copying. Anyway, it's not a first generation copy: that turned out OK. What I did was to copy the copy, then copy the copy of the copy . . .'

'Hang on,' I said, 'I've got to sit down.'

Kathy switched on the TV and set the video recorder running.

'Now look at this. At first I thought I'd got the

cassettes mixed up – this wasn't *The Omega Plan* at all. But then . . .'

I watched the black-and-white fuzz blizzard across the screens as the leader ran through, then came zig-zag torn curtains of colour that drew aside to show a beautiful beach of clean, pale sand; the sky was a tranquil blue and floating in it I saw a vague moon, half-full, as though sunk deep in quiet water. It was our moon.

The beach curved off in a broad, smooth sweep to distant dunes and hills that were draped with a bright glowing green – it might have been moss, or new grass, or something else entirely. The sea was mill-pond still, tideless it seemed, tideless and safe with no storms to wash away boats or cast up dark monsters.

In the distance stood slender cycad-like trees, and from between these trees the only moving objects in the whole picture gradually appeared: two people, walking together, making their way down the hillside to the beach, but never coming close enough for the details of their faces to be visible.

But I could imagine what they were saying . . .

I'm glad I'm with you, Simon. I never really wanted anyone else.

I feel the same about you, Louise. I couldn't stop staring from the first time I saw you.

Now you can stare as long as you like. We've got forever, after all. . . .

I said, very quietly, to Kathy: 'Have you used up all the slubber now?' She nodded.

'But I thought I'd fetch some more. Fancy a walk?'

'You've got to be joking!'

She looked at me curiously.

'No, why? There's more work to do. Can't you

119

see the link, Simon? Von Neumann machines make themselves; slubber recreates the world from which it came – but it suits us too, right? Just the two of us . . .'

I started to argue, to question, but Kathy just laughed happily, took my hand and almost dragged me back out of the house.

I'd been right in thinking the rain had set in for the day, although by now the bland greyness of cloud was almost rained-out, a final fitful drizzle bringing on an early night.

'It won't take us long. An hour there, an hour back.'

I was doubtful. And a bit worried too, to recognize in Kathy the same kind of uncontrolled curiosity I had noticed in Chris. That was precisely it – when you saw a little of what slubber could do, you were led to wonder where it might end. Or if it *did* end . . .

'Well, only if you carry me when I get tired.'

'You're a pal, Simon. Thanks.'

Yeah, that's right. Soft-hearted Simon, everyone's friend.

We took a couple of plastic buckets with us, and a torch, a big grey heavy one that was covered in rubber and shone with a strong white beam. We needed it too. Twilight was upon us by the time we left the road and took to the shingle beach. The tide was on the turn, swinging in dark water the same gloomy colour as the sky, and the wind off the channel took all the feeling out of my nose, then my fingers.

'I hope it's not like this tomorrow!' Kathy yelled at me. She was just a yard away, but her face was only a pale white blotch and her words, like torn scraps of paper, flew away on the gusts.

'That's one thing slubber can't make – sunshine to order!'

Kathy shouted back: I half heard it . . . Sounded like, 'Not yet, Simon, not yet.'

At Blackshales we stood again on the whale's back of dark rock overlooking the little bay. Beyond and farther up the coast, the lights of Westmartin cast an orange underglow on the sagging ceiling of the clouds. Closer in, whitecaps sparkled briefly; rain glinted slickly in the beam of our torch.

'Still here,' I said, 'but look at it!'

The bad weather had damaged the slubber structures, some of them quite badly. Many of the tree-things had crumpled like corn stalks, while the pillar box anemones closest to us had collapsed into ruined stumps.

'I think the water's washing a lot of it out to sea,' Kathy said. 'You know, if we have another storm like the last one, there'll be nothing left here.'

'Closer to the cliffs, in the rockpools: more protection there. Perhaps the slubber won't be diluted.'

I saw her smile in the dimness, just a fleeting impression of it, then she turned to make her way across the rocks.

I began to shout for her to be careful, but before I spoke the first word I saw her slip, lose balance, and disappear in a flail of arms. The torch vanished behind a boulder, though a moment later I caught sight of it again, half submerged in a rockpool.

Kathy was on her back, mouth opening and closing comically like a fish. I almost laughed, until I saw the skin stretched tight on her face and the shock in her eyes: their pupils were all black, like buttons.

'Kathy . . .?'

I wondered what was wrong, while dread like slushy ice trickled down my neck and back. She might have done something to her spine, fractured her skull, broken a leg . . .

I slid the torchlight down her body. One hand in its red fingerless glove lay limply in the water, and some of the dye must have seeped out because—

I flicked the beam down further and saw that her right leg was bleeding, bleeding too much. It was bent at the knee, but at an odd angle and below that her jeans were torn and a jagged spike of bone had come through the tear.

I nearly lost the torch again. My hands felt too weak to grip anything. I was like a hollow shell, empty and fragile and incapable. I didn't feel sick or anything, just kind of trapped in indecision.

Then Kathy started to make sounds, little whimpering noises as though she was having a bad dream. I heard my name.

'Si – Simon . . . Simon. Oh, it hurts. Oh, it hurts me, it *hurts me*!'

Her crying rose to a screaming, snatched away in the night. I scrambled down to her, pressed my face close to hers and told her not to worry. And she screamed, nails on glass, it went on and on . . .

'I've got to go and get help, Kath—' she clutched at me as though if I left her I might never come back, or that when I did it would be too late.

'I *must* leave, Kathy. I'll run all the way, OK? And look, I'll put the torch here. Keep it shining towards Seabeck . . .'

After a few seconds her stranger's face nodded. Her hand edged down over my hand and found the stem

122

of the torch and gripped it. Now her screams had calmed to deep sobs that shook her each time.

'Come back,' she said, close to my ear. 'Come back, Simon, OK? Come back.'

'I'll come back, less than an hour. You've not seen me run in a crisis!'

I tried to raise a smile from her, but got instead a terrible agonized grimace. Kathy must have bitten down on her tongue, for her teeth and lips were streaked with blood.

I left her, taking care over the rock, jumping down on to the shingle, then pumping my feet into a clumsy jogging run. The thought struck me that her torchlight would be invisible because of where she lay; I turned into the brunt of the wind and saw only an ocean of dark with Kathy adrift in it somewhere.

'Oh no, Oh no, she'll die. She's going to die.'

There was the cold, and the awful mess of her injury, there was the tide, there was her fear and shock. She was alone, I'd left her alone.

'No! She *won't* die! No – no – no – no –'

I used the word like a chant, helping to pace my run, not trying to go too quickly because at a certain speed my shoes sank down in the wet shingle and the run turned into a trudge. I went carefully, steadily, and counted two thousand no's before I saw the lights of Seabeck. Another two hundred and I was on the road home.

Half a mile out I remembered the phonebox, and saw the homely glow of it almost at the same time. I'd thought it strange that a phone should be stuck way out here, but Kathy had told me that in summer, when the beaches were packed, it was used constantly. I begged for it not to be out of order.

Inside, away from the wind, my head sang dizzily and I began to shiver. I lifted the handset and nearly cried when I heard the buzzing of the line. I dialled the house and Mum answered.

'Fetch Dad, quick Mum—' I shouted when she started asking questions. 'Just do it! Please, just do it . . .'

Dad came on, cool and business-like, expecting an emergency. I told him what had happened.

'I'll get in the car and drive out. I'll pick you up at the phonebox—'

'No Dad, I'm going back. She's by herself and the tide's coming in pretty fast. Just hurry up!'

I heard him start to argue, so I banged the phone down and barged out into the cold blackness.

Now came the journey back. I was already tired, and beginning to feel queasy and faint. Something that felt like oil churned in my stomach and my face was cold, but hot stars gushed in my head. I saw them, fat wet yellow stars popping before my eyes.

I thought I was going to be sick, so I stopped, bent and propped my hands on my legs. Nothing came, I just gagged drily, but felt better for it anyway.

When I looked up, the dizzy-stars were clearing. All except one, that jiggled sharply ahead, swinging to and fro, to and fro. The torch thrown about in the sea!

Couldn't have been, the tide was not that far in. And besides, the movement was too regular, as if—

'Kath? Kathy . . . Kathy!'

I ran towards the light, not understanding it, until the star grew and I could see a shadow shape behind it that became Kathy.

I wrapped my arms around her. She calmed my

shivering and I calmed hers. She was laughing, couldn't stop.

I pulled the torch from her and shone it down to her leg. The jeans were torn all right, but the flesh was whole and well.

And then I began to realize what had happened. The thought was bigger than the night, bigger than the sea that filled the night. Kathy smiled.

'It was like a friend, Simon,' she said. 'It made me better. The best friend in all the world.'

Chill Factor

Mum had a bath and hot tea waiting for us when we returned. Dad had phoned her from the beach and told her it had been a false alarm; he'd said it with a kind of you-know-what-kids-are, half-angry grin on his face, though his eyes said something different. They kept glancing at Kathy's torn jeans and trying to understand the lack of injury. The denim was stained, although most of the blood had been washed out by the sea-water. The first thing Dad had done was to look for deep cuts or fractures, but there was nothing: no bruising or scarring, no pain . . .

Back home Kathy took her bath first, while I phoned through to her parents and explained that we'd been out beachcombing and that she'd be staying for supper. The story sounded flimsy, but at least not incredible like the truth would have been.

Afterwards Dad got the coal fire stoked up in the lounge, then cleared off. I heard him and Mum talking quietly from the kitchen, maybe trying to puzzle the thing out ('Simon doesn't normally over-react, Greg,' she'd be saying), but soon the voices faded and stopped. Dad would be smoking a late pipe, perhaps re-reading the paper; Mum might be washing up, might be staring out at the night with her thoughts far away.

I stared at Kathy.

She sipped at her tea and gazed into the flames letting them make pictures for her – I wondered of what.

She was the first to break the silence, and I was glad of that. It was not the comfortable, peaceful silence you might expect at a hearthside, nor were either of us frightened. What had happened had happened and both of us were still here . . . Mr Barrett would have called it a 'reflective silence'.

'I've been thinking about hospitals,' Kathy said at last, very quietly, not looking up at me. 'And you know, we won't need them any more . . .'

Her brown eyes were twinkling, flame-orange glints in their darkness. Her hair shone from its washing and her face looked flushed in the firelight. She was wrapped up in one of Mum's big dressing gowns and seemed very calm, not happy or sad, but pushed beyond both.

'When I was eight,' Kathy went on, half to herself, 'Mum took me to Westmartin General to see Auntie Vye. I knew she'd been ill for a long time – actually for as far back as I can remember. But when I'd visited the time before that, Vye had still been at home and things didn't seem so bad. She could still smile then . . .

'Well, Mum didn't explain too much, but I've found out since that Auntie Vye had cancer. Dad said, "She was riddled with it, Kath." Isn't that the most awful picture you can imagine—'

Now Kathy did look up and what was there in her face startled me. I nodded like a little kid being told off.

'Reminds me of bad cheese or something.' Kathy said what I was thinking.

'Anyway, there was I still expecting Auntie Vye's bright smile. She had all her own teeth and her smile was the youngest thing about her. I wondered how many million smiles she had given in her life. Not any more.

'A doctor showed us through to the intensive care ward, and together with the ward sister we went to Vye's room. You know, I couldn't see Vye at all, just this kind of skinny skeleton in a big white bed surrounded by metal boxes and small TV screens and drip trolleys. The green blip on the screen was the only thing that told us she was alive. Her mouth was a little bit open and her face was white, white as the bedsheets. I was terrified to touch her because I thought she'd be cold: I didn't kiss her when Mum told me to . . .

'We stayed a while, and Mum and the doctor spoke so quietly I couldn't hear anything of what they were saying. In the end Mum nodded and put her arm around my shoulder. I remember her looking over to the bed and saying, Goodnight Vye. But I knew it meant "goodbye". I thought that was silly, because whatever had made my Auntie Vye was already gone. What was left was empty.

'She died in the night, Simon, and . . . the funeral was grey . . .'

Tears quivered on the brim of Kathy's eyes. I gulped at my tea to hide my emotion, then shrugged, feeling clumsy.

'Yeah, hospitals are pretty depressing. Smell, too. But like you say, if slubber had its way we wouldn't need them any more . . .'

I said it, but the idea didn't carry any weight. I couldn't quite believe it, despite what had happened to Kathy. I chuckled glibly. 'Hey, Dad would be happy to get rid of his medical insurance payments!'

'That's just it,' Kathy said. Her expression had not changed. 'If slubber could preserve us, maybe keep us from dying, our whole lives would be changed.'

'One big party! And—'

'No, Simon. No!' She shouted it, cut me off dead. 'If it happened, we wouldn't be *us* any more. Don't you understand that if slubber gives us everything, we won't need to *try*!'

I realized suddenly that Kathy was angry. It shocked me. Her face was hard with fury and outrage, and the firelight bloomed red on her skin.

'That's just it – we depend on slubber for it all, and we will not be ourselves. We will not be people anymore!'

Tuesday, November the fifth brought a bright blue morning, bluer still for the rain-puddles that lay on pavements and in gutters reflecting the sky. The air had that metallic smell, close to frost, but there was no wind. I was glad. The chill factor from any breeze would have dipped the temperature below zero. And I hate being cold.

I saw Kathy sitting several rows down the bus on the way to school, but for some reason held back from speaking to her. She seemed so quiet, lost in the quietness, as though radiating the message that she wanted to be left alone.

Once at Rowley Mead, with the bus-kids dispersed, I ran after her and caught up near the tennis courts.

'Kathy!' She waved and stood waiting until I was standing at her side. 'OK? Fit for this evening?'

'Yes . . . Yes, I was just thinking, that's all.'

'I'd give it up if it makes you feel like this!'

I realized that this seed of good cheer was falling on stony ground, so I wiped the grin off my face and we began walking again, slowly. I decided to ignore the faint catcalls drifting over from the English base.

'Anyway, cheer up, eh? Penny for your thoughts.'

'I can *make* pennies now,' she said quietly, 'for nothing.'

So *that* was it. 'I get your thoughts for free, then?'

At last came a weak and unwilling smile.

'Go on like that and you'll crack your face.'

'It's just that I feel I owe a debt for being alive. But who to? Oh, I'm grateful to you, Simon. You were brilliant. But when I was lying out at Blackshales in the dark and the cold, I – I thought I was going to die. I've never been so frightened in my life. And the pain was awful, it kept hammering at me, and growing all the time. I thought there'd come a point when I'd sink under it, be overwhelmed; then that would be it: then I'd be dead.'

'It sounds terrifying,' I said lamely, remembering my fear rather than Kathy's ordeal.

'It was, but before it got to that, I felt someone was with me. One minute my hand was in the freezing water, the next it was as though someone was holding it, someone warm and friendly. Someone who could help.

'I saw it all in my head,' Kathy went on, 'but where the torchlight shone on the rocks, everything looked normal. Then this – presence – seemed to lay a warm coat over me, and sat beside me for company. My body became warm and the pain faded away, like, from a scream to a whisper. Do you understand?'

I nodded.

'After a while, I was well enough to stand up. I grabbed the torch and ran after you. The one who was with me stayed by me until I saw Seabeck's lights in the distance, then he was gone – back inside my head, or wherever he came from.'

'Did you see him?'

'Once,' Kathy began, than caught herself. 'You'll think it's stupid. You'll laugh.'

'Come on Kathy, you know me better than that,' I lied, and she spotted the smile.

'It was . . . Well, I have this uncle who lives in Australia. Actually he's Mum's brother, and quite a bit older than her. Every Christmas he sends us a box of *glacé* fruit – apricots, pineapple, you name it. Dad and I can't stand the stuff, it's so sickly. But Mum wolfs it down. Anyway,' Kathy smiled, 'I've only ever seen Uncle Phil once, years ago. He came over and stayed for a week. And you know, Simon, there was such love in his eyes all the time he was with us . . .And on the Friday before he left, he held me tight and said he loved his little Kathy so much . . .'

Kathy's lip quivered and her eyes sparkled with tears; not unhappily, I thought, but with a deep fondness.

'And you saw him again, at Blackshales?'

She nodded.

'He told me he might never get to hug me again, so he was going to make *that* hug big enough to last him through the years . . . So I owe *someone*, right, Simon? But it can't be Uncle Phil because he's ten

131

thousand miles away. And it can't be the slubber because that's just – nothing, it's . . .'

'What we make it. That's all.' I whispered. The lion walked through my head. 'Slubber is only what we make it, just like life, eh?'

'Just like life,' Kathy said, and turned away from me. 'I'll see you tonight.'

'Yeah. Oh, but wear jeans, OK? It'll be cold out, so make sure you wear your jeans . . .'

At school and all through the day, excitement was in the air, though dampened a bit by the hard-sell warnings about fireworks in Assembly, the Guy Fawkes project work in Art, the talk on the history of gunpowder by Mr Brunton in Integrated Studies, and so on . . .

At breaktime I noticed Claire Goodson putting her bag in the French room ready for next lesson. She was alone, so I took my chance (and my life in my hands!) and went up to her.

'Claire . . .'

She glanced round brightly enough, but her expression soured as soon as she saw who it was. I put up my hands in surrender.

'Please, I'm only here to apologize. And to ask one question.'

Her face stayed hard and she didn't offer any kind of friendliness; and that disturbed me, because Claire bounced through life and usually didn't waste a single second worrying about what people said. Something had stabbed into her deeply. She said,

'Don't bother to apologize. What do you want to know?'

'Only who it was that told you I'd said those things.'

'Why does that matter?'

'Because I *didn't* say them. I think you're great actually — but I know there's no point in trying to convince you I'm on your side . . .'

'Not really,' She looked away again and reached for something in her bag. Her plastic jewellery — surely a trademark as well as a kick against the school rules — clattered on her wrist. Today her bangles and earrings were blue.

'Then just tell me and I'll push off.'

'So you can spread more rumours about the person I mention.'

'No, so I can defend myself against her — and maybe prevent other people from being hurt.'

'Oh, so noble Simon!'

Anger flared up in me then. 'All *right*. I'll tell *you* who slandered you. It was Louise Williams, yes? Am I right, or what?'

Claire didn't reply. I thought in fact she was going to push straight past me, and maybe land one of her incredible right hooks as she went. But instead, she seemed to lose the inner pressure of her fury suddenly; she sat on a desk, shook her head and wiped her eyes.

'You know, I never thought *any*body could be quite so vindictive. I mean, not you. I believe you didn't spread those lies—'

'Thank you for that!'

'And she did it, not to get at me, but because she didn't want anything happening between us.'

'Me and you? I was stunned and bewildered and pleased all at once. Claire nodded.

'Because,' she went on. 'Louise wants you for herself. I don't know why — and don't take that wrong — but she's the sort of girl who's so single-minded that

133

once she's decided on something, she goes for it. And God help anybody who gets in her way.'

When I didn't reply, Claire added, 'Do you understand what I'm saying?'

'I understand. And I don't know why either. I mean, I'm not Superman, right?'

We both laughed and the day around us seemed normal again, not tight with hostility. I thought about Kathy and guessed, as everything slotted into place, that she'd be Louise's next target – and for the same reason as Claire.

'I'm sorry,' Claire said, 'for flying off the handle. I guess I made a right fool of myself!'

'Naa, you added to your reputation as one of the world's Amazons. And I'll tell you, I'm sorry too for all this trouble. It's, um, a pity we can't be friends. You'd make a good friend, Claire . . .'

The girl blushed, but not as much as I did.

'I'm sort of spoken for now.'

'I didn't mean like that, I meant just friends. Mind you, I wouldn't've said no to what you're thinking of.'

Claire giggled and was transformed into her real self, all cheeky backtalk and bubble. She pushed herself away from the desk and we walked outside together.

'I may be an Amazon, Simon,' she said, 'but I'm not Wonder Woman. One boyfriend at a time is enough. Pity there aren't two of me.'

Yes, I thought, and thank God there's only one of Louise Williams.

No one dawdled in getting away at the end of the afternoon. All through the area and down the coast bonfire parties had been organized, and kids shouted last-minute plans and instructions as they boarded buses and cycled away.

By seven o'clock that evening the first skyrockets were crackling upwards. I went out into the garden and stood on the top terrace to watch. There was a thin moon following the sun that had already set way out to sea, and the sky had cooled to the colour of deep ice. Stars sparkled along the coast and in towns across the channel. People were busy and excited and having fun.

I walked back inside shivering.

Mum, Dad and I left the house together soon afterwards, Dad struggling with his burden of beer-cans, a fragile quiche that Mum had made, and his annual small box of fireworks.

Before we reached the Williams' house I saw Kathy leaning against a garden wall, waiting for us. Dad took a look at the huge bag of rockets she'd brought – at first dumbfounded and with his mouth open, then with a gathering annoyance.

'Hey, I paid over three quid for this puny boxful. How come—'

'Greg,' Mum said, with perfect timing and tone. She understood Dad perfectly. 'You'll get to see them anyway.'

'That's right,' I agreed, innocent-eyed, 'after we've had ten seconds' enjoyment watching the ones you bought, eh Dad?'

'Cheers,' he said nastily, but he didn't moan again.

We heard the party music bumping from several doors away; over it and above it came shouts and some laughter. Fireworks were already being let off generously from the back garden – a rocket cracked its fires and geysered sparks above us, making me jump.

John Williams had strung a cable of coloured lights around a holly tree near the patio. Beneath them people moved, half shadows and half firelit pink silhouettes. Someone raised a glass: with the flames beyond, it seemed to be filled with a red liquid light.

'Let's party,' I drawled in my best imitation Californian accent.

'Right,' Dad agreed, irritation forgotten. 'I might as well take all of this stuff straight round the back. Grab me a pint and we'll rendezvous at the garlic dip – five minutes.'

Plans made (though once inside they'd be abandoned), Dad hefted all the bags and walked down the house-side pretending to struggle manfully.

Mum rang the front bell and Mrs Williams answered. I hadn't seen her for days and was surprised to see the strange caricature that her face had become – an uneasy mixture of polite cheerfulness laid over a deep frustration and sadness. It struck me that preparing for this party had been a worry and a chore, not the fun it was meant to be and should have been.

'Come in.'

Somehow, the invitation sounded like an apology.

The house was warm, every light was on, and rooms and hallways were filled with little clutches of people all holding drinks, chatting, laughing; mouths replying politely to conversation while eyes roved, taking everything in.

'People have *dressed up*,' was the first thing Mum said, obviously worried by it. She glanced down at her own baggy cords and the thick checked shirt she had borrowed from Dad – sensible clothes to stand and watch fireworks in.

'Oh,' I said, 'so they have.' I was thinking more of Kathy. She was openly staring at the women in their smart dresses and discreet but expensive jewellery, her first feelings of shock turning into anger towards me, because we both knew what was about to happen. Soon enough Louise was going to swish along in her latest outfit, looking as gorgeous as a filmstar (making sure she had a couple of the Harpies with her, of course). She would not be obvious enough to jeer. Instead, she might make a point of looking Kathy up and down, smiling slightly at her plump legs in their faded jeans. Maureen would put a hand up to her mouth and pretend to be coughing; a third Harpy might hurry back to spread the word that old frumpy Kathy had fallen into another trap . . .

'Oh well, never mind.' Mum's face assumed its I-won't-be-put-off expression. 'Elegance comes from the inside anyway.'

She headed for the drinks' table.

'Kathy,' I started to say heavily, not quite knowing how to proceed, but preparing for the embarrassment of a row just five yards and five minutes into the party.

I might have been able to cope with that too, but not with the way Kathy's face crumpled. She started quivering, wiped at the big tears that had risen to her eyes, and shook her head from side to side, backing away as I stepped towards her.

'Doesn't matter, Simon, OK . . . It doesn't matter. Just don't bother to be sorry . . .'

Temper flashed through me, not because Kathy was blaming me, but because she sounded beaten and kind of hopeless. I wanted suddenly to hit sense into her.

'Oh come on! You think I'm sorry, do you? 'Cause Louise tricked you into wearing your scruffy gear while she prances around like something out of Hollywood? Does it matter that much, anyway?'

Kathy hesitated, shrugged and dabbed at her wet eyes again in a gesture that reminded me of a little girl who's fallen down and grazed her knee. That image made my mind jump to the sight of Kathy's smashed leg at Blackshales. She'd trusted me then, trusted me to leave her before we'd realized that the slubber would take all the danger away. She might have died. I might never have seen her again.

'Louise has made me feel as stupid and as ugly as I have ever done: fat and gullible, clumsy, naive—'

'That's enough!'

She tried to step away again, but I lunged forward and grabbed her arm and pulled her towards me. I held on tight. 'It's true! Don't bother lying—' She began to struggle.

'It's true she's made you feel like that – but it isn't true you're *like* that. Kathy – listen!'

She calmed down, and then blushed as she noticed people looking at us.

'That's Louise's game. Haven't you realized? To own people or to beat people. It's stupid. She's got looks, brains, nice clothes—'

'See!'

'But what else? All those mates of hers hang around because she's strong, and because they're scared, not because they like her. If one of them crossed her, she'd eat the girl alive. Same goes for Louise, if she left the gang. She puts people down because she has to be the best, on top, leader of the pack. Oh, she'll get whatever she wants, Kathy, except happiness . . .'

'Yeah . . .' Kathy looked bitter. 'And what do I get?'

'You get me,' I said softly, 'if you want.'

That stopped her dead, although I hadn't said it for that. In fact, I hadn't planned to say it at all. And now my head was pounding and I felt I was standing on a high wire, wondering when the fall would come.

Slowly, as though the sound was being turned up on the TV, I became aware of people talking around us and the heat of the room, the smell of lavender. The moment had gone and I still didn't have an answer.

'You know,' I said with nervous humour – my turn to tremble now – 'you've smeared mascara all over your face.'

Kathy laughed, a warm and natural laughter, then stepped up close in front of me. I saw a fleeting shift of mood in her eyes as she put her hands on my shoulders and kissed my lips, and knew without having to glance round that Louise was coming down the stairs behind me.

Later we talked, about all sorts of things, and when I tried to persuade Kathy to go home and change if she wanted to, she just shook her head.

'Your mum's got it right,' she said. 'Elegance comes from the inside. Though if it's all the same to you I'll watch the fireworks from the window. It'll be pretty cold outside tonight.'

'Looks likely,' I agreed. Then I noticed Chris across the other side of the room. 'Hang on,' I told Kathy, 'I'll be back in a minute . . .'

I hadn't seen Chris for days, not since we'd met in his greenhouse and he'd shown us his latest 'experiments'. Although Kathy herself had explored plenty of possibilities, it was Chris and Louise that worried me. I wondered how far beyond hamsters they'd progressed by now – and the phantom of my almost-hands growing into reality in Kathy's garage drifted through my mind.

'Hi, Chris,' I said cheerfully. 'How're you doin'?'

He gave me a kind of suspicious sideways look and then glanced round to see who else might be watching. Everybody in the room seemed occupied, listening to music, or chatting, some responding to Mrs Williams' call that hot food was ready in the dining room.

'I'm all right. How are you?'

'Fine, man. Hey, how are your cactuses coming along? Have they grown teeth yet?'

It wasn't a particularly funny quip, but Chris burst into giggling laughter: overloud, sounding somehow false and unconvincing.

'Well, em . . .'

'Can I take a look at them . . .? And how's old Hammy, the duplicate hamster, getting on? Ha, you'll be into cats and dogs at this rate—'

'Shut up—' Chris said, hissing the words venomously. His mood of dodge-the-question dropped away like a mask, and underneath I saw hard, raw anger – and fear too. The kid was scared witless.

'What's that?' I must have looked gormless with my wide eyes and raised eyebrows, but he'd taken me by surprise. 'All I said was . . . Oh, Jesus . . .'

I followed Chris's gaze across the room, peering between pairs of legs and into shadows. He was expecting it to be in the room, but I found it first.

140

The cat was sitting on a footstool that someone had pushed close to the TV set. And it was staring at us.

'Listen, Simon . . .' Chris put out his hand to touch my arm, and his fingers were trembling. 'Come into the other room. Come on, I'll tell you there.'

Off he went, glancing behind like some over-the-top stool pigeon in a bad gangster movie. If he hadn't been so obviously frightened I'd've laughed.

We went through into his parents' study. The lights were off – Chris kept them off – and because the place had been empty for hours and no extra heating turned on, the air inside was still and cold enough to make me shiver.

'I can see what homework grade I got,' I said to cover my own nervousness, then wondered what sort of an explosion would follow if John Williams actually caught us in here.

Chris didn't bother laughing or even replying. He sat down at one desk chair, and I at another. The chairs creaked comfortably under our weight.

'So you duplicated your cat . . .'

'Louise did. Honest, I never wanted to do it. I thought the hamster trick was fun . . . But Tweedle, well, she's our cat. There's only one of her, really . . .'

That brought back the conversation I'd had with Kathy and raised so many problems and puzzles that I didn't pursue it. I asked, 'How long did the copying take?'

'A few hours. I thought it'd be ages, but when I went down in the afternoon – this was a few days ago – I could see . . .'

'Yeah?'

'There was bones hanging there in the slubber, touching but not joined yet by muscles. Its heart was

141

a faint red patch, just like a bit of pink mist. But its green eyes were clear, even that early on: bright and clear, Simon, staring like hard marbles . . .'

Chris's voice began to catch. I could imagine him reliving the moment as he explained it to me. Back there in the greenhouse, those eyes with no body around them were staring at him. And they *knew* what they were looking at.

The slubber, I realized then, had its own intelligence and purpose. All the vague bad feelings about it that had bothered me for the past week came together in that one thought. The slubber knew what it was doing. We were making it into things, but at the same time it was changing us as well, for its own reasons, with its own plans.

'OK,' I said, 'calm down. Haven't your mum and dad got suspicious, seeing *two* black cats around the house?'

Chris gave a low, quiet laugh that did not sound quite normal.

'Ah, but you never *see* both of them. That's the weird thing. Tweedle was around a lot of the time at first – our Tweedle, that is, the real one. And I saw very little of the other one. But now, *that's* in the house and down the garden all the time, always looking about. And – and I haven't seen Tweedle at all today. I wonder, Simon, if . . . I wonder . . .'

Chris broke into sniffles, making little helpless moaning sounds, as though he'd just broken a piece of his Mum's best china and now could only wait helplessly until she caught him and punished him.

'Well, we'll look for Tweedle soon, if you like. Don't worry, we'll find her. She's probably tucked away and hiding from all these fireworks . . .'

'Yeah . . .' Chris looked at me in the darkness and wiped his nose across his sleeve. 'Yeah Simon, right.'

I shook my head.

'I don't know what Louise is playing at! Didn't she realize that this stuff might be dangerous? It was all too easy, that's the trouble. Making something for nothing was just too easy, too tempting. When I get my hands on her I'll—'

Chris's face suddenly grew brighter, from a shadowed half-shape to a white patch in the growing light. Around me details of books ranged on shelves and papers in untidy piles began to appear out of the gloom.

The door eased open silently, but no one came through.

Then Chris shrieked, not so much in startlement as dread.

'Simon!' He pointed. The black cat was in the study with us. It had found us out, and now glared balefully, knowingly, in our direction.

'Get out of it!'

My hand swept across the desktop and scooped up the first book it touched. I hurled the thing at the cat. The book went flying in a mad flutter of pages and landed short.

The cat didn't budge, not an inch. It stood its ground and did not take its gaze from us. In the green eyes I began to see other eyes glowing; and around the small cat shape a larger more powerful image began to form, like a gleam of gold fur and great bulking of huge muscles.

I took Chris's hand.

'Come on,' I said firmly, and led him across the

floor, skirting around the cat which had swung its head slowly to follow our progress.

'It's going to bite us!'

'No it's not! It isn't ready yet to make its move. Slubber hasn't *spread* far enough yet – it's not in Government labs, or factories, or people's houses . . . It's not strong enough yet.'

And the cat let us by without making a move. Close beside it lay the book I'd thrown, an open butterfly-spread of pages with the spine uppermost. It was Darwin's *On the Origin of Species*. I laughed at that, and the laughter made me want to throw up.

'What are we going to do?' Chris wanted to know, once we were back in the warm company of people.

'You stay around here,' I told him. 'Stay safe. I'll find Louise and sort something out with her, OK?'

Across the room Maureen (the harpy) stood looking gorgeous in her blue dress and silver jewellery, wine glass in hand, all very sophisticated and cool. The slubber would eat you alive, girl, if you ever found out about it . . .

'Hey, why don't you ask her for a date?' I wondered, trying to get Chris to calm down. He gave me a sickly little smile.

'Why don't *you*?'

'She's not into fossils,' I said; I'd worked *that* out all by myself, and enjoyed Chris's frown.

'I'll see you later,' I said.

Louise wasn't around downstairs. I spotted Kathy in the kitchen, face aglow, laughing with Mum as they helped themselves to generous ladlefuls of punch (Mum was going to have a wicked hangover in the morning). Kathy caught sight of me, waved, and started forward. I shook my head and turned away before I had time to see her change of expression. I went upstairs into the quietness of the landing and cautiously pushed open doors until I found Louise's room, then stepped inside. It was the first time I'd seen the place, and the sweet smell of it made my heart beat faster.

It was a modern girl's bedroom: duvet on the bed, desk nearby, boxy squarish dresser and chest of drawers against another wall done out in white and red. There was a TV/video and midistack system built into a unit opposite the bed. Louise's dresser was cluttered with cosmetics bottles; she had no hero-posters up on the walls.

It was her room, but it said nothing *about* her: Louise was not in here, not in any sense of the word.

I wondered why, and was still wondering as I closed the bedroom door and turned to find Louise standing three steps away, hands on hips, glaring at me balefully.

'Decided to have a little snoop around, Simon? I thought you'd rather've been downstairs necking with your new girlfriend.'

Her words came out hot and angry. A week ago I might have choked on a mouthful of excuses, but right now making excuses to her wasn't at all important.

'Listen, Louise, it's about the slubber and – and what you're doing with it.'

'What *I'm* doing with it? What do you expect me to do with the stuff – take it to the authorities, and earn my Girl Guide's badge for good service and honesty?'

'You're going too far,' I said quietly. 'In fact, I think we went too far on the first day we picked the stuff up. It's using us, Louise. We'll come to depend on it more and more; slubber will end up everywhere, a part of everybody's life—'

'Not before I get what *I* want!'

'Until in the end we can't exist without it, and then it will have us.'

'It's the answer to all the problems,' she insisted.

'No! It isn't – this isn't a benediction, it's an invasion!'

'It's what you make of it. Like life, right?'

Her smile was pure malice.

'Have you told your father about this?' I asked changing tack. Louise gave a little bubbling laugh of derision.

'No way. Daddy just hasn't got the imagination to use it properly. You know what he'd do? He'd duplicate videos and TVs, cars, maybe, when he gets *really* ambitious: set up a nice little business for himself so he can escape from the drab routine of his existence. It's pathetic!'

'And what you're doing is frightening. Have you *seen* that cat you've made?'

'Little Tweedle-Two? What's wrong?'

'It isn't a cat for a start. And where's the original?'

'Around.'

'Around where?'

'Look, Simon, the slubber's here, on Earth. We can't get away from that fact. And whether it kills us or cures us depends on who utilizes it first, and with imagination.'

'Really, and what are your plans?'

Louise shrugged. 'First, I think, I'm going to make something of myself. I don't want to be Father's little pride and joy, working my way obediently through college, then set myself up in a cosy career, then get married and have a couple of nice little children, then get bored and old and then die!'

Her voice rose as she spoke, until at the end Louise was almost shouting at me. Her body was shaking with the force of her determination, and I think at that moment she frightened me more than the black cat had done.

'Louise . . .'

She turned her head away from me, her eyes glinting. It gave me pause to notice how her hair shone, how easily and well she wore her pale yellow party dress, and how skilfully she had put shadows around her eyes to make their blue stand out so strikingly. She knew I was staring; Louise never missed a thing like that. Her sudden, growing smile set me tingling as though she'd touched me.

'My plans depend on who's with me,' she said quietly, 'at my side. Understand?'

I said nothing. She let her hands fall, and tilted her head a little to one side.

'I mean, we could achieve a lot before other people got their hands on the slubber. Don't you ever think about fortunes, Simon? Don't you ever dream?'

'Sometimes.' Now my throat was dry and the ground suddenly unsure beneath my feet. I saw that she was offering so much, and that it would be so easy to accept it. So easy, so tempting . . .

'No reason why we both shouldn't benefit.'

'There will be no benefits . . .' I said it like a final defensive gesture before the ultimatum, the last chance; what I'd been waiting for since I'd first met Louise Williams.

'How about it then? Come on, Simon, what do you want? Say what you want, then take it. Come on . . .'

She held me with her eyes and started to put out her hands towards me.

'No – no, that's not the way!'

The words burst out and released me. I pushed past her and saw incredulity start to transform itself into something much nastier.

'That's it then, Hallam,' she yelled. 'You've blown your last chance. Life is going to get pretty difficult after this, you hear me? You're a *loser*, Simon. You've got nothing! You don't even interest me!'

Her voice rose almost to a shriek, the words coming after me like stones. I'd expected her reaction and it didn't upset me – it scared me to death.

I made my way straight to the kitchen, found Kathy and pulled her aside. She had her sleeves rolled up by now and had been busy helping Mum and Mrs Williams to serve up the eats.

'Oh, so you've followed your stomach's advice after all! I'd been wondering when—'

'Kathy, listen,' I said. 'I haven't time to muck about. Go home – go straight home – and burn what's left of the slubber. The stuff's dangerous and we must get rid of it. Come *on* now, move . . .'

'Wait a minute.' Kathy twisted around and stood firm, to stop me pushing her towards the door. Her face was flushed from the kitchen warmth and the punch she'd guzzled – she was smiling.

'Please, Kathy, this is vital . . .'

'The slubber in Dad's garage has died.'

'What?'

'Or whatever you want to call it; ceased to function, lost its powers . . .' She saw me gaping and laughed.

'There's a frost tonight, a sharp one. I noticed the

148

slubber in the bowls was very thick and treacly earlier; then just before I came out, when I went to fetch the rockets, I saw a skin of ice over it – only it wasn't ice at all. The slubber had crystallised. It's dead. I tried to tell you earlier without your parents overhearing, but you went dashing off who knows where and—'

'Kathy, I love you!'

She didn't have a chance to react (to look surprised or smack me in the mouth), before I leaned forward and kissed her firmly on the lips.

'Simon, people are looking!'

'Let them look. Don't you see, it means the slubber still on the beach is finished too.'

Leaving only the stuff in Louise's greenhouse, I realized.

'I'm going now,' I told her, 'but I'll be back soon, OK? Don't worry, it'll be all right now. And Kathy, you look pretty good in those jeans!'

She smiled wanly, doubting me. But I meant it.

I let myself out into the back garden and grinned as the cold air began to snap at my nose and finger-tips. Behind the glare of the bonfire that was in full blaze, and the showering glitter of fireworks, a few pale stars were shining in a clear black sky.

Dad was there, enjoying the show amongst the crowd. He saw me and waved. I waved back but did not go across, being too intent on John Williams lining up half a dozen milk bottles to use as launching pads for a fleet of rockets – Kathy's rockets; the ones she'd manufactured from raw slubber.

'Ladies and gentlemen,' Williams said with an air of great ceremony, and really enjoying himself. 'This is to be the finale of our little display, which I hope you've enjoyed. I am reliably informed by my wife that hot food is being served indoors, so we'll get this over with and then eat. Here we go!'

A few people applauded, playing the game. Williams made an exaggerated bow and deftly touched his lighted taper to the base of each rocket.

One in the middle fizzed first, hissed harshly as white fire spurted from it, then whipped upwards on a wavering path, high into the sky.

It burst spectacularly into a flower or green sparks, each of which crackled into further gleaming fragments as it disintegrated. With a final bang, the heart of the rocket exploded and lit the garden below with a rich coppery light, as bright as a camera-flash.

Some people gasped, half a dozen were prompted into clapping again at the sight. The other rockets flared and flew, each erupting gloriously.

But they were all green, identical, each with a copper star at its heart.

And the crowd shouted and laughed, clapped and pointed.

Mad, I thought. They're all mad. Mad in England. All of them, every one.

Mad in England.

Once the fireworks had finished people began drifting indoors, suddenly feeling the cold. I hung around on the fringes, waiting for the garden to clear. And as the last stragglers stepped through the patio doors into the house, I ducked behind some bushes and followed the path down towards Chris's greenhouse. The stars watched me as I went.

I felt strange as I traced the faint line of paving stones down in the darkness; a bit guilty I suppose for not trusting Chris and Louise – who were my friends – with the secret and responsibility of slubber.

I was also uneasy, because my mistrust of Louise went further. It was not a huge step of the imagination to dream of more than cats made from the stuff, but it was a great leap of daring. And Louise imagined. And Louise dared . . .

The shape of the greenhouse defined itself out of its background of shadow; a few distant firelights glinted back off the glass, and as my eyes grew sensitive to the gloom I was able to see, vaguely, other shapes beyond. Things were still growing in there, and moving. Or was I mistaken?

I stood at the doorway, making myself as still as the air. Now I could feel a faint heat radiating from the building. I touched one of the panes and found it to be mildly warm: Chris must have had the heating full on for that to happen. Inside, it must be stifling.

For a second or two I thought about turning back, maybe finding Kathy and telling her what was going on. Perhaps Dad would be able to do something, help in some way . . . the police ought to be told, the Government should know . . .

All of that would take time, would be the wrong thing to do. As soon as people discovered slubber, they would never let it go. And it, I realized, would never let *them* go. How stupid, to think that we could take and take from the slubber, without having to give anything back.

I pulled open the sliding door and took a careful step inside.

Green grew around me. I could sense it, smell it, rather than see it directly. The walls of the greenhouse seemed to melt away into great distances and I was standing on an endless plain. Strangely elegant trees swished nearby in the night. Perhaps, somewhere above, weird diamond shapes were drifting. In the distance might be a lake of purplish water, its surface disturbed only by gentle ripples as though something had just submerged. Soon it would be morning here, and into a paper-white dawn sky a sun like a polished coin would rise.

Something brushed by my leg, something softly powerful, silent and bulking. I could not even hear its breathing, but its voice spoke to me clearly in the still places of my mind.

Don't be afraid of me, you just haven't discovered yet what you want.

I didn't think it would be like this. I thought spaceships would land. You know, flying saucers with death rays or something. Robots, maybe.

People would be frightened. Better a small beginning.

Is this what you're really like? Like a lion?

Each would see me differently. A lion is strong, noble, fearless—

Dangerous.

Only to its enemies. It is what you want? Everybody can have what they want. What do you want?

Everything, all of it . . . No! I've got what I want. I mean, Kathy and . . . Mum and Dad are happy enough, aren't they? They can't live forever, but—

Can't they? Is that what you want?

I—

The sun is coming. Soon it will be here and the new day will have arrived.

Then we'll never get rid of you!

Wait.

Then we'll never be free of you!

I jumped backwards as a huge heavy shadow plunged by, just missing me. And as it did so I sensed that there was another shape within it, a part of it, something more real and solid.

I was caught off balance as teeth like swords clashed in front of my face, and what looked like a thin white hand pushed me in the chest. Eyes like no eyes I had ever imagined stared for a second into mine – but they changed, became green and triumphant and horribly familiar . . .

I tripped over the lip of the door frame and fell backwards on to the grass, crashing down so that I was winded.

I felt sure that nothing came after me; it was too cold out here, I realized that suddenly. The relief of it, and the *nearness* of what had almost happened, made me shudder. The slubber couldn't work below zero. I was safe in the frost.

I scrambled up without taking my eyes from the open greenhouse doorway. I could feel the waves or anger and violence in my mind: the lion was roaring silently in my head, roaring out its failure and pain as the cold penetrated the matrix of the slubber and killed the last thoughts lingering there. I wondered fleetingly if the things that had already been *made* from slubber would be destroyed, either because the main bulk of the stuff had been, or because, whatever it resembled, it was still slubber at the heart and had never encountered the alien cold of Earth. Time to worry about that later.

Louise would never forgive me, I knew. Whatever dreams she'd had were finished too. Suddenly I didn't care. I'd done it and that was that.

Kathy would forgive me, though, and that mattered. She had seen what I had; she'd understand, even though her Uncle Phil was just a ghost, like my lion, like every dream that did not rely on the ambitions and skills and weaknesses of ordinary human beings.

I walked back up the path slowly, pausing at the garage to switch off the power that ran from the junction-box there to the greenhouse. Then I hurried up to the house.

And the stars watched me as I went.

Ebb Tide

There was no way I could sleep that night. I kept seeing lions in my half-dreams and in the patterns of the wallpaper. Eventually these emerged as doubts that the slubber was really finished – but it had to be; as Kathy had said, the frost was severe. By six o'clock, when the dawnlight had strengthened enough for me to see into the garden, the glass was white with a sprinkling of stiff crystals.

Mum called me as usual at seven. I washed, put on my school uniform and went downstairs for breakfast. Mum's eyes were red and heavy with the hangover she'd given herself, and when she put the bowl of muesli in front of me, she almost threw up. I resisted asking for eggs and bacon to follow.

I ate hurriedly, checked my school bag to make sure I had the right books for a Wednesday's lessons, then proceeded to duck school for the day . . .

I wrapped up warm and walked straight round to Louise's house.

Mrs Williams answered the door, looking pale with vague, sleep-puffy eyes.

'I thought I'd call for Louise before she goes to school, Mrs Williams. And thank her for inviting me last night.'

The lie slipped out easily, and with it the smile.

'Oh, um, Louise . . . She went for an early walk, Simon . . . to the beach.'

'Oh, right. Thanks. Is – anything wrong?'

'I don't think so, why?'

'No reason,' I said, not wanting to give away the reason that I thought Mrs Williams was scared. And she seemed confused, too, as though she'd woken up from the same kind of nightmare I'd had.

I was about to trot out some stupid apologies and excuses, when I saw movement beyond Mrs Williams in the hallway.

The lounge door must have been ajar, for suddenly the black cat glided out, sat at the foot of the stairs and regarded me solemnly. I knew it for what it was: there could be no doubt about the strange intelligence in its eyes. Well, I thought, it's answered one question – the things created from slubber were not destroyed by the cold . . .

'And how's Chris?' I went on.

'Well, he's fine. Come in, if you wish, and see him.'

'He's all right?'

'Yes!' Her voice had an edge to it now, and she looked impatient. I tried the smile again, and it didn't come out so successfully this time.

'No, um, thanks anyway. I think I'll walk down and find Louise, if you don't mind.'

'Not at all, Simon. Good morning.'

She closed the door and went back into the depths of the house. Through the frosted patterned glass I could still see the unmoving shape of the cat, and I was sure it went on watching until I was down the street and out of sight.

I walked hard for over an hour, by which time the cold had sunk through my anorak to my bones. The sands were deserted: not even dog-walkers had turned out on such a frozen morning. Ahead, the coast road to Dunton Point was a dull grey strip between verges of pale motionless grass. The sky was hazy with mist, and through it the sun was rising in a pink patch of light that was broader than my outspread hand.

One car passed me on the way, swishing along from Westmartin and probably on its way to Reabridge and the motorway beyond. It churned up a freezing flood of air that burned my face like splinters and poured cold through me, so that I had to stop for a minute to catch my breath.

I reached Blackshales by nine. By then the sun was fully up and the rocks and pools looked beautiful – beautiful because they were normal again, except for streaks and traces of transparent crystal, all that remained of the slubber.

I was totally satisfied, but walked on a short way to make sure that the whole beach was the same.

In the distance, perched on a rock quite close to the spot where Kathy had fallen, a yellowish shape caught my eye. It was small, hunched down, not moving . . . For one terrible second I thought that the golden lion had not been destroyed – that it sat there with its jaws open and waiting, sensing me coming up slowly behind . . .

Then in a blink I made sense of it. The shape was not that of a lion at all, but of a person sitting with back turned towards me. A person wearing a fawn dufflecoat.

'Louise!'

I ran across, scrambled up the side of the rock and sat beside he.

'Hello, Simon.'

I didn't expect her to look at me, let alone forgive me, so I felt pleased that she was answering me at all.

I stuck my hands deep down into my pockets and stared at the long reach of sand and stone that led to the sea. The tide was out. A few gulls had ventured back to the beach and stood like white carvings on the breakwaters.

'I'm, uh, I'm sorry, Louise.'

'Nothing to be sorry about.'

'I know it put an end to your plans – but the damn stuff would've put an end to *us*, otherwise. Anyway, we had an adventure out of it, eh?'

She made a sound like a sigh that might have been a stifled laugh or a gasp. I angled round to look at her, but long veils of blonde hair hung down to cover her face.

'Hey, maybe we could sell the story to the papers and make our fortune that way!'

Louise didn't answer. I guessed that she was probably more upset then she'd admit, so I edged closer and put my arm around her shoulders. I was meant as a friendly gesture only, but it brought a feeling of loss and of excitement that was unexpectedly strong.

'Come on, you've got it all – brains, initiative, good looks. You'll have no trouble getting what you want in this world. You haven't missed your chance. . . .'

'Simon . . .'

She turned towards me, nuzzling her face into my neck. I felt her lips cool on my skin and saw all the traps ahead of me that I thought I'd avoided.

'Hey, look . . . I don't think we . . .'

'You're right,' she said, 'I haven't missed my chance.'

Her manner unnerved me. It was too calm. Too – cold.

'I think we'd better get back. Maybe catch a late bus to school, eh? Your parents will be pretty mad about all this.'

And then she did laugh, and it was a hard brittle sound like nothing I'd ever heard before: it scared me.

'Did you – um – grow something else in the greenhouse, Louise?' I could feel my heart going now, like a tripswitch letting loose the panic.

'Grow – something?' she wondered, playing her game out to the end. The low gold sunlight shone on her and made me think how pretty she was; that butter wouldn't melt in her mouth, as they say.

'Do you want to make me say it? I know what you've wanted, Louise! But to make – yourself . . . It wouldn't be right!'

She turned and snuggled up to me, kissed my ear and said:

'No hard feelings, Simon. But Louise is at home.'

I sprang away, pushing wildly, but she caught me and stared at me, smiling. I'd seen that smile before: it was horribly familiar. And those eyes. Not Louise's blue eyes, but eyes of green that held an awful and single-minded purpose.

My hands were sweeping madly to find a stick, a stone, anything at all. But the world was already lost in the gaping span of a lion's jaws, all sound smashed by the terrible noise of its roar.

All Pan books are available at your local bookshop or newsagent, or can be ordered direct from the publisher. Indicate the number of copies required and fill in the form below.

Send to: **CS Department, Pan Books Ltd., P.O. Box 40, Basingstoke, Hants.   RG21 2YT.**

or phone: 0256 469551 (Ansaphone), quoting title, author and Credit Card number.

Please enclose a remittance* to the value of the cover price plus: 60p for the first book plus 30p per copy for each additional book ordered to a maximum charge of £2.40 to cover postage and packing.

*Payment may be made in sterling by UK personal cheque, postal order, sterling draft or international money order, made payable to Pan Books Ltd.

Alternatively by Barclaycard/Access:

Card No. ☐☐☐☐☐☐☐☐☐☐☐☐☐☐☐☐

Signature:

Applicable only in the UK and Republic of Ireland.

While every effort is made to keep prices low, it is sometimes necessary to increase prices at short notice. Pan Books reserve the right to show on covers and charge new retail prices which may differ from those advertised in the text or elsewhere.

NAME AND ADDRESS IN BLOCK LETTERS PLEASE:

....

Name ——————————————————————————

Address ——————————————————————————

——————————————————————————————

——————————————————————————————

——————————————————————————————

3/87